MW01258633

OVERTAKEN

Also by K.F. Breene

OVERTAKEN

BY K.F. BREENE

Copyright © 2016 by K.F. Breene

Print Edition

All rights reserved. The people, places and situations contained in this ebook are figments of the author's imagination and in no way reflect real or true events.

Contact info:

www.kfbreene.com

Facebook: facebook.com/authorKF

Twitter: @KFBreene

CHAPTER ONE

XANDRE SLOWLY MADE his way through the stone hall before climbing the steep steps to his strategizing chamber. A light mental touch brushed his mind, making him stop abruptly. He placed his hand on the wood banister and waited. When the touch wasn't repeated, he continued up the steps.

"One of the Inkna has violated my trust," he said calmly. At the top step he stalled, not bothering to look back at the member of the Inner Circle following him. "Find him. Put him on display."

"And if he is powerful?"

"Maim. Permanently. I care only about their minds and their ability to reproduce. Anything else can go."

"Yes, master."

Xandre heard only a soft scrape of his man before he felt the presence drift away. Even the soft scrape was telling. Xandre had been in one place too long. His protectors were getting bored. Listless. They needed tasks to keep their minds active and their skills honed. Xandre had to think about that.

He entered the quiet space and grimaced when the heat from the window wafted against his face. He took the large chair at the top of the room, as uncomfortable as it was hideous. A king of old had sat in that place at one time, deep in the recesses of history. And so Xandre sat on it today, proving his claims of power by the symbolism of the grand chair. In his titles and how is minions addressed him. In his brutality over those threatening to rise up against him. All of it was nothing more than show. A needed show, of course. Like the nobles with their silly hats and their expensive finery— they were only actors on a stage. It amazed Xandre every day that nobody saw through it. That a common- er could have all of those things with nothing more than the will to take it, yet the commoner cowered instead.

Xandre sat and surveyed those who were gathered around him, waiting. "What is the latest news?" he asked them.

"The Chosen has her own network," his leading man, One, replied. "They are springing up across the land, fighting with what little they have. It is becoming a problem."

Xandre crossed an ankle over his knee. "I did not foresee her efforts taking this long. Time has worn away our effectiveness." He sucked at his lip. This was a grievous oversight that now could not be helped. He could not rush her. When they met, Xandre wanted her to be at her best. "Continue our efforts as best we can. She is the key. With her on our side, or dead, it will be easy to regain control. Sheep need only a shepherd; any will do."

He drummed his fingers against the pockmarked wood of the armrest and let his gaze drift toward the arrow slit acting as a window. Putrid-smelling air drifted through, hot and sticky. It was a vile part of the country that unfortunately suited his plans. He longed to return home.

He took a deep, calming breath. Patience had plentiful rewards.

"What of my orders?" he asked, tearing his mind away from distant places.

"They are in the process of being carried out. Our armies are on the move, gearing up for battle. We need to get moving if we hope to meet them before she gets there."

Xandre smiled to himself, excitement surging. It was finally so close. All these long years he'd waited, and it was all about to come to fruition. "My place is right here."

Abruptly, he stood from the robust seat in the ringing silence. The soft sound of a foot shifting, of fabric rubbing, caught his ears. Containing the delighted laughter, he strolled to the arrow slit. Sparkling waters glistened in the intense sun, surging toward the base of the cliff far below. Around the front of the castle, hidden from this vantage point, was a crumbling and pockmarked wall screaming of battles waged and inevitably lost. Still, it was easily defendable, overlooking a murky, swampy sort of land that was defense in and of itself. If his immediate plans failed, she would find him, he was sure of it. This was a challenge fit for Shanti Cu-Hoi.

He almost hoped his next attempt *did* fail. That way he could study her a while longer. He wondered: if she did have to approach him, would she brave the swamp-lands? Or take to her roots and approach by boat, scaling the treacherous cliff and into Xandre's borrowed back garden? She was such a fascinating creature. So resourceful. So unexpected. She was the highlight of his dull days.

Turning around to face his Inner Circle, their per-plexity hidden behind blank expressions and hard eyes, he clasped his hands behind his back. "You may ask your questions."

"Thank you, master," One said. He paused for a second, no doubt collecting his thoughts, hopefully making them as concise as possible. "I am given to understand that we are continuing to gather our troops in preparation for a large-scale battle?"

"Yes."

One's lips tightened marginally. "So, we are staying

here, and will not be joining the battle."

"Correct."

One's shoulders tightened, annoyance at missing the opportunity to work at his trade and waste away here instead, indefinitely. Yet his mind would never deteriorate. Although boredom coated his thoughts like a heavy film, he would not break and act out of character, Xandre was sure of it. Had tested the theory mercilessly. It was why One gained both his name and position.

Silence filtered through the room again as One processed his thoughts. He was not a quick man to speak, by nature, and even less so in these situations. Xandre's patience for stupidity could only stretch so far, and all of them knew it. Finally, his head tilted downward incrementally. "Would you lower yourself to hint at your plans, master?"

"She cannot be beaten in a large battle." Xandre leaned against the wall. "Her people are not like others. Twice I have sought to annihilate them completely. The first time, so long ago in their tiny villages, I was surprised. So I studied. I planned. With the second battle I took the field, yes, but still I did not take the tribe."

Xandre looked at the ceiling and chuckled. How surprised he'd been. He'd sought the prize of prizes, and when it could've been in his clutches, she evaporated like fog in a forest fire. As elusive as a phantom and as delightfully troublesome. "They, as a people, put all their trust in that young woman. Aged beyond her years, powerful in more than just the Old Blood, she was elected to lead her line into the next generation. So wise, her people. They could've found no one better. *I* have found no one better. She is perfection. Look what she did in the Shadow Lands! Genius at work. I couldn't have achieved more."

More fabric rustled, Xandre's explanation not solid enough for their taste. The simpletons that they were, they did not see Shanti Cu-Hoi for what she really was. They thought she had luck on her side—that pinned down in one place, she could easily be beaten with just their ring of warriors.

What fools.

"She will know I am not heading into that battle." Xandre pushed away from the wall and crossed to the door. Not hearing a command to the contrary, the warriors filed in behind him, barely better than house-broken dogs. "So she will try to ferret out where I am hiding. If left to her own devices, our roles will be reversed. She will become the hunter, and I the hunted." He smiled to himself, the excitement nearly breaking free again. "Of course, it is my job to maintain the status quo. She will remain the hunted, if you do your jobs."

They descended the stairs, his heavy tread echoing

through the hollowed-out space, and silence behind him. Around the bend, with his footfalls muted as it fell on a plush blood-red rug, he continued to the back garden.

"You have orders for us, master," One said.

"I do. A small team of you will retrieve Shanti Cu-Hoi and bring her here. Her group are close—your journey will be an easy one. Hopefully the capture won't kill you all. Should you fail, however, and are still alive, you will report back and we will allow her to find us. You will not be harshly penalized should you fail in this. I almost expect that outcome."

After a slight pause, in which Xandre was sure One struggled with his irritation at being thought second best, One said, "We have told no one of this place. It will be impossible to find you. She might be moving toward the battle now. Should we not send a messenger to spread a rumor of your whereabouts and bring her back in this direction?"

"Oh my, no." Xandre waved the suggestion away. "Then she will know I am luring her. No, no. She must discover it on her own. And rest assured, she is headed our way. She has to rescue her people from my blockade. That'll keep her put for a moment. Just a moment, though. The sands are running through the hourglass."

Xandre smiled as they stalked to the south side of the castle, where a small outcropping of benches and stone seats faced a crumbling defensive wall. Beyond stretched a gulf, blue as far as the eye could see. If the weather hadn't been so horrifying, and the swamp so disgusting, the area might've been a lovely one, almost like his home.

A scarred man glanced up from a book, his face perfectly blank and his body completely lax, showing no hint of aggression. He'd almost been killed by the Graygual when they had raided his village. Rabid and on the verge of breaking. Xandre saw immediately what the strongman needed—revenge. A summons to the Graygual in question, a sword for the scarred man, a closed-off courtyard, and a gruesome fight to the death had taken the last little shred of humanity the man possessed. What remained could be molded to Xandre's needs, and with his extremely rare and necessary power, he would keep Xandre safe from Shanti Cu-Hoi's potent powers.

Xandre nodded at the man. "He'll go with you, of course. Without him you would be dead before you got within earshot."

The man glanced up, took in Xandre for a moment, and then returned to his book.

Xandre took a seat behind the man before leaning back. "You had better get working," he said over his shoulder. "She moves quickly and the whole land is rallying behind her. If you hope to capture her, you'll have to hurry before she beats you back here."

"Yes, master."

"It is so close now," Xandre said softly. The scarred man glanced his way, but knew not to speak. "And I cannot foresee what will transpire between us."

CHAPTER TWO

S HANTI STARED DOWN at the pass, frowning in consternation as the lines of Graygual made their way along. "Why are they leaving their posts?" she asked, observing the slouched posture and soiled uniforms. They looked haggard, one and all. "And where are the officers?"

"Probably took off when they heard we were coming." Sanders spat off to the side, sparing a glance for the Graygual below them before looking at the quietly assembled army behind, now made up of Shadow, Shumas, Westwood, and some from the Wanderer Network. Food and supplies were becoming a problem with the growing force. They would need to pass through a large city to get everything they required.

Shanti sighed and ran her thumb along the smooth wood of her bow. "I don't understand why Cayan doesn't want to kill them."

Sanders plucked a stalk of grass from the ground and stuck it in the corner of his mouth. "They're leaving because they received orders to leave. The captain wants to see where they are going."

"They are a large host of stinky, filthy men with deplorable morals—we'll *hear* about where they go. We don't need to see."

"Deplorable, huh? What's with the big words? Trying to show off to your new followers?"

Shanti barely kept herself from glancing at the city people, hellbent on treating her like some sort of royalty. She grimaced and thought very hard about punching Sanders.

"Don't do it," he growled. "I can see you're thinking about it. Don't do it."

Shanti shifted, crouching as she watched the Graygual trudge by. Not one of them looked up.

Curious, she picked up a small rock and lobbed it down the side of the sloping ledge. It bounced and tumbled, dislodging a few more rocks and some dirt. A mini landslide sprinkled the ground next to one of the Graygual's feet.

He didn't so much as glance over.

"We would rip through these people." Shanti squinted as she draped her arms over her knees and looked out at the setting sun. "Xandre's armies are deteriorating. Not enough fresh food, I'd wager. Poorly trained men. Maybe men missing their homes. No female sexual relief for this lot, and if there were, it probably wouldn't be voluntary. They have been reduced to animals. Worse, maybe. Broken."

"Hence the reason I am sitting here, in a pile of dirt, listening to your uplifting observations while my men wander around with their dicks in their hands, worried about the next battle but bored in the meantime. I'd really like to be home with my wife."

Shanti glanced back at the stern-faced men and women, waiting in groups for orders. Not two days before, the Graygual army had occupied the area where they now stood, watching the narrow mountain pass to ensure no one went through. On the other side of the mountain range waited a group of Shanti's people.

Hopefully they were waiting, or else Shanti would have to track them down and waste valuable time.

"Speaking of Junice," Shanti said, lowering her voice, "I was sorry to learn of her miscarriage. It must've been a blow."

"That damn twin of yours shouldn't stick his nose where it doesn't belong." Sanders looked away, pain radiating from him. His wife had been barely pregnant when Shanti first met them, but within their many battles and travels, somewhere along the way Junice's body had rejected the new life.

"It was my fault, actually," she said, feeling guilt rise up. "Rohnan has been paying closer attention to people's emotions since Daniels' murder. He asked me about your pain—it took me a while to remember what the source of that pain might be. I'm sorry about that. I should've remembered and consoled Junice when I was in the city."

Sanders huffed. "Not that it's any of your business, but it's been long enough now. She said it was for the best. Trying to care for an infant in this shithole of a land wouldn't be easy."

"I'm sure she will get pregnant again. She just needs your—"

Sanders held up a hand and shook his head. "Stop right there. I know where to stick my dick, thank you very much."

"Well, some men get the holes mixed up. You're not real bright. I'm helping."

Rough laughter burst out of Sanders. He squelched it immediately before looking down at the army. This time a few vague eyes went skyward, but nothing came of it. "Great heavens, you are a piece of work."

"Once it happened by accident. I couldn't sit right for a couple days…"

"Nope." Sanders jumped up, clearly not concerned about those passing below.

"Cayan is a large man. I wasn't ready—"

"Sayas, take over," he barked, stalking away. "She is insane."

"*What happened?*" Sayas asked in their language as he settled down beside Shanti.

Three Graygual looked up, their faces gaunt and eyes hollow. Moments later they returned their attention to the ground in front of their feet, their minds turned off like their willpower.

"Sanders needed a distraction. Any news?"

"The captain is discussing tactics with the Shadow Lord and Lucius. Tulous has joined them, if only to help bridge the gap for Poano." The happy-go-lucky glimmer in his eyes dulled. *"If she is still among them."*

"She will be," Shanti said, her own doubts stuffing the air between them.

"Rohnan muttered something about the captain missing Daniels acutely. The captain is worried, though doesn't show it. Rohnan is staying there to monitor the situation, which is probably making the captain aggravated."

"He's used to Rohnan, at this stage."

"Has to be, right? He wants to mate you, and Rohnan is basically your brother. The captain is stuck with him."

The end of the line marched past, leading the last few carrier mules. Food bags looked mostly empty, and the canvas from tents that weren't tied down was covered in stains, affirming Shanti's thoughts on the shape of the army.

"If we just wait it out, Xandre's armies might fall apart without our help." She stood, looking out over the hilltops.

"He'd still have more people than we do. How are we going to defeat him, Chosen?"

Shanti blew out a breath. She had no idea. *"C'mon, let's find Cayan and get on the way. I'm anxious to see our people."*

"WHAT'S THAT, SIR?" Leilius asked, inching away from the high-powered commanders and hard-eyed Shadow. He'd never felt easy in the captain's presence, and even less so among the Shadow, who made weird jokes about skinning and boiling people. Leilius was positive that the foreigners were responding to the bedtime stories intended to scare Westwood Lands children into behaving, which Gracas had told them about, but the Shadow joked with a little too much gusto for Leilius' taste.

"This is the job you've been trained to do," the captain said, thickening Leilius' tongue with his hard stare. "The city of Belos is only a ways up the road. I want you to get the lay of the land. See if it's occupied."

A ways up the road? Leilius would have to follow the Graygual at a safe distance through the mountain pass, hoping there were no robbers, and then it was a huge distance from there on open road if the maps he had seen had been anything to go by. Leilius had never been this far southeast, but it seemed stark and bare, for the most part. There would be nowhere to hide.

"But sir," Leilius said, raising a finger. "The towns-people are bound to know who I am, right? I'm kinda tall for this part of the world, and people from the town we conquered left for other places. I'm sure to see someone who recognizes me. Because, you know—it's not a big deal, really—but I was kind of known there…"

No flash of knowing passed over the captain's eyes.

"I helped out that old woman. Did S'am tell you?" he tried again. His legs started to shake under the captain's commanding stare. The attempt to get out of this journey was not going well.

"Shanti has assured me that you can hide yourself, even in the midst of family and friends," the captain said, thankfully breaking the tense silence.

Leilius cursed S'am and her belief in him. "Yes, sir, but—"

"Good. I want you to find Burson if you can, but most importantly, send a pigeon to us with any infor-mation you can glean. We badly need supplies, but I don't want to risk another battle. If there are Graygual, I need numbers and positions. Do you understand?"

"Yes, sir. If I may ask, sir…is anyone going with me?"

"I'll be sending Boas with you. He is darkening his hair now."

Was that gulp audible? Leilius wasn't sure, but as he

croaked out a "yes, sir," he definitely heard a couple snickers from those gathered around the map. He would almost rather go alone than with a Shadow and their serious manner of joking about cannibalism.

THREE HOURS LATER, riding some excellent horses and mostly in silence, they made it out of the mountain passes and onto a hard-packed dirt track big enough for one cart to travel at a time. Given the lack of tracks along the sides, however, it didn't seem that carts often traveled that way. At least not enough to leave lasting marks.

Trees thinned further as they made their way along the natural slope of the land. Scraggly bushes crouched along the sides and yellowed grasses waved in the thick, warm breeze.

Leilius wiped the sweat from his forehead and stared out in front of them, where a plume of dust rose in the air. He could just see the line of enemy making their way north and sighed in relief.

"Why do you sigh, little boy?" Boas asked with a twinkle in his eyes.

Leilius hunched in his saddle.

Boas was partially quoting the line "Why do you lie, little boy?" part of a nursery rhyme that ended in a Shadow person stealing naughty children in the middle of the night and roasting them over a fire. *Be a good boy and you have nothing to fear, Leilius,* his mother had always said. *Only bad little boys need to worry about the Shadow people...*

Very graphic, those nursery rhymes, and unlike the rest of the Honor Guard, Leilius had always had an inventive imagination when it came to danger. The problem was, actually knowing the Shadow now, the real stories were ten times more terrifying.

"Their army is going a different direction than we are." Leilius watched the ground, observing the recent dents and scuffs of hooves and boots.

"Let's hope that is not because they don't want to double the size of the army in Belos, huh?"

"Kind of strange to pull them out of there right when S'am is ready to go through, right?" Leilius glanced back at the retreating mountain pass. "It's almost like she passed some kind of test, and now the Being Supreme—"

"Call him by his name. Do not give him the power of a title."

Leilius cleared his throat. "It is almost like Xandre is giving her a pass to the next thing."

"Or he is saving his men, knowing she would've demolished them. *Should* have demolished them. The captain wants to see their next move. Where they station." Boas sniffed. "Xandre will not so easily show his hand. The captain is missing his strategist, I think.

He is not thinking things through."

Leilius felt a pang of loss for Daniels. "The captain always thinks things through. Besides, who cares if they go? What's a few hundred more Graygual?"

"A few hundred more to defeat when things are dire, that's what. You are young—you haven't seen much of battle. A few hundred can tip the scales in a close battle."

"Not wishing to incite a fistfight in which I'll surely lose, but I've probably seen more large-scale battles than you. But what I meant was, Xandre has a whole land of people who will fight. A whole land. Those few hundred will just increase the weight on the scales already tipped in his favor. I agree with the captain—we can learn something from their movements. More than we could learn from their death, at any rate."

Boas' face turned in Leilius' direction. The horses clomped on, oblivious to the tall, lean man now staring at Leilius unflinchingly. After a tense few minutes, in which those eyes didn't divert, Boas said, "Westwood has thick roots. You are a headstrong, stubborn sort of people. Shanti chose well."

Images of what this man was capable of flitted through Leilius' mind. He had once seen Boas rip the throat out of an Inkna. He *ripped the throat out* with his bare hands! And now the same man was close enough to reach out and grab him in a fit of anger. Or throw him off his horse then stomp on his head. Or any number of things that Leilius wouldn't be able to come back from...

He shivered and looked the other way, fighting his indulgent imagination. "I wonder how many Inner Circle guards Xandre has."

After another quiet moment, Leilius heard, "That is the real question, I think. A whole land of starving men with swords is one thing, but a host of excellently trained, probably well taken care of, expert fighters is..."

"It is a solid defense even if we get past all the other obstacles," Leilius finished, feeling despondency settle over him. It had been happening a lot since news of Daniels had reached him. Their big victory had been immediately diminished. They'd thought they were safe behind the large walls and tight defenses.

Not only had the enemy snuck in without being seen, but they'd taken out two skilled swordsmen, grabbed the prisoner, and left just as quietly. It was a wake-up call. Nowhere was safe. They were dealing with someone who knew no limits, someone who could think his way over any hurdle, and move his pawns accordingly.

He shook his head as another thought struck him. The Inner Circle had been allowed close to S'am in the last few months. They'd followed her, and certainly been the party that had freed the prisoner…which meant there was no reason why they weren't watching S'am now. Three of those men stalking around, with the prisoner to disguise their minds, was more dangerous than hundreds of sickly Graygual.

Leilius looked around wildly, his mind's eye seeing silent, stalking men everywhere—crouched in the shadows of bushes, or sucking in their guts behind the thin trees. "We should've brought more people."

"Why?" Boas asked.

"Because we've just separated from the herd. Predators always go after the loners who wander away. We might as well have a target on our backs."

CHAPTER THREE

"THERE THEY ARE!" S'am exclaimed, a rare child-like excitement ringing through her voice. "Look!" She threw out her hand, pointing at a small collection of glowing lights of fires in the distance. Her people clearly weren't worried about the enemy. They were making no attempt to hide themselves.

Marc wiped his eyes and glanced back at the distant mountains, springing up like colossal teeth in the darkening sky. They'd barely waited for the Graygual to clear out of the pass before readying their horses and soldiers and hiking down. While S'am hadn't known exactly where her people would be camped, she'd had a general idea and headed in that direction.

"I wish they were further out," Xavier murmured from his horse beside Marc's.

"Why?" Marc slapped at a bug buzzing around his face.

"Because it doesn't look like the Graygual are inter-ested in protecting this area. It'd be nice for a few more days of peace before we get back to fighting." He rolled his shoulders.

"I'd rather get it all over with. Once and for all."

"Do you think there will be a once and for all?"

Marc looked at the moon, large and full in an expansive sky speckled with stars. "Eventually. We might die getting there, though. That's the bad news."

Xavier huffed. "You're becoming as jaded as Sanders."

"Now we know why he is jaded."

Their band of fierce warriors and random followers continued on in near silence. In the moonlight, Marc could just make the backs of those ahead of him, clearly ready for an attack. Xavier might've felt safe way out there, but Marc did not. Not many of them probably did. They wouldn't be safe until Xandre was dead, along with all his minions.

The glow of the fires grew as they neared. Their horses picked up speed as the leaders pushed on faster despite the darkness. It must've been the Shumas, eager to meet people they thought they'd never see again. The figures around the fires stood, the light flickering against their lean bodies. A touch pressed against Marc's mind, like when S'am checked on him. He doubted this was S'am, though. The Shumas were making sure there were no surprises.

S'am and Rohnan leapt off their horses and ran at the fires. The rest of the Shumas quickly followed, delaying everyone else. Laughter and talking burst into the quiet night as the two groups met.

Non-Shumas waited awkwardly on their horses at a distance. Marc felt awkward.

"At least we keep adding the best of the best," he mumbled.

"Is that what you call the loud woman who keeps grabbing my junk and promising me a free ride?" Xavier growled. He glanced over his shoulder, but did not appear to see who he was looking for.

"I'd probably be annoyed if every woman I met wanted to get a piece of me," Gracas said from behind them. "But since they act like I'm diseased, I'd take the ride, and say *thank you* when I was done."

"Nothing is ever free." Xavier shook his head as a group of Shumas walked toward the front of their line of horses. The captain swung a leg over his mount and gracefully jumped down. A few female gasps preceded a rattle of speech that sounded suspiciously like "Do you share?"

Marc grimaced, thinking about the large prostitute who constantly leered at Xavier. "She'd use you, rob you, maybe stick a knife in your ribs, or perhaps chain you up for her own personal benefit. I try not to go near her or her women. They are too cunning by half, and know exactly what it is they are selling."

"We all know what they are selling. If the captain

would let me buy, I would," Gracas said. "He says I'm too young."

"It's not what they are selling that you have to worry about; it's what they take in addition to the agreed-on price." Xavier shook his head again. "No thank you. I'd rather go about all that honestly."

"Maybe I would, too, if I was a dopey-eyed pretty boy like you." Rachie shifted on his horse, which then stamped its foot.

"Better a dopey-eyed pretty boy than a slack-jawed idiot who smells like ass," Xavier retorted.

"Dismount!" Sanders barked as he made his way down the line. The plane of his face flashed their way, hiding the heated and impatient gaze that was bound to be looking out of it. "Let's go. Get the horses squared away, get some dinner on, get tents up—you know the drill. We're here for the night."

"I miss my bed," Rachie moaned as he swung his leg over his horse and dropped down like a sack of pota-toes. He rubbed his thighs. "I never want to see another horse again."

"It's a helluva lot better than walking." Gracas punched him for no discernible reason.

"What the hell, Gracas?" Rachie swung but Gracas turned slightly at the last second, lightning fast. Rachie's fist sailed through the air. He took a jarring step, pivoted, and kicked. His foot connected with Gracas' thigh.

Gracas hit the dirt as Xavier stepped in, pushing Rachie back and bracing for Gracas' retaliation. "Stop. If Sanders doesn't brain you, S'am will sort it out. I doubt you want that."

Both guys slowed. Rachie wiped the corner of his mouth where a dribble of blood leaked out.

It was then Marc felt the presence, like a weight pushing against his back. He hunched, lowered his head, and backed toward his horse without a word. Behind him, as he'd thought, stood the captain, tall and broad and full of lethal muscle. Without looking up, Marc knew the captain's intense gaze was trying to bore a hole in the top of his head.

"What's going on here?" the captain asked, looking them over.

Xavier's eyes rounded and his spine went straightened. "N-nothing, sir," he squeaked out before clearing his throat. "They're just tired and not thinking, sir. We're about to take care of the horses."

Gracas struggled to his feet. Rachie looked anywhere but at the intense man standing in front of him.

"Don't embarrass Shanti in front of her people."

"No, sir," Xavier said as the captain moved on. "Of course, sir." They waited a minute, watching him walk down the line, before Xavier slugged Gracas in the shoulder. "Nice going."

SHANTI WATCHED THE HONOR GUARD as they slunk away with their horses in Cayan's wake. They were wound up, fearful, and anxious. Like most of the army. No one liked the unexpected, especially when it didn't make sense.

As if hearing her thoughts, Rohnan said, *"The issue with the Graygual just leaving isn't sitting right with everyone."*

Pahona, their best strategist and a formidable fighter despite her short stature, turned her attention to Rohnan. *"They just left? Without fighting?"*

"Yes," Shanti said, fighting the urgency as she turned back to the more than two dozen fighters she'd once thought she'd lost. She allowed a moment to drink them in, their familiar faces flickering in the light of the nearby fires. She took a deep breath and sighed. *"It is good to see you all."*

"Why are you sitting out here in the open?" Kallon asked. *"It appears that you are inviting the enemy to advance."*

With that, the overall attitude sobered. Pahona shifted and moved, looking back through the crowd. *"Bring up Alexa."*

Shanti felt her confusion even as her heart surged when Cayan started back toward her, satisfied with his check-in but trying to hide the unease boiling deep within him. She couldn't help looking back, catching the sway of his shoulders and his graceful movements, indicating the excellent fighter that he was. Energy sizzled between them when he reached her and ran a warm hand down her back. As she turned back to her people, a strange, grounded sense came over her. Her family, her people, and now her mate were all together. They stood in the wilds of the world, in a barren hell not far from danger, and still she felt a surge of hope.

After all this time, and all the traveling, she'd finally brought together the best the land had to offer, and now she would pit them against the best Xandre could produce. When it came to experienced, excellent fighters, and potent *Gifts,* she outweighed him.

She could win.

She could beat Xandre.

Her heart swelled and fire roared through her body.

She could win. And would. Then she'd make Cayan plant a garden outside their home, within the Westwood Lands, and they'd try for children. Xandre had tarnished her past, but he wouldn't steal her future.

"What are you thinking, love?" Cayan asked in a soft voice.

Her people had all fallen quiet, no doubt feeling the energy heating her blood.

"Our destiny awaits," she said in a hum, the lightning of her power crackling. Cayan's power surged in response. "Let's find Xandre and end this."

A cheer rose up behind them, Cayan's men yelling out their approval. Shadow nodded their heads. Esme, the Shadow Lord, grinned, her eyes flashing in the flickering glow.

"Can we eat dinner first?" Sanders asked with a dry voice. "Maybe get a little shut eye before the charge starts?"

Everyone laughed and the moment died away. *For now*, Shanti thought. The desire to fight, and to win, was still there. These men and women were more than ready. They were eager.

Shanti assessed the girl they'd brought forward. She blinked in disbelief and leaned forward, not expecting the young woman standing in front of her. The last time Shanti had spoken to her had been well before the battle that chased her from her home. Then, Alexa had been a gangly teen, just budding into a woman.

"You remember Alexa?" Pahona asked.

"We're going to need translation if you talk about anything essential," Cayan said. "I am learning, but they speak quickly."

"I will do it," Rohnan said.

"I do." Shanti nodded at the young woman. *"You've changed."*

"I have worked hard every day, Chosen." Alexa stepped forward, earnest. *"I will not make you sorry for*

keeping me with the fighters."

It hadn't been Shanti's choice. The prophecies had a hand in Alexa being kept from safety with the younger children. That was what the elders had said, anyway.

"*She has developed* Seer *abilities,*" Pahona said gravely.

"Ah crap, not another one," Sanders blurted out after Rohnan translated. "Burson was bad enough."

"*The problem is, her abilities are unreliable,*" Pahona continued. "*They seem to result from extreme duress. After uttering the prophecy, she has no recollection of her words. If no one is there to hear her, or if her words are drowned out, they are lost.*"

"*That is not ideal for battle,*" Shanti said. "*How are her fighting skills?*"

"*Excellent. She has made a place for herself, despite her age. She has a strong* Warring Gift *that she uses gracefully with her fighting.*" Pahona shifted, uncomfortable. "*My worry is that she will be in the heart of battle, freeze up with an upcoming prophecy, and either be run through, or her words will never be heard. If she is the turning point in a situation, then we could have an issue on our hands.*"

"Put her with Marc," Cayan said without hesitation. "He often drags the Honor Guard to the edges of battle, and they could use someone with mental ability watching their backs. When she freezes, he'll see it and call one of the others back to save her."

"*What is this Honor Guard?*" someone asked. Shanti couldn't make out who, but suspicion rang through his words.

"*I am training them. Here…*" Shanti turned, looking for them among the horses.

"I got it," Sanders said, and stalked away.

"*I'd like to try him in a fight,*" Pahona muttered, watching Sanders disappear into the darkness. "*He is a surly sort, is he not? Prone to temper?*"

"*I'd be careful there,*" Shanti said, unable to prevent a smile. "*He rules his temper; it does not rule him. He uses it like an effective weapon. And he has a wife. Rohnan, bring them up to speed with the Westwood Lands' social rules. I don't want to backslide.*"

Shanti barely heard Kallon mutter, "*Prudish.*"

"Hurry up," Sanders barked, shoving someone in front of him. "I'm hungry."

"What does that have to do with us, sir?" Marc asked. "We're not in charge of cooking."

"What happens when you question senior officers?" Sanders growled, grabbing Gracas by the scruff of his neck and moving him along. A horse neighed as they passed.

"A kick in the hole, sir," Rachie answered.

"That's right, nitwit. A kick in the hole."

"Sorry, sir," Marc mumbled.

The ragtag crew assembled to one side, the girls in the group wisely remaining silent and on the other side of the boys, out of Sanders' immediate reach.

"They were a distraction at first," Shanti said, looking them over with a critical eye for the first time in a long time. Since she'd first known them, they'd filled out and owned their bodies. Mostly confident, if sometimes still clueless, they stood straight and broad, tall and thick, like the rest of their people. Most sported stacked muscle and the fluid grace of a fighter, only a few, like Marc and Xavier, looked at those assembled in front of them with assessing stares. The girls, too, had gained muscle and an awareness of their person, knowing what they were physically capable of, and used to pushing past their boundaries to survive.

They'd come a long way, this crew, and had earned their right to be in the army.

"They were a project, at first," she continued. *"They've been with me since I stumbled onto their doorstep. They've seen a lot of action, they know how to work with us, and they are still alive, which is saying something."*

"How are they going to understand each other?" Sanders asked, bracing his fists on his hips. "If she spouts off some helpful prophecies, it won't matter if they can hear her or not; they won't be able to understand her."

"I can speak their language," Marc mumbled, his face pointed at the ground. "I've been working hard with Rohnan."

"He is very smart. Picks up new languages very fast." Rohnan nodded his approval.

A strange, equine growl rent the night, followed by the sound of men yelling. Shanti sighed and shook her head. "That damn bastard of a horse. He *still* won't let people see to him."

"I've tried punching him, Shoo-lan," Sanders said. "Like you do. He tries to kick me. Don't let it be said that I shied away."

"Yeah, you did," Rachie said. "You ran when it tried to kick you." As if he realized he'd just voiced his thought, his mouth audibly clicked shut.

"Cayan's plan is a good one," Shanti said, back on track. *"We'll put her with the Honor Guard. They are used to our way of doing things. She can protect Marc until she has a premonition, in which case he can protect her while screaming for help."*

"I said I can understand the language," Marc murmured. *"I know you're embarrassing me."*

"Alexa." Shanti waited for the girl's hard eyes to hit her own. She wasn't overjoyed about being sent to be with people her own age, Shanti bet. That would last until she saw them actually fight. *"Xavier is your commanding officer, which means he gives the orders.*

He's smarter and faster than he looks. Underestimate him, or any of these Westwood Lands guys, and you'll be sorry. However, they will often underestimate you. They are not used to working with women, even now. Take advantage of it. If they will not hit you, make them sorry."

A sly grin crept up her face. *"Yes, Chosen."*

"Xavier." Shanti shifted to include him. "This is Alexa." She indicated whom she was speaking about. She hadn't needed to. Xavier was staring with a slack jaw and intense eyes. In fact, a lot of the guys were. "What's the matter?"

"If you guys don't keep your hands to yourselves, that girl will cut off your dick and kick it around the ground, do you hear me?" Sanders barked.

"Didn't need to be said, sir," Xavier said, straightening awkwardly. "I was just taken aback."

"They'll work it out," Cayan said, laughter in his voice. "Are you finished here? I'd like to help you with your horse, then we can discuss what we need to do over dinner."

Shanti frowned at him. Why he wanted to help with her horse, she had no idea. She relayed what he'd said to her people and let Cayan lead her away.

His fingers entwined with hers. "You have a new fire within you," he said into the night. Large horses loomed off to the right, tied to whatever was available, and eating. Men moved around and between them, finishing settling them for the night.

Off to the left, tents were going up and fires started.

"Are we sure we want to advertise our whereabouts in case anyone has followed us?" she asked.

"With this much mental power, it would take a large host to take us. We'll hear them coming if that's the case. I'm not worried."

Shanti let it drop as she came upon a city dweller giving her horse a lot of distance.

"I couldn't do anything with him, ma'am," he said. He had joined them as part of the Wanderer Network, claiming to have a certain magic with animals. Joke was on him, clearly.

"I'll take care of it." Shanti reached her horse and slapped him. He struck out, trying to catch her with his hoof. She stuck up a finger. "Now we're on the same footing. Behave!" He chomped at her digit.

Gritting her teeth, wondering if this would be another battle of wills, she stared at him, waiting to see if he needed another slap. Miraculously, he bobbed his head and huffed.

She got to work, taking off his saddle while Cayan readied his feed.

"We have all the pieces now," Shanti said to Cayan. "All the players, I should say. My people, the Shadow, you... We have a lot of power behind us."

"We don't have information. That is what we are still missing." Cayan stared at the Bastard as he approached, playing tough. The Bastard stared back, not playing at being surly.

"Just put it down and let him walk to it, Cayan. Help me with the saddle."

"What help do you need?" Cayan asked, coming up beside her.

She handed him the heavy item. "Your muscle. I'm tired."

"We'll hit the closest town and look for information," Cayan said, taking the saddle without complaint. "It looks like Xandre is amassing his armies. I want to see if he keeps adding to one location, or if he is planning to section them off into a few."

"What will the difference tell you?"

"Likely not as much as it would've told Daniels." Pain radiated through Cayan. Shanti left the Bastard to eat and slid her hands up Cayan's chest before looping them around his shoulders. He leaned into her. "That was what he had been studying before he was murdered."

"We can't replace Daniels," Shanti said as his face dipped to hers. She closed her eyes as his hands ducked under her top and roamed over her skin. "But Pahona is an excellent tactician, and a few of the others work well with her. We can use his notes and see if we can piece things together. We are not lost."

"I know," he whispered. "We will come out of this alive, you and I. Whatever his plans, however large an army he throws at us, we will still come out alive."

She smiled. "I know."

CHAPTER FOUR

"THEY'RE GAINING ON US!" Leilius clutched the reins of his horse and leaned forward, his breathing rapid. "How did you not feel them coming? I thought people couldn't sneak up on you."

The city loomed in front of them, the welcoming torches on the gates twinkling. Behind them, five Graygual with drawn swords on huffing horses were in pursuit.

"I knew they were back there. I didn't want to panic you."

"It didn't work. I'm panicking. I am really panicking!" He urged his horse faster. "C'mon, c'mon. Run, damn you!"

"Don't push him too fast. This road is smooth, but you never know if he might hit a divot and break his ankle. Horses can't see in the dark."

Leilius chanced a look behind him. The Graygual were gaining, swords gleaming in the moonlight.

"We're not going to make it. We have to stop and fight. Otherwise they'll just hack us down."

"Good plan." Boas was too calm by half. Clearly they were outnumbered, or he would already have used his mental power and wiped them all out. In times like this he really missed the might of S'am and the captain. "Should we stop now, or would you like to run a little more?"

"Why are you so calm? We don't stand a chance against them!"

"You should never go into battle with a frenzied head, young Leilius. It will derail your confidence, and that will kill you. Let's fight now. Whoa!" Boas pulled the reins to stop his horse.

Leilius did the same thing, almost losing control and falling. He regained his composure and jumped from his horse, hitting the ground with a stagger and ripping out his sword.

"No, no, you must stay on your horse or you will be run down." Boas waved him back.

"*Stupid!*" Swearing at himself, Leilius gritted his teeth and ran back to his horse. He had never been very good at fighting—the captain *knew* that. Why had he sent him with just one man?

The thunder of hooves shook the ground. Leilius' horse neighed and reared, forcing Leilius back. A Graygual headed right for him, his sword out. Nowhere to go, nothing else to do, Leilius stepped forward and braced himself, ready to dodge left and swipe at the animal as it passed.

Bearing down on him, the horse screamed. The animal reared, lifting its front feet into the sky and kicking wildly. The Graygual flew, one arm windmilling, while his sword hand remained largely steady. Clearly this group was trained.

As the Graygual hit the ground, Leilius was there, digging his sword into the man's ribs.

Another Graygual came right behind the first. Leilius dodged the hooves of the flailing animal in front of him and surged for the second. He slashed, slicing down the side of the horse.

"Sorry," he muttered as the animal screamed. He hated hurting the innocent, regardless of whether they were human. It reared, but the Graygual stayed on, balanced. This one was definitely well trained.

The second the horse's front hooves touched the ground, the Graygual struck downward, aiming for Leilius' head.

Reacting blindly, he rolled. Something tugged at his tunic. The sword passing by!

He thrust upward, on one knee, and then the tip of his sword found a home in the animal's belly. The horse screamed again as Leilius squeezed his eyes shut and ripped, ending the poor thing's life a little faster—causing suffering was no fun.

The horse collapsed, but not before two feet landed

with a thump right beside him. His heart pounding wildly, he jumped and slashed, with no real control. His blade miraculously stuck in soft flesh!

"Behind you!" Leilius heard.

He jumped up, spinning around, just missing a blade coming at his head. Its trajectory changed immediately, now arching down toward his shoulder. At the last second, he twisted. The blade glinted as it narrowly missed. The Graygual cried out, dropping his sword into the dirt. The man sank to the ground and began to writhe.

Leilius yanked his head upward, looking for Inkna looming in the night. Instead, as the last screams died away, silence rained down.

"What's happening?" Leilius asked quietly, seeing that Boas stood off to the side, straight and broad, oozing confidence. The reality sank in. "Oh good, you used your power. Thanks."

"The Chosen was right, it seems. You are adept, if a bit clumsy still. I apologize for that last strike. I did not think you'd get out of the way in time. I should've let you continue the fight and claim your victory."

All Leilius could do was shake his head in frustration. He didn't need a battle victory to feel good about himself. An ale and a warm bed afterward would be plenty. He would rather Boas had taken care of all of those Graygual and then moved along to an inn.

"As for what we are doing," Boas continued, stalking toward his horse. Why he'd gotten off to fight by hand, Leilius did not know, but he wouldn't be asking. "We're taking a moment to bask in a battle won."

"I thought we were done for."

"You can always see what someone is made of when they are under pressure. Pity about that horse. C'mon, we'll take the rest of the Graygual animals and sell them. They'll fetch a fine price."

"Can you just handle it next time this happens?" Leilius threw a leg over the saddle. "I'm much better at not being seen than fighting."

"We shall see."

The rest of the ride passed in silence, with Leilius' frown firmly in place. He had no idea where those other Graygual had come from, except from *behind*, and didn't trust they would be the last. He'd been challenged with his fighting prowess, and wondered how he'd be challenged once in the city. If it was anything like that last skirmish, it wouldn't be pretty.

"City is closed at sundown," a man yelled from the top of the wall next to the artful metal workings of the gate. A collection of crude boards covered the other side of the gate, ruining the facing and preventing visibility into the city. "You'll have to wait until morning."

"Do you deny the Graygual entrance?" Boas called up, his stare unwavering.

The man leaned an elbow onto the wall, peering through the darkness at them. "We ain't got no choice in the matter. If we don't let them in, they cause a lot of problems."

"I see. Rest assured, friend, we're just honest folk that got held up by bandits. If not for that, we would've been here by sundown. There's just the two of us. We just want to sell these horses and be on our way."

The man's gaze settled on Leilius. "He don't talk much."

"I just want a hot meal, a pint of ale, and a soft bed," Leilius said, in a temper. "If you don't let me in, I'll abandon these horses and climb the wall where you can't see me. I'm tired."

Boas stiffened. The man paused for a moment, his expression lost to the night, before bursting out laughing. "Can't begrudge a man an honest answer. Okay, then."

The man's head disappeared from the top of the wall. After a silent beat, metal clanged and a crank sounded. One gate drifted open wide enough to allow them through.

The flickering glow from the torches stationed on the sides of the guard station highlighted the well-worked saddles and groomed, healthy horses of the Graygual.

The guard stood atop a platform in front of a large

metal crank. He whistled, his eyes trained on the excellent horse stock. "You'd be wanting to go straight to the Ha-Ra Inn with those horses. No one else will be able to afford them."

"Thank you for the information." Boas handed up a coin.

The man gestured Boas on impatiently. After he'd closed the gate, he turned back and pointed at the captured horses. "Those from the bandits you spoke of?"

"Yes."

The man's eyes roved over the animals before turning to Leilius and then Boas' horses. "Different stock to the ones you're riding, but similar origin…"

"They are also from Graygual, yes," Boas said. "None of which are still alive."

"Cat's out of the bag now," Leilius mumbled. A flicker of movement caught his eye. He glanced up, only to see a blur disappear behind from a rooftop. "You better have enough range for bystanders with bows, because I don't dodge arrows as well as I do sword thrusts."

Boas gave him a constipated look as the guard shifted.

"You're not from around here," the guard said.

"No," Boas answered. "Can you point us toward a good inn?"

The guard squinted. He pointed off to the right. "Head that way until you get to the blacksmith. Turn left. There are a few inns right up that way. Ha-Ra Inn isn't far beyond that."

"Thank you, good sir." Boas nodded and clicked his tongue to get his horse moving.

"Mind yourself," the guard called after them. "Outsiders are watched pretty closely around here."

"He does not favor the Graygual," Boas said as they walked their horses away. Hooves on cobblestone echoed against the buildings. "When I said I killed them, I felt his mood shift."

"I doubt many people like the Graygual."

"True. But he was not afraid. That is good."

"We should've asked him how many there were in the city. It would've saved us some time."

Boas glanced down an alleyway. Leilius couldn't see his eyes, but the way his head turned as the horse walked on told him he was looking at someone.

"See anything?" Leilius asked softly.

"See? No. But someone is there, lurking. They are up to no good. There is crime in this city."

"There's crime in every city."

"True."

When they turned left, smaller dwellings slowly turned into storefronts with hanging signs. While the usual city grime was evident, this one seemed cleaner than most. The streets were mostly swept, shops lined their windows with their wares, and signs boasted fresh paint.

"S'am once said that the Graygual officers make the townspeople keep their town clean. I wonder if some higher-level officers were here." Leilius leaned to the side, trying to peer in a window. Knives and various weapons called to him, asking him to buy something sharp and light. "I need to get a new knife tomorrow."

"The guard at the gate wouldn't have acted the way he did if the officers were still here. So then, if they were once here, why did they leave?" Boas watched a drunk man stagger down the road. The man burped loudly before staring down Boas.

"Problem?" he asked in a gruff voice.

Boas didn't answer, just continued to stare.

"Don't pick a fight, please," Leilius murmured. "Let's just get to an inn."

"He is spoiling for a fight. Seems a waste not to engage."

More people wandered the streets now, most of them swaying from their card games and drinking. One man had a buxom woman under each arm, only pausing in his talking to take in their delighted laughter. Their efforts to keep him upright were unmistakable.

Boas huffed out a laugh. "He will pay them to tuck him in."

"I'll doubt they'll go that far. They'll probably drug him and just drop him on his bed."

"You are very knowledgeable for one so young."

"At first I was interested in the stories Tauneya's women told. Kind of exciting, know what I mean?"

"No."

Leilius scowled at him. "Well, anyway, they started getting really raunchy when they found out I was a virgin. I couldn't get away from them then. Now I know all the swindling tricks, whether I want to or not. Any desire I had for a prostitute has been shattered."

"I wonder that you ever had any in the first place. They don't even excel at pretending. They are nothing more than a warm body for a desperate man."

"Clearly you have been a desperate man, huh?"

"No, but I was curious. The question was answered. I had a rash to show for it."

"Why would you share that?" Leilius shook his head and pointed at the first inn up the way. "That place looks okay."

"It looks expensive. We'll go further."

"The cheaper ones have fleas."

Boas smiled. "You and they will have something in common."

"I'm not the one that just admitted to a rash."

"It went away."

"Yeah, sure. That's probably what everyone says."

"Yes."

Leilius ignored Boas' grin. He was probably lying about the whole encounter. One never could trust his stories when he had that grin.

Yelling drew Leilius' attention. Two men fell out of a doorway, wrapped in each other's arms and writhing. They rolled over before one got his arm free and started pummeling the other. A woman screamed and ran out after them, holding her skirt with one hand and a mug in the other. She stooped and struck the aggressor on the head. He grunted and slowed, allowing the other man to get free and jump to his feet.

The freed man brought his foot back before delivering a kick, catching the downed man in the ribs. The woman grabbed the standing man's shirt sleeve and started to pull him away down the street.

"That is the right place. Let's stay there." Boas started toward the stables attached to the inn.

"Nope," Leilius said, crossing his arms. "No way."

A big-bellied man filled the entrance to the inn. A hard expression coated his flat face. He crossed his arms, much like Leilius had, and leaned against the doorway, looking out.

"No way," Leilius said again under his breath, hunching a little. He was on a fine horse, leading two other fine animals, in front of what must be the roughest inn in town. There was no way he'd blend in.

With a change of mind, he straightened and

dropped his arms, now holding the reins with feigned confidence in an air of nobility.

The man in the doorway spat. He wiped his chin with the back of his hand before recrossing his arms. Smears stained the white apron spreading across the expanse of his stomach.

That man wouldn't be impressed by much, Leilius had a feeling. He might just go back to hunching.

"Let's go." Boas sauntered out of the stables with his natural killer's grace. The man in the doorway's facial expression didn't change. "There is room for all the animals."

"No," Leilius said in a low tone. He didn't want the man in the doorway, who was probably the cook, to hear. For all Leilius knew, the man would get offended, pull a knife out of nowhere, and throw it at Leilius' head. "Let's go back to the other place."

"Here we go." Boas took his horse's reins.

"No!" Leilius said through clenched teeth. "This is *my* show. *I* call the shots, and I say we're not—" Pain rolled through his body and seized up his jaw. Waves of agony vibrated his bones, freezing him in place. Boas took the opportunity that he had obviously created to calmly lead Leilius around the side and to the stables. There, without letting up on the body-consuming horror that coursed through Leilius' veins, Boas pushed his shoulder and knocked him off the horse.

CHAPTER FIVE

"WE'LL NEED TO board this one as well," Boas said to someone wearing shit-stained boots.

"Is that guy okay?" someone with a young-sounding voice asked.

"Yes. He's just suffering from a momentary case of idiocy. Soon he'll think with his brain instead of his shriveled nut sack."

"If you say so," the stable hand said.

Another pair of boots walked over and stopped by Leilius' head. Boas looked down on him. "Are you playing dead?" The pain receded, and Boas bent with his hands on his knees. "I have not seen that before. But look, it clearly works."

That was why Leilius always fell back on that approach.

He shook off the pain. "I realize you want to stay here because the men are obviously drunkards, and drunk men talk…" Leilius opened his mouth wide before rotating his jaw to loosen it up. "But when they are fighting, they don't say anything worth listening to."

Leilius straightened out, jittery with the remnants of pain that the mind took longer than the body to forget. "We'd be better off in a less violent place."

"Fighters are wary of those they cannot easily dominate. They steer clear enough to stay out of a fist's reach, but not so far as to miss weaknesses. They will know the most about the Graygual, I should think. Besides, you are not limited by the inn. You can go wherever your heart desires, as long as you bring back information."

Instead of heading into the inn through the stable door, as normal patrons would've done, they walked back around to the street. Boas stood there for a moment, staring straight ahead.

"What are we doing?" Leilius asked, slinking to the side.

"Just looking." Boas glanced right, stared for a moment longer, before turning in that direction and heading toward the inn door. He stopped in front of the man in the doorway. He'd made no move to clear to the side. "Do you work here?"

The man shook his head.

"*Do you work here?*" Boas repeated in the traders' dialect.

"*No. I wear a dirty apron for the love of it,*" the man replied.

"*Do you also stand in doorways, blocking patrons, for*

the love of it?"

The man surveyed Boas for a moment. His arms lowered slowly and he took a step back. *"It is not wise to think you are the best warrior in the room before you have entered the room."*

"This is true. Luckily, I think I am the best warrior in the whole city. Since I have already entered the city, and have not yet found my equal, I am confident this room will be no different."

The man turned without a word, leading them further into the hovel that did not, even remotely, match the relatively well kept exterior. The banister of the staircase had pockmarks and missing spindles. Suspicious brown patches stained the floor, hinting at the results of various fights. Through an archway with peeling paint lay an expansive room with rickety tables and chairs, a couple of booths, and a large bar lining the back. Jeers and laughter rolled through the smoke-filled air. Glasses clinked. A woman cackled.

The man gestured toward a ruddy-faced woman behind the bar who was cleaning a glass. Her breasts were pushed up to her neck and held there, ample cleavage for any eye to get lost in. Of course, there were probably weapons lost in there too, hidden until the need arose.

"Maggie'll get ya sorted," the man said, walking behind the bar and looking out at the rowdy game players.

Wood screeched against the floor. A man stood, knocking over his chair. He swept the cards to the ground and yelled something in a language Leilius had never heard before.

The woman's gaze focused, tracking the disturbance. She muttered something.

The man shrugged and leaned against the bar, watching two men square off by the fireplace.

"How many rooms?" the woman asked, scanning Boas and then Leilius. Her gaze touched each thing of value, big and small, on their persons.

"Two," Boas answered in a bored voice. "Boarding for six horses."

The woman's gaze locked with Boas' as yelling erupted behind them. She didn't seem to notice. "Six horses, you say?"

"Yes. Graygual horses. It would be best that they remain in my possession."

"It would be best if they were not in my stable."

"Better that you keep them safe than if you allow someone to take them."

The man, who could have been the woman's husband, shifted. His gaze wasn't on Boas, though. It was on Leilius.

Leilius edged away a little, unsure of why he was suddenly the object of scrutiny.

The woman tsked and raised her eyebrows. "Such a

big ego for so slight a man. This city looks nice, but it is rough. I think you'll learn that the hard way."

"Why does it look so nice, then?" Boas asked.

"For someone with a few Graygual horses, you don't know too much." She pushed two keys across the bar. *"That might work out badly for you in the end. You're in room eight. Your friend is in seven. Pay upfront. I don't want to be out of money if you turn up dead."*

The man was still looking at Leilius. It was becoming disconcerting.

"Two meals, two pints, and two baths." Boas laid out more than the amount needed. The woman's stare intensified. *"Keep your silence, and there will more."*

The woman huffed and wiped the money off the bar, muttering something. Boas grinned as the man slowly took two mugs from a shelf and began filling them.

"She doesn't think I'll last the night." Boas looked out at the common room. "Where will you start?"

"Bed. It's too late to get anything meaningful now. I can start in the morning."

The mugs landed on the counter with solid *thunks*.

"The Chosen will be eager to get on the way. We'll work tonight and send a message early."

"Sit. I'll get you some gruel." The man wiped his hands on a dirty towel and turned toward a half-door and the kitchen beyond.

"Gruel?" Leilius whined.

They sat at a table in the corner of the room. The gruel tasted about as good as it looked, and after Leilius choked his portion down, he wiped his face on his sleeve and glanced at the sleeping man at the table next to him. "Will you be coming with me?"

Boas finished his pint. He wiped his mouth and set his mug to the side. "In a way. I'll be near you, but not with you."

Leilius rolled his eyes. "Fine. I'll head out, then. Where will I meet you?"

"Depends on what you find."

"Do you make my life more difficult intentionally?"

"Yes."

Why the captain had chosen Boas, Leilius had no idea. It was a hindrance more than a help, especially when he left Leilius to fight instead of just stopping the battle before it began.

Annoyed, Leilius reached the front door and saw the familiar figure standing in the doorway. As Leilius approached, the man looked back, met Leilius' eyes for a moment, and then resumed his previous pose. *"I know you."*

Leilius paused, now standing behind the girth of the man.

"It is safe for the Wanderer here. We keep our eyes out." The man crossed his arms over his chest, still

looking away. *"We are doing our duty."*

"How do you know me?"

"Your description has been passed along. Word is that you, and others like you, help people. You travel with the Wanderer. We're here to help, though the missus will probably still make you pay. She's a hard one to talk around."

Leilius shifted. *"The Graygual are gone?"*

"Yes, as far as I know. They pulled out as one. We didn't chase them; they left on their own. There's talk of a big battle about to be waged. It is away in the west." The man turned, leaning his back against the door frame. He coughed into his fist, then left his hand there, picking at his nose.

"There are rumors," the man said into his hand. *"Shapes moving in the night, barely seen. Just lately. The gates haven't seen anyone. Could be just talk. Fear."* He flicked his finger. Whatever was on it flew off.

Leilius grimaced and looked away.

The man went at it again, his hand covering his mouth as he indulged in cleaning his nose. *"Keep your eye out. If you need information, or help, ask after Easy Bernice."*

"That's the name you came up with? Easy Bernice?"

The man wiped his finger on his apron. *"Your friend is not what he seems, eh?"*

"No, and unless a bunch of Inkna come through, he

doesn't even have to lift a finger to be the best warrior in this city."

"Ah." The man wiped his face, covering his mouth again. *"He is one of those. The strongest only until his power is taken away."*

"He is still excellent, even without that. You are standing in a darkened doorway. Who do you assume can read your lips?"

"He is excellent, but maybe not the best." The man turned, finally glancing at Leilius. *"Better safe than dead. Leaking knowledge is as good as dead. Let it not be said that I plunged the land into ruin. Now go. Chase the shadows. Make way for the Wanderer."*

"A little over the top," Leilius muttered as he drifted into the night.

He moved along the wall, opening up his senses to what lay in wait. Something tugged at him immediately, a presence drifting behind him. It didn't take a genius to figure out that Boas had taken up stalking him. Why he didn't want to look around together was anyone's guess.

Moonlight glimmered atop a rivulet of water leaking from a shop drain and into the cracks of the cobblestone street. Away from the inns, the noise of the city died down. Something scurried underfoot. Leilius froze until he identified a cat leaping up onto a fence and quickly jumping over.

He wound his way to the guard station, wondering

about the vigilance. There he saw the man from earlier, still standing on the wall and looking out. Leilius could barely see his head moving, scanning from side to side.

Wondering about the ease of getting into the city any other way, he slunk through the quiet streets until he reached the wall behind a row of houses. Getting over the small, rickety fences was easy, and scaling the barrier, twice his height, wouldn't be too big a challenge either, not with the vines and trees crawling up and reaching over. So much for the gate and guards.

The star-filled sky twinkled above, stretching out over him like a blanket. He marveled for a moment, never getting tired of the beauty of a clear night. That presence lurked just up the way, no doubt wondering what Leilius had gotten up to.

Sighing softly, he took off down a small lane, glancing at the dark windows of shabby homes. As he continued along, the dwellings improved until they were quite large and stately. The city had social levels, and judging by the front yards and walkways, most were occupied. They'd struck it lucky with the Graygual that had inhabited their city.

Growing steadily bored, Leilius wandered back toward the strip of inns, the only place still lively so late. At the corner of the strip, with the glow of the interiors spilling out into the street, something new stroked the edges of his mind.

He stopped and slid into a shallow shadow, ready to watch and wait. A man laughed as he stumbled out of a building ahead. He patted himself down and looked around, almost as if something had gone missing. Before he continued, another man walked out behind him, straight and tall.

The tall man's hand slowly came away from his body. Metal glinted in the moonlight as he neared the first man. With a sudden movement, the tall man plunged something into the first, and a hoarse scream broke the tranquility. The tall man shoved the other to the ground and delivered one more stab. He straightened up and ran, heading straight for Leilius.

Fighting the instinct to flinch closer to the corner and the deeper shadow, Leilius froze. The screaming tapered off as the tall man kept coming, blade at his side, head moving from side to side. He wasn't intoxicated, which meant he had an agenda. He was wearing black, but his clothing was all wrong for a Graygual, as was his build, which was lanky and bony. Voices sounded as people stumbled out of the doorway and bent to the now moaning man.

The tall man dodged around the corner five feet from where Leilius stood, and stopped, breathing loudly. Something slid against the wall, probably the man's back, as the people down the way carried the injured man toward the door. Those not employed looked around, as though the murderer could be seen with such a vague attempt.

A head slowly came out from the corner, the breathing still ragged, fear-induced. He should easily see Leilius—hell, he could reach around to *touch* Leilius.

Still Leilius did not move, not even for his knife.

A long moment passed. Shouts drifted away. The laggers drifted out of the night. The head retracted, and shuffling announced the murderer slipping away.

At that moment, something caught Leilius' eye. Off to the side, a small something disappeared around a bend, at eye level.

Thinking of Boas, Leilius squinted into the murky black, waiting for it to reappear.

"Shall we—"

Leilius struck sideways without thinking, his heart throbbing in sudden terror. His hand was knocked away, sending his knife clattering to the street. A strong hand hit his chest, pushing him against the wall.

"Don't chase it," Boas said softly, looking down the lane where the man had fallen and likely died. "If they look out, they'll see you."

"Where the hell were you?" Leilius clutched his chest, gulping for air.

"I moved in close when you were preoccupied with the killing. I applaud you for letting the murderer walk away. I thought your people were do-gooders."

"We are, but a stabbing in a bar with gambling and heaven knows what else is their own fault. It's none of my business."

"Right you are. In case you feel guilty when the fear has left you later, just be glad that I killed him moments ago."

"With your mind, or…"

"Obviously. I am not able to be two places at once."

Leilius' gaze jerked up to the place across the way. Nothing moved. "Do you sense anything out that way?" He pointed.

"No. All is clear."

"A moment ago?"

Boas was silent for a moment. "Not that I'm aware, but a rodent got by me earlier."

Leilius squinted through the night. He'd thought it was the wrong height for a cat, and certainly bigger than a rodent, but the mind played tricks when in the middle of a dangerous situation. He couldn't trust just one sense.

He sighed and started along the wall, watching to make sure no one came out with torches and pitchforks, on a witch hunt for a murderer. He didn't want to be the first thing they found.

"I thought I'd call into a couple of the inns before I went off to bed," he said when he was far enough away. "This city is quiet. The guy at the inn said there are no

Graygual here, and if he were wrong, the Graygual would be patrolling."

"I agree. It looks like Xandre pulled his forces. He's preparing for the last battle. We'll need to get moving to catch up."

CHAPTER SIX

"CITY IS CLOSED at sundown," a man yelled down from the wall. He popped his face over for a moment, and then quickly pulled it back in.

Trying to push away her urgency, Shanti glanced behind her at those chosen to stay in the city. The rest of their large group, always growing due to the word spreading through the Wanderer's Network, waited a little to the north, setting up a camp and tallying supplies.

The small crew with her now had ridden all day, helped set up the camp, before continuing here to meet with Leilius and Boas, who had sent a message that the way was clear.

"All seems quiet here, but you never can tell with Xandre," she said to Cayan, who waited beside her with a hard face and upward-pointed gaze. She could feel the annoyance rolling through his body. "We might not have the time to wait."

"Want me to climb the gate, grab that guy, and dangle him above the ground until he agrees to let us in?"

Sanders asked. His hand braced on his leg and his arm muscles flared. Intense aggravation and impatience drifted from him.

"As opposed to just knocking him out and opening it yourself, you mean?" Rohnan asked.

"Yes, gorgeous. Hence my saying all that."

"We mean the town no harm. We merely want supplies," Cayan called up, his stare intense.

"I don't make the rules. Come back at sun-up." The man's hand extended over the wall long enough to motion them away.

"What the hell is the difference between now and sun-up? Sunshine is unlikely to make this lot any merrier," Sanders said loudly.

"Sanders," Cayan said, shifting in his saddle. "Get us in."

"My pleasure, sir." Sanders swung a leg over his saddle and dropped to the ground. "Shanti, do they have arrows pointed at us?"

"The only defense for this gate is a single guard." She let her *Gift* sink into the city, feeling the emotions and overall vibe. It was late, and most of the activity had slowed as people drifted to sleep, but she found areas of vigilance. Churning minds, sharp and alert, sparked in various areas. Two of those minds she knew. Leilius and Boas were making their rounds. The rest, though, didn't speak of a peaceful life. She wondered if they'd present a threat of any kind. Perhaps some remaining Graygual were lying in wait, hiding their identities.

"Where are ya?" Sanders punched through the gate, knocking a board away, and stuck his foot in it.

"I've got a sword!" the gatekeeper yelled. An extended arm waved a blade over the wall.

"Well, look at that. We're twins. Only, mine is bigger. Tough luck." Sanders climbed the wall without difficulty, leaving room along the side in case the gatekeeper jabbed.

"I don't know what you're so worried about. We're wearing blue, not black. We're the good guys!" Sanders reached the top and leaned over. A smile spread across his face. "Hello."

"No!" The sword prodded the empty space between the man and Sanders.

"Why would you be watching the gate if you can't use a sword, I wonder. That sounds ridiculous." Sanders kicked another board away from the wrought iron gate so he could get a firm hold with his feet before ripping out his sword. He bashed the gatekeeper's sword, easily knocking it from the man's hand. "If you had just opened the gate, this would've been so much easier."

With one hand and sword still out, Sanders edged along until he could jump onto the platform behind the wall. "C'mere."

"Commander Sanders," Cayan barked. "Open the

gate. There is no need to dangle him over it."

"Hear that?" they heard from behind the wall. "You just got lucky. Sit over there. We're not going to hurt you."

"Who are you?" the man asked in a shaking voice.

"We're the people who are going to rid this land of the Graygual, that's who we are. And you need a new post, because you're no good at this one." A loud crank sounded and the gate shuddered into movement. It drifted open, revealing a large space beyond, with cleanly swept cobblestone and blazing torches to light their way.

"How long ago were the Graygual here?" Shanti asked as she kicked the Bloody Bastard. The blasted horse jerked his head down, yanking at her arms. He didn't budge. "I will get down and walk, you filthy horse. Do you want that? You'll be the only horse without a rider. Everyone will laugh at you."

"He can't understand you." Sonson laughed. They'd left the Shadow Lord and Portolmous in the camp to organize their fighters and keep all the groups complacent. While they were working together well, fights and skirmishes sprang up over the smallest of things. Esme was well used to dealing with it.

"Oh yes he can. This animal knows when I'm making threats. C'mon!" Shanti kicked the Bastard's sides. She braced herself, expecting him to spring forward.

Instead, he calmly walked, like a normal horse. It meant he was saving his attitude for another time, when she least expected it. "He is such an ornery bastard."

"He does what you tell him, and you're not happy. He does what you don't tell him, and you're not happy." Sanders sniffed from the top of the wall where he waited with hands planted on his hips. "Just like a woman."

"The only time he complies pleasantly is when he's setting me up. If you weren't such a blockheaded idiot, I wouldn't have to constantly tell you that." Shanti glanced along the quiet lane, where candle stands flickered a ways before the poles went dark. "As I was saying, how long since the Graygual were here?"

The man wiped his face with his hand. "Most of the Graygual left more than a week ago. Only a few were left behind." His voice quivered.

"He fears us. He's mistrustful. This isn't the way to make friends," Rohnan said softly.

"Shut the gate when everyone is through," Cayan said. "Hand the man back his sword and stand him up."

Shanti noticed a new siding on an old house, and various other renovations to make the city look nicer, confirming Leilius' thoughts that those stationed here had been higher-level officers.

"Th-thank you, good sir." The guard winched when Sanders handed him back his sword. He took it gingerly.

"Take the sword, man." Sanders closed the man's grip around the handle and flexed, grunting as he did so. He shook the man's arm, in some sort of manly show, before releasing and then slapping the guard on the shoulder. "Hold your weapon with confidence. Now, we're not going to hurt you, but you don't belong in this post. Why are you here?"

"It's not your job to fix the defenses of this city," Punston, one of the Shadow men, said.

"That is a stupid thing to say. This man wouldn't stop a trader. We could be sieged in the blink of an eye." Sanders' gaze hadn't dislodged from the guard, who was trying to shrivel backward from it. "Well?"

"At first we tried to keep the Graygual out, but men lost their lives doing that. We couldn't stand up to them. It made everyone afraid. After they left..." He shrugged. "I was the only one to volunteer."

"What happened to the few Graygual who were left behind?" Cayan asked.

The man shrugged again, but his back straightened marginally. "I don't know, sir."

"Confidence surged through him after that question," Rohnan said as he walked his horse to the far side of the lane, scanning. "He probably does know, at least in part, and is proud of the outcome."

"Good for you." Sanders clapped the man on the back. "Stand up for yourselves. Listen, if any Graygual come back, do you have an alarm?"

"I will feel them. Let's go." Cayan walked his horse down the street, prompting those around him to follow. Shanti remained where she was, looking at the strange boarding they put against the gate to make it harder to climb.

"All due respect, sir," Sanders said, not leaving the wall, "you might not. Not if they have that scarred prisoner with them." He stared after Cayan and received a backward glance and then a nod. Sanders turned back to the man, waiting for the answer.

"We have an alarm of sorts. But it won't help." The man's chin waggled as he shook his head. "They always have a few Inkna with them. Even if we could keep them out, which we can't, we can't fight them."

"Man that alarm. Trust me on that one. A loud one. As long as we're in this city, you ring that alarm for your life. Then run like hell if you have to. Do what you gotta do, but you let the city know. Got it?"

"Y-yes, sir."

Shanti couldn't see it, but she bet the man swallowed hard. Lesser men had a hard time saying no to the Westwood Lands army, whether they had any idea what they were agreeing to or not.

"Good man." Sanders stepped up to the edge of the wall and surveyed what lay beyond. His gaze then scanned the top, running along it.

"Easily climbable," Shanti said, knowing what he was looking for.

Sanders turned back. "For a few, yes. For an army, no. Not if we have any sort of warning."

"With a few ladders they'd be over it in a heartbeat." Shanti waited for Sanders to descend and get on his horse before directing the Bastard to walk with him. The horse complied easily again, which was not a good sign. She had no doubt that he was planning something.

She glanced behind her, making sure the select few of the Honor Guard made it through with their new charge. Xavier rode a little in front of Alexa, who had a straight face.

"So Xandre pulled his army after our recent victory." Shanti let her words hover in the air as she sped the Bastard along, wanting to catch up with Cayan. "That doesn't feel right."

"He's compiling his resources. Trying to prepare a solid front." Sanders motioned to Cayan. "Does the captain know where we're going?"

"Don't ask stupid questions."

Sander sniffed. "You can talk. Your whole life is a series of stupid questions."

"I don't like this," Cayan said in a low voice as they moved closer, his eyes facing front but his power blanketing the city. "There is a void area. Do you feel it?"

Shanti focused on the one area of blackness in a sea of colorful minds. Nervousness churned in her stomach. "Yes," she said.

"It could just be Burson. He was supposed to be in this city about now."

"It might be, but we've been snuck up on before. I don't want that happening again. I was thinking of dropping off the Bastard and going to check it out."

"Not alone, you won't."

"Which was why I didn't head out the moment we entered the city," she replied dryly. "I didn't want to hear you bitch."

Cayan glanced her way, and she had no doubt his dimples showed themselves, if only for a moment. "Soon this will be over, and you'll be forced to put on a dress and join the Women's Circle. You'll cook for me and do my washing, wait on me, and do everything I say, like a good little wife. Are you excited about your new life?"

Sanders barked out a laugh. "Sir, I do not envy you if that's your desire. You'll wake up right before the knife enters your throat."

"He's just being funny. He knows *he'll* be the one doing all that." Shanti snapped her head right, just in time to see a tail disappear behind a barrel. Cat. Even with that disturbance most likely being Burson, she couldn't shake the feeling that something wasn't right.

Xandre's movements had never been obvious, and he'd always been one step ahead of her. There was something in the works, she knew it, and when it struck, it would be right under her nose. "He'll cost a fortune in fabric for the dresses, though. Silk slippers will have to be made specially."

"You two have a strange version of foreplay." Sanders glanced up at the rooftops. "I would like to have brought your cats. I got used to them prowling the night."

"People would end up dead all over the city." Shanti saw the sign of the inn they were looking for. A man waited in the doorway, his apron smeared orange, his arms crossed over his chest, and his face as hard as granite. "That must be Leilius' favorite barman."

"Speaking of Leilius, where is he?" Sanders jumped down from his horse.

Shanti did too, grabbing a tight hold of the Bastard's reins. "Other side of the city, close to that void. He's stationary, but that void is not. It's heading toward him. We need to get moving."

"*Too many,*" the barman said, shaking his head slowly. "*Not enough beds.*"

"*We'll be sharing rooms.*" Cayan let his mount's lead dangle on the ground and stalked closer to the man. His horse, perfectly trained, stayed put.

"*Still not enough rooms. I got three. Two with two*

beds, one with bigger bed." The man's eyes darted to each person, nine in all.

Cayan looked at Shanti. "Did the letter say if Leilius and Boas were sharing?"

Before she could shake her head, the man stepped forward, his stare finding her face. He braced himself in the door. *"I did not know. Forgive me. The wife is right; I can be dense. Please. Come in. We'll find rooms."*

"Finally she's good for something." Sanders patted his horse's flank.

"We need to move, Cayan. Let Sanders sort this out," Shanti said, monitoring the void.

"Sanders, get the animals organized." Cayan stepped away from the man and into the middle of the lane. Someone shouted down the way before starting to sing loudly. "Have something to eat, but hold off on the baths. I'm not sure what we'll find."

Sanders hesitated in leading his horse around the side. "Should we all go, sir?"

"No. Not this time. We'll send a message to those with the *Gift* before we engage."

"If we can," Shanti murmured.

"Let's go, love." Cayan motioned her to get moving. "Hand the reins to Sanders."

Shanti locked eyes with Sanders for a moment. His gaze flicked to the Bastard. Then back.

A wicked grin curled Shanti's lips. "Not man

enough to do your job, Sanders?" She uncurled her fingers from the Bastard's reins. "Or was that a dumb question?"

"That's why you don't insult women—they can be vindictive when they want to be," Marc mumbled. He was waiting patiently beside the barn, clearly staying in cover so he wouldn't be forced to go with Shanti.

That void moved ever closer to Leilius, slowly stalking. Her love of putting Sanders in a tight spot had to be cut short. She jogged backward, making sure the Bastard didn't follow her. Still acting the "good horse," he didn't, watching her instead.

"What's got into him?" She turned and started jogging, Cayan at her side immediately. "I have a very bad feeling about that horse."

"Not as bad as I have about that void. Do you think Xandre would send out his secret weapon so soon after we captured him?"

"Why not? Xandre had no trouble taking him back." They ran down the lane, dodging the drunks who were making their way home.

"Come to Daddy," someone called in a messy slur of southern dialect. A man stepped out from the wall with his hands out, reaching for Shanti.

She veered quickly, right into him. She punched him in the gut before head-butting his face, cracking his nose. She hooked her toe around his ankle and kicked out, pulling his leg out from under him. As he fell, she hammered a foot into his side. *"Don't speak to women like that. It isn't nice."*

With a burst of speed, she was back with Cayan, who had barely slowed. They turned a corner and were dunked into darkness.

"It's probably a good thing I didn't understand what he said." Cayan's voice had turned rough.

"Definitely a good thing. You would've spoiled my fun."

Boas, who had been as immobile as Leilius, though some distance away, suddenly started moving. Slowly, he made his way closer to the younger man.

"Boas is moving in position to protect," Cayan said quietly, increasing his speed.

"At this moment, I hate that your legs are longer." Shanti sucked in breath, not liking the energy it was taking to keep up. If the Inner Circle prowled these streets, she'd need all her energy to face them.

A shock of alarm colored Leilius as anxiety pooled around Boas. Boas surged forward before both of their minds blinked out, consumed by the void.

CHAPTER SEVEN

S HANTI PUT ON a burst of speed. Anything could be happening with that bubble of nothingness. If it was the Inner Circle, Boas would be hard-pressed to take one down, and Leilius not able to at all. Any more and their graves would be the hard cobblestone of the street.

They rounded a corner and both flattened themselves against the wall, slowing despite the mad desire to hurry. They were close now. If they made a noise and gave themselves away, the Inner Circle would kill quickly and escape. Otherwise, their enemy might toy with their prizes for a time, giving Shanti and Cayan a chance to intercede.

It could still just be Burson. She hated this not knowing—not being able to plan—when the lives of her people were in the balance. Cayan held out his hand to stop her. He glanced up at the rooftops before scanning to the sides. Shanti did the same, seeing no movement. Feeling nothing.

"Split up," Shanti whispered softly in his ear.

He looked at her, his face hard. Tendrils of fear

wormed through him, his thoughts of losing her warring with logic.

A moment later he nodded and leaned toward her, his mouth glancing her ear. "We'll come at it from both sides. You go around the block that way." He motioned toward the right and hooked his hand around. "I'll wait here until you're in position. We'll box that void in."

Without complaining that he was trying to keep her safe by sending her the long way, where she could keep control of her power until the very end, she peeled off to the side before grabbing a drainpipe and scaling the wall. Without much effort, and feeling Cayan's shock, she pulled herself up and onto the mostly flat roof. Going all the way around would be a waste of time. He should've known she wouldn't go for that.

Quick and light-footed, she moved toward the void, hopping from one roof to the other. Nothing hindered her. No movement caught her eye. At the edge of the nearest roof, she looked down, hearing the soft hum of male voices. Shadows cut across the deserted street. The words on the night breeze offered no shape that she could discern, an unfamiliar language, or perhaps just too far away.

Another voice took up the conversation. A little louder, but not enough for her to catch its meaning, only enough to reveal the speakers' position.

At least that was something.

K . F .   B R E E N E

Careful not to make a sound, she moved in that direction, staying low. She'd bet Leilius had heard the conversation and moved closer, dragging Boas in his wake. That meant he'd be in their vicinity somewhere.

She felt Cayan rounding the corner as she worked toward the speakers, neither of them yet in the void. She crouched again, right above the speakers, but still the words remained a mystery, the murmurs too low. A blast of awareness came from Cayan, a sudden sense of urgency. He was ready to move.

She peered over the edge of the roof. The brim of a hat moved and a boot scraped the ground. Across the street, tucked away behind a barrel, something lurked, she could feel it, deep in the shadow. Its focus was on the street, not her.

Glancing to the side, she saw another drainpipe a short distance from the speakers' location. It would have to do. She had to get down somehow.

Perhaps going around would've been the better idea.

Impatience rang out from Cayan. Why, she had no idea. There was no fighting. Why rush things?

Doing another quick scan and seeing nothing, she crawled along the edge of the rooftop and swung herself over, tensing when her knife hit the metal of the pipe. She froze.

The sound of voices dried up. Silence dripped onto

the street as the moonlight glowed along the cobble-stone. Fabric rustled and a thrill ran up Shanti's spine, anxiety and danger arresting her. She didn't know who those men were, but they were trouble. She'd bet her life on it.

But were they trouble for her?

More fabric rustled. Her arms burned from holding herself on the pipe. The itch of eyes on her fizzled between her shoulder blades.

As if the night released its breath, the words began to flow again. Shanti let out a soft exhale and started to lower herself down. The itch still bothered her, though. She'd been seen. She had no idea by who.

Cayan's *Gift* disappeared. Like someone stealing her breath, her *Gift* blinked out a moment later. The words continued. Those two men weren't involved in this silent battle. They had no idea that predators lurked in their midst.

Anxiety poured through Cayan and Shanti's shared plane of awareness, something made possible by their *Joining*. She took a deep breath, willing calm and adjusting to the lack of power. Not long after, Cayan did the same.

Her feet touched the ground with a gentle scrape. When the talking continued, she eased out her sword and a knife, preparing to throw the knife as she stalked forward. The itch between her shoulder blades grew more intense. The subtle movement of the speaker drew her eye, but she quickly dismissed it.

"*I don't like the feel of things,*" she heard, the words still low but finally taking shape.

"*I need to get moving,*" the other said, shifting.

The first man stood tense, looking around him. Even to someone without training, the number of deadly people in the very small area had to give a person pause.

"*What's the matter?*" the second asked, looking Cayan's direction.

"*Nothing. Let's go.*" The man pulled a knife. The blade glinted as he turned toward Shanti.

Moving quickly, she backed away along the wall, putting some distance between herself and the trash cans. It was a suspicious area. They'd look hard at those shadows, which wouldn't be enough to cover her. Instead, she chose a more open place, pressing herself into a small corner between two houses. Her arm and shoulder stuck out, as did most of her foot, but if they didn't eyeball it too closely, they'd pass right by.

"*Did I mention, someone got in after dark last night,*" the second man said, slowing with the first as they passed the cans. As Shanti expected, they peered through the gloom. Beyond them, across the street, a movement flickered. "*Two guys.*"

"*I know. They are staying at Budo's place.*"

"He say anything about them?"

"No. He never does."

"I don't trust that one. His time might be up."

The two men passed Shanti slowly, their eyes roaming the street. One of them glanced at her small nook, and even paused for a moment, but almost as if his brain couldn't process the abstract shape, he kept going, muttering to the other one.

Movement flickered along the way, a different location to the one she'd seen a moment ago. A shape broke away from the wall, running.

Cayan's large frame darted across the street, fast as lightning. He'd grab that one, and Shanti would wait for the other.

A moment later, she was rewarded with another flicker of movement, and the glint of moonlight briefly flashing on metal. The lurker didn't leave the shadows. He must have known she was there, and that his movements would've been seen, as obvious as they were in the stillness. Was she being baited?

Someone screamed. Leilius?

Heart thumping, Shanti still didn't move. Someone babbled, a high-pitched, terrified sound. It echoed off the walls. Slapping feet hit the street. People were coming to help. If there was a move to be made, it was now.

Shanti stayed where she was. That was her move—

to wait and see. People didn't bait fighters and stay in the shadows. That person was trying to force her to act, or hiding someone else needing to get away.

"*Who's there?*" someone shouted.

"*You're surrounded!*" another claimed.

They ran through the street, cutting out her vision of the person for a brief moment. That was all it took.

The shape was running by the time the clueless do-gooders had passed. Putting on a burst of speed, she crossed the street and followed the lithe shape around a corner. She saw an elbow disappear around another corner.

Taking it wide in case the enemy lay in wait, she barely avoided the hands reaching for her. She turned and slashed, catching a limb that couldn't get out of the way in time. The man moved to give himself room. His sword swung up and out, slashing. She tapped it aside almost lazily and lunged. The dark shape moved. Her sword cut air. She yanked it up and blocked a downward strike she knew would be coming. The man's shape lowered, nothing more than dark patches against a murky background. A sliding noise made her jump, avoiding the foot trying to take out her feet.

She swiveled and turned, angling so he would be against the better-lit backdrop of the street, giving her the benefit of stronger sight. Tall and lean, he moved like a dancer, stepping in with a sword strike. She blocked and brought her sword back, pulling back at the last moment so she barely caught skin. He flinched, giving her just a moment to surge forward and crash into him. She took him to the ground, bringing the knife to his throat and digging it into his flesh.

"Please tell me you didn't turn traitor and I need to kill you," she said, recognizing his lax limbs. He'd stopped fighting.

"I didn't turn traitor and you don't need to kill me," Boas said. "I think you've gotten better, if that were possible. Apart from climbing off roofs. A blind man would've seen you."

"Who is covering our *Gifts,* or doesn't that concern you?"

"Burson. He was creeping up on the same person Leilius was listening to."

Shanti's mouth dropped open, but her knife didn't move. "Burson?"

As if in answer to her question, the veil on their *Gifts* dropped away. Leilius' brain image popped back on her map. The kid was calming down after being terrified. Cayan's was there, too, amused.

Amused was good.

She sat back, releasing Boas. "Obviously I'll kill you if you're lying."

"It wasn't so obvious before this little skirmish." He sat up stiffly before rubbing his elbow. "Now I know better."

"No. Unlike the Shadow Lands, when you tried to sneak up on me first, you don't have the advantage of knowing the terrain you're attacking in here."

"It's just streets and houses. I know how streets and houses work. We'll agree to disagree that you know how to get off roofs as well as I do, though. That is a glaring hole in your prowess."

Shanti stood and dusted herself off. "Elders help me, you're annoying."

"Yes."

"What happened here?" Cayan asked over his shoulder. Leilius peeked out from behind the wall as Boas heaved himself to his feet, moving slowly.

"Boas was having a little fun. This was his second chance to take me down by stealth. He failed." Shanti stowed her weapons.

"Here's some salt, dear wound." Boas brought his elbow up to look closer.

Shanti flicked it.

"Ow, woman!" he said in his language, backing away.

"Is that Burson?" Shanti pointed at the draped figure.

"Yes. He's heavy, so let's go." Cayan turned away toward the inn. When Shanti was beside him, she noticed two men holding small knives heading back the way they'd come. Their eyes were wide as they stared at Cayan. It seemed as if they were considering helping the unconscious man who was being carried away, but couldn't get their limbs moving.

"They meant well," she said. "That's the main thing."

"Burson kept trying to get away," Cayan said. "And while I realize I should've let him because of his *Seer* abilities, Leilius was screaming and carrying on, and I had no idea what was happening with you. I figured a light punch would stun Burson and I could sort everything out. Unfortunately, the punch was a bit harder than I'd intended."

"I didn't realize it was the captain when he ran after me. Then he caught me from behind." Leilius clutched his chest. "My life flashed before my eyes."

"He is prone to exaggeration, this one," Boas said. *"It is fun teasing him."*

Shanti rolled her eyes. *"Yes, but you'll give him nightmares."*

Boas laughed heartily. Apparently that was a bonus.

"If he didn't want to be in our presence, how could Burson not realize we'd be here?" Shanti wondered.

"Maybe he did, but he needed to be here, too." Cayan turned onto the street with the collection of inns, bathed in light. "That's the problem. We don't know. He's been off on his own, sending us instructions, but we have no idea what he's been doing. I'd like to find out."

"I think first we need to find out why he wanted you to leave him alone. He was always annoying, but just as often right."

"I had that thought too. That's why I tried to stun him."

"And failed." Boas grinned.

"Let's hope the damage can be undone," Shanti said, uncertainty unfurling within her.

CHAPTER EIGHT

S HANTI WALKED INTO the common room with fatigue dragging at her. Her crew all looked up as she entered, dirty and disheveled. Their eyes were serious, but their plates nearly emptied. They might've been concerned, but it certainly wasn't holding up their suppers.

"What's the story?" Sanders asked as she sat down. He shoveled a potato into his mouth, the piece so big it filled his cheek.

Leilius scurried to the barman, in charge of finding a place to put Burson until he regained consciousness.

"It was Burson. He's in the city." Shanti grabbed Sanders' mug of ale and took a gulp, nodding in hello to Pahona and Rohnan, who shared his table. Rohnan didn't nod back. He must've been sulking because she hadn't taken him to find the void.

"Careful. That ale isn't the best. Makes you lose an eye," Sanders said around his full mouth.

Shanti coughed as the bitter brew scratched at her tongue. She passed it back. "What do you mean, makes you lose an eye?"

Sanders grimaced, with his mouth puckered, his face scrunched, and one eye squeezed shut. He pointed at the closed eye. "It's that bad."

Shanti laughed as she glanced at Leilius, now gesturing toward her and holding up fingers. He was probably ordering food, and hopefully baths.

"Who is this Burson?" Pahona asked. Her plate and Rohnan's were clear, leaving nothing but tiny scraps.

"Since when are you a slow eater, Sanders?" she asked, eyeing what was left on his plate and feeling her stomach pinch in hunger.

"That's his second helping," Rohnan said, shaking his head. "He was done with the first before we were halfway through ours."

"I'm hungry." Sanders speared another potato and shoved it into his mouth.

"You're a glutton." Rohnan's lips turned downward.

Sanders shrugged. He'd never minded name calling.

"Burson is a potent *Seer,* but more importantly, he has the ability to cut out the *Gift.*" Shanti reached for a carrot on Sanders' plate. He slapped her hand away.

"What do you mean, he *cuts* it away?" Pahona leaned her elbows on the table, studying Shanti.

"That's rude." Sanders pointed at her elbows with the tip of his knife. "Elbows, elbows, strong and able, get your elbows off the table. This is not a horse's stable," he half sang.

"What a lovely little tune." Pahona turned her attention back to Shanti.

"Figures." Sanders huffed. "You people were born in a barn."

"He can create a void of power, if he chooses to." Shanti stole another sip of the horrible ale. It was better than nothing. "He can block off an enemy while allowing an ally to use the *Gift,* if he wants."

Pahona's face lit up. "What a remarkable *Gift.* That will greatly help us. The Inkna will be utterly useless."

"They have one too." Shanti watched as Leilius worked through the tables to her. A man reached back and grabbed Leilius' shirt. Before Leilius could react, the man frowned at him and let go, going back to his card game without an apology or explanation. "Their guy is more willing to help, however. Burson didn't want to come back with Cayan."

"The captain persuaded him, huh?" Sanders nodded to himself.

"He accidentally knocked him out, actually."

"Same thing."

Shanti raised her eyebrows in a silent question when Leilius stopped at the table.

"He's fixing your supper, S'am," Leilius said. "And the captain's. After that he'll have baths ready for you. He knows who you are and is in the network…" Leilius straightened and looked around. "Remind me later to tell you the code word."

"We have missed so much," Pahona said. "We had heard of the Wanderer, but had no idea what it meant."

"Can I go?" Leilius asked quietly, glancing behind him as Boas entered the common room. The men at the gaming table nearest him all looked up, tracking Boas' progress.

"Join the Honor Guard, Leilius." Shanti waited for him to nod before leaning back in her seat. "What of the Bastard, did you get him squared away?"

Pahona and Rohnan both started laughing. A dark look came over Sanders' face. He popped the last piece of meat into his mouth before pulling up his shirt sleeve. An angry red bite marred his skin. "He dodged my punch! Like a human!"

"Yes, he's quick. Not as easy to hit." Shanti smiled with pride. "He's a fighter."

"He's an asshole."

"A *good* fighter, yes." Shanti laughed. "You finally got him in there?"

"With help, yeah." Sanders took a gulp of his ale, lost his eye to the resulting grimace, and leaned back with a hand on his stomach. "In fairness, I think he was tired. I've seen him put up a bigger fight."

"He's planning something awful, I can tell." Shanti watched Cayan walk in without Burson. Half the gaming tables looked up. Silence spread through the room and more eyes came away from their cards. It was almost as though they expected Cayan to run at their tables and upend them before starting a huge brawl.

"I got the same thing when I walked in." Sanders wiped his forehead. "I ate too much. I pity the person sharing my room."

Pahona scooted away a little with a sour look on her face. She glanced down at his seat—or, more likely, his butt.

Cayan sauntered past the quiet tables, grabbed a chair at random, and pulled it up to sit beside Shanti. "Burson is on the floor in our room." He nodded to the others at the table. "A few people were kicked out of their rooms to accommodate us, I hear."

"Boas picked the mangiest inn he could find." Sanders sucked at his teeth.

"Less questions this way." Shanti sighed in delight as the barman emerged from the kitchen with two steaming plates. A surly-faced woman followed him out with two more, no doubt for Leilius and Boas.

As the barman passed the gamers, someone grabbed the back of his shirt. *"I need—"*

The barman kept walking, not even slowing. The man in the chair hadn't let go in time, and his arm wrenched. He fell sideways before grabbing his shoulder. He sent a baleful look at the woman passing behind. She glared down at him. There'd be no help from her.

"Here you go. I put you in the best room." The barman lowered a heaping plate in front of Shanti. *"Please, you tell me if you need anything. But be careful in the city. There are still enemies out there."*

"I will, thank you."

"The water is being heated for the baths now. Nice and fresh. You just let me know when you're ready. And if any of these men give you problems"—the barman vaguely gestured toward the gaming tables—*"you let me know."*

"Thank you. I'll be fine."

"Yes. Of course." The barman glanced down at Cayan. *"Of course."*

With a nod, he was off, stepping around the surly barmaid, who headed for Leilius and Boas.

The night passed quickly. After the decent, hot meal and hotter, glorious bath, Shanti and Cayan climbed into bed while Burson lay on the floor, tied up. The next day they went about ordering supplies and selling off the Graygual horses they didn't want, trading some of the ones they'd captured for those they'd been riding. The city was flooded with people going about their day, buying goods from the stalls, or taking a stroll with their children. It was a completely different vibe to the city than during the night, with honest families rather than lonesome, gambling drunks. While eyes and emotions were wary, these people did not carry around horrible scars inflicted by Graygual misdeeds. They'd truly been lucky with the type of officer that had settled in their quaint town.

For all that, Shanti occasionally spied a man crouching on a rooftop, bow and arrow in hand. Another lounged in an alleyway, watchful. Their gazes tracked Shanti and her party consistently, picking them out of the crowd easily and watching their progress.

"Where were those watchers last night?" Shanti asked as they made their way back to the inn.

"Leilius said he's seen a couple, though Boas hadn't felt them. I'm anxious to ask Burson why he'd hide the watchers from the *Gift*." Cayan slowed as Alexa stalled in the doorway ahead of them. Xavier stood behind her, his hand out to direct her inside.

"I don't want you at my back," Alexa said, her accent thick but words clear. Shanti wondered when she'd learned the language.

"Ladies first. It's how we do things. Go." Xavier shook his hands, trying to corral Alexa in.

"You put women in vulnerable positions so you can have the upper hand?" Alexa scowled. "What a disgraceful sort of people. I am glad I am not one of them."

Shanti grimaced. That wasn't a great way to make friends. Not that Shanti had any right to judge. She'd been surly at best when she had first met the Westwood Lands people.

"She reminds me of you," Cayan said in a deep tone, clearly reading her mind. His hand curled around her waist. "I was just as besotted as Xavier seems to be."

"*Aggravated* is the word you're looking for with Xavier, I think," Shanti said, leaning against Cayan's hard body. "Aggravated and about to break."

"Exactly."

"What's going on?" Sanders roared, pushing people to the side so he could stalk toward the inn door.

"Alexa won't go through, sir," Xavier said, irritation ringing clearly though his voice.

"Fine. You go."

"I'm not going to push a woman to the side and step in front of her!" Xavier, his hands still lifted like a sign directing the way, shook his limbs again. "Please *go*! Ladies first."

"I'm not a lady. I'm a fighter."

"You have the parts of a lady, and that means you're a lady. *Go!*"

"This is ridiculous." Sanders pushed Marc out of the way and grabbed Alexa by the nape and britches. Before she could react, he hoisted her up, swung her, and threw her through the door. Without skipping a beat, he turned, punched Xavier in the stomach, doubling the younger man over, and gave him the same treatment, only Xavier rolled through the door, too big and heavy to actually throw. It was a testament to how much size and muscle Xavier had gained.

"Leilius," Sanders barked.

"I'll go in front of girls, sir, I don't care." Leilius scurried forward. Maggie, one of the Honor Guard chosen to enter the city, burst out laughing.

"Fine." Sanders waved him through. "Get the dinners going. I'm hungry."

"Yes, sir," Leilius yelled over his shoulder, jogging.

Sanders swung his gaze around the group trying to enter the inn. "Let's move!"

As one, experienced fighter and young alike jerked into motion, filing in without hesitation.

"This is why I always bring him," Cayan said softly, stepping to the side with Shanti so everyone could have their chance to receive Sanders' fierce gaze and thinning lips. "He makes my life easier."

"What are you looking at?" Sanders stared down gawking passersby. Two younger men started and then quickened their pace.

"Should we check on Burson before or after supper?" Shanti asked.

"After. My patience has run out from haggling for supplies." Cayan guided her through the door with a hand on her lower back. She had changed from when she'd first met him.

"You didn't haggle; you told them what you wanted and stared them down until they folded." Shanti laughed and stepped through into the common room. Card games were already being set up by sober, and somber, men, with Boas at one of the tables. Sanders would probably be joining him before long.

"It took all the patience I had." Cayan stepped away. "Grab a table and I'll get some ale."

Shanti stopped next to one of the gaming tables, looking over the setup. Though she'd been in a great many common rooms during her long journey, and watched the play, she'd never actually sat down and joined in. With her *Gift* it would be cheating, and even without, she could often read people better than they knew their intentions themselves. It wouldn't be fair.

She glanced at Boas, waiting patiently. He winked.

Boas didn't care about fair.

"Well look at you, pretty lady." A man lumbered through the door. His long beard sparkled down the middle, wet from the spilled ale currently sloshing from his mug. *"No skirt, eh? Oh. You're one of the independent types. Inspired by that ridiculous woman parading through the land."* He laughed heartily, his heavy footfalls speaking of a slow mover.

At the bar, Cayan turned and leaned against his forearm, watching the newcomer. Though his face was closed down in a hard mask, he made no move to rush over and defend her honor. He'd changed a lot since they'd first met, too.

She prevented the grin from curving her lips.

"All these women nowadays think they can strap on a pair of pants and boots and run around with the men." The man sniffed, his thick stomach popping out. *"It's disgusting. You have a place. It's in the home, right, men?"*

The men seating themselves nodded and muttered, *"Yeah."*

At a table near the far wall, Maggie stiffened in indignation. Pahona, sitting next to her, looked at the man in confusion. Shanti, more experienced with this mindset than either, held on to her straight face.

"There's another use for women, though, isn't there?" the man continued, stopping a little too close to Shanti, lust sparking in his eyes. His bulk overshadowed her, and the smell of stale ale and pipe smoke took away a little of her joy. She hated that smell.

Raw rage surged through Cayan. Shanti didn't have to look to know he was flexed from head to toe, barely keeping himself from turning this man into a sobbing mess.

"You need a man to teach you your place." A slimy smile crept up the newcomer's face.

The men around the table smirked and chuckled, fire alighting in their eyes. One nudged another. Boas, at the next table, grinned and lowered his cards, watching with the same joy Shanti felt.

"Show you how good it feels to submit." The man reached low, going right for Shanti's crotch.

She punched him in the gut at half power, slapped his hand away, grabbed his ale, and slapped it onto the table next to her. *"I'm not interested. That's your only warning."*

Preventing the smile of anticipation was becoming a challenge. She knew he was too stupid to heed the warning, and too dense to gauge the fighter in front of him. Her rebuff would fuel his rage.

What a blast.

Disgust crossed his expression before lust and anger fused. The need for control and dominance took over, both carrying sexual overtones. He'd explode with aggression soon. Shanti only hoped some of the men at the table came to his aid, and that none of her group bothered to get up.

"Oh, you're begging for a lesson, aren't you?" He snatched at her crotch again, his hand jerky, ruled by his testosterone. His other hand grabbed for her upper arm, probably so he could drag her into a corner.

"Just like you'll beg for forgiveness, yes." She grabbed his reaching wrist with one hand and jammed her other forearm down onto his with all her weight. Something popped. He grunted, his teeth grinding. Before he could

yell, she peppered his body with hard punches, hitting the soft areas that would render him immobile. She stepped back and kicked up with all her power, crunching her foot into the apex between his legs.

His breath wheezed out, but before he could bend, she grabbed his forearm, spun, hooked her shoulder under his, and used her momentum to fling his upper body over her back. He crashed down onto the card table. The wood squealed before the legs snapped. Cards, drinks, and man all clattered to the ground.

Shanti braced herself, waiting for an assault.

The men at the card table hopped up from their seats and staggered backward with wide eyes. They looked at the groaning man on the ground, at the broken table, and then finally, slowly, their gazes landed on her. No one spoke. The whole common room had fallen silent except for Sanders' chuckling.

"When he regains his breath, he'll apologize for ruining your game, I'm sure." Shanti wiped off the front of her clothes, more for show than anything else.

Boas stood, handed her his mug of ale, and slapped her on her back, also for show. She took a large gulp and tried not to grimace. It was foul stuff, definitely gone off.

The common room cheered. Guys laughed. A prostitute near the corner nodded in approval. A warning flared from Rohnan.

Shanti passed by the barman, who was standing with a straight face and crossed arms. The barmaid stood behind the bar, also watching, anger in her bearing.

Shanti handed over two gold coins. *"Buy a new table and bar that man. He's bad for business."*

"He was here to send me a message, I have no doubt. He's one of the cheaper mercenaries in this town." The barman shrugged.

What Shanti had heard the night before came back to her. *"It's because of me. They don't want you housing me. We can easily—"*

The barman waved the thought away. *"I am threatened constantly. My wife, Nossie, does not need to wear pants to get the job done. A bottle broken over someone's head works equally well as throwing them on a table."* He took one of the gold coins. *"For the table, since it wasn't self-defense."*

Shanti laughed and gave a slight bow.

"I am Budo," he said. *"Anytime you need a room, I will accommodate you. When you have money, pay. When you don't, that's okay too. That is how we help each other in the Network."*

She bowed again. *"Right now, a warm meal would be enough."*

"It's coming. We've tapped a new barrel of ale for you." He walked her to the table where Rohnan waited

uneasily.

"You didn't need to." She looked down at her brother's grim face.

"Yes, we did. Your man—the big one at the bar—insisted. Not even Nossie wanted to say no to him. He has a way about him." Budo looked back where Cayan had just procured two mugs. *"He is paying handsomely for them. He is exactly the man I would expect to capture the Wanderer. You could not have found one more terrifying."*

Shanti was struck mute for a moment. That wasn't the word she would've used for Cayan. Although, if they'd been talking to Cayan when Shanti was dealing with the bearded idiot, it made sense.

"The man there, in the corner," Rohnan said, his voice pitched low for her and Budo's ears alone. He nodded toward a lanky fellow half sitting in shadow, watching the proceedings of the room. *"He is here for a stealthy kind of violence. The target is most likely you."* Rohnan's light eyes hit Budo.

Again Budo waved it away. *"That man is one of the more expensive mercenaries. Who sits by himself, in a corner, in shadow, and does not expect sober people to notice him?"* Budo huffed out a laugh, though his face didn't show his mirth. *"Simpletons. Maybe we'll just kill him. I am getting sick of their kind."*

Muttering to himself, he wandered back to the bar.

With a sigh, the kind that came after a long day where much was accomplished, Shanti settled into her seat. They still needed to hash out what Leilius had overheard, which was little more than the direction Xandre's armies were headed. The people of the land were trying to track him as much as Shanti and Cayan were, keen to know where the next act of devastation would appear.

Leilius suspected those men from last night were more interested in the spoils of war than protecting the land from it. They'd met in this city looking for easy pickings and finding things mostly in order. It seemed they attributed that to the Wanderer's appearance, and not the type of Graygual that had occupied it.

"Simpletons" was right.

"S'am!" Marc rushed in through the common room door with dirt on his face and eyes wide. Rohnan jumped up, reading the intense distress. "Your horse broke free. He kicked the stable hand and ran out. He's loose in the city."

CHAPTER NINE

"**D**OES NOTHING EVER go right for me?" Shanti lugged herself out of her seat just as Cayan reached them. "My horse has escaped. I have to go bring him back."

Cayan hesitated as Rohnan stood. Shanti laid a hand on Cayan's shoulder. "I'll take Rohnan. You eat and then talk to Burson. He is probably ready to talk now, after being tied up all day."

Still he hesitated. She rolled her eyes. "The city is clear. Eat." A good pat to his arm, and she was walking out of the common room to find her blasted horse. "I knew he was planning something."

Marc rushed out after her with Leilius and Xavier in tow.

"What are you guys doing?" Shanti asked, glancing back at the others. Alexa and Maggie both jogged to catch up.

"We thought we could do a little training, since Sanders won't let us play cards or drink ale." Xavier walked just a little behind Alexa, which annoyed her no end, though she was clearly trying not to show it.

"Why can't you drink ale?" Rohnan asked.

Leilius huffed. "He said ale makes people sleep too soundly, and the *adults* should get the privilege of drunkenness."

Shanti nodded. She wasn't going to argue with that.

"I'm going to get my horse. It took off with yours." Marc looked down a side street, and then jumped when someone wandered out, pulling up his pants. "That explains the stale urine smell I've run into all day."

"What is your take on Burson?" Shanti asked Rohnan. They'd checked the room at various times throughout the day, trying to get him to say why he needed to leave, or even what he'd been doing. Each time, he'd smiled at the ceiling, or frowned at the ground, but said nothing. Rohnan had sat in, but, of course, couldn't get anything without the use of his *Gift*.

"I don't know." Rohnan looked around at the Honor Guard. "Don't you usually disperse and try to sneak up on her later?"

"Yes. Go hide." Shanti shooed them away.

They took off at a run, Alexa almost dragged by Maggie, having no idea what was happening.

"How long will it take them to realize I don't intend to stay out for them to find me?" she asked with a smile.

"Not long. They've learned that lesson."

Shanti let her *Gift* settle more heavily over the city,

trying to locate any groups of people displaying a flash of fear or irritation. The Bastard would already be roaming the streets, stomping and trying to bite anyone who got close.

"He has always been secretive, Burson." Rohnan looked down a side street. "Remember, in the Hunter's camp, he was tortured and still didn't talk. If he means to keep his silence, he will."

"I'm half inclined just to let him go, if that's what he wants. He's only helpful if he's speaking."

"I would imagine the captain feels the same way, don't you? I think he is uncertain why he has kept him as long as he has."

Shanti nodded, knowing that was true. "Where is that blasted animal?" She started to jog, just to get this underway faster. The presence of Xavier came up on the left, his body completely hidden. If she hadn't felt him, she would've passed by without a second glance.

"Well done, Xavier." She felt a flash of fear across the city, followed by an emotion that seemed like *opportunity*. "I think we have him."

She turned the corner and increased her speed, aiming straight for her horse. It wasn't long before she heard loud neighs and the clattering of hooves. "I have him. He's running east."

"Should I go behind him and shoo him your way?" Rohnan hefted his staff, as if he was going into battle.

"Probably wise. Branch off in two blocks. He's slowing in an area without many humans. I don't feel another animal near him, either. He's just out for a pleasure ride."

"He has been tied up a lot. Made to be with horses he despises, and has had no one to battle with. He's probably going a little insane."

"Now I know why people think I sound crazy when I talk about that horse." Shanti motioned Rohnan right, and she continued straight on. Leilius hid just ahead of her, somehow choosing the right path though he couldn't feel her target. Impressive.

"I can see your arm and hand, Leilius," she said as she jogged by. "Those things will give you away as a person."

The arm pulled in.

"Too late." She reached the corner and slowed, registering another void inside the city. Frowning, she glanced back in that direction, one slightly north of the inn. Cayan must've acted on the conclusion she and Rohnan had come to. Hopefully he'd also set someone to tail Burson. That, more than anything, could reveal what the man would say under duress.

Another neigh rolled through the night.

Someone ran into the street up ahead of her, carrying a net.

A net for a horse? She shook her head and slowed,

curious about how that was going to work out for the man.

The Bastard came into view, eating something out of a plant box in someone's front yard. The man, his net held out wide, walked toward the horse with his body hunched just a little, making himself smaller so as not to spook the horse.

Little did he know that that particular horse didn't spook.

The void took a new path, headed her way.

The Bastard looked up as the man walked toward him. The man said something, though Shanti couldn't hear the words.

Leilius' presence crept closer as well, with the other Honor Guard members all converging on her. Maybe they would try and overtake her. They hadn't tried that method in a while.

The Bastard shifted position, turning to face his stealthy attacker. The horse stamped a foot and huffed. The man said something again. His net wiggled.

A blast of alarm surged through the city, Cayan reacting to something. As the horse let out his strange equine growl, Shanti straightened up, terror dripping down her middle.

A small void was still near Cayan, covering a tiny area. One head, she bet. If she hadn't focused in on Cayan, she could easily have missed it. *Had* almost missed it. In the size of the city, one tiny void was nothing.

The larger void had almost reached her, someone that must've been covering a group of people. Someone that wasn't Burson.

Horse forgotten, she faced the void that was coming, scanning the area and looking up. They would be able to feel her mind, and she was a long way from the inn, but if she could stall, and lead them on a chase, it would give Cayan and the others time to reach her.

Pulling in her *Gift*, focusing just on a two-block radius, more tiny voids popped into awareness. Tiny bits of nothing she could barely feel. She was surrounded.

Flak, she silently swore, feeling Rohnan more than a block away, on the other side of the Bastard. Her *Gift* cut off.

"That's not good," she said in her language, eyeing the wall next to her. Unlike before, this was a double-story residence. Not as easy to climb.

As she stepped toward it, hellbent on trying, a man dressed all in black stepped into the mouth of the street. A glance behind revealed the same picture. Xander's Inner Circle. If she tried to climb, they'd catch her easily.

Neither could she fight both. One would give her enough trouble.

She ripped out her sword, turning toward the man

at her back, away from the direction the void had come. She ran straight at him. Footfalls she barely heard sounded behind her. The chase was on.

The man now in front, his sword in hand, slightly bent his knees. Calm and cool, he waited patiently for Shanti to reach him.

She did, battering at him with a coarse swing and ramming him with her body. He fell away easily, by design, and grabbed her arm. She turned back and slashed, wasting valuable time, making him flinch.

Breathing calmly, knowing she had to keep her head, and more importantly, get out of there, she ran again. A group of three black-clad fighters turned the corner at a sprint, cutting her off. The one behind stepped diagonally, blocking her way to her horse and Rohnan. The last, whom she'd initially run away from, slowed up to complete the circle.

She was surrounded by excellent, lethal fighters. One she could take. Two she could stall. Five would kill her easily.

"*You've outsmarted me,*" she said, speaking their language. "*Where are your Inkna?*"

The face of the fighter in front of her turned down in disgust. "*We do not need Inkna.*"

"*Oh. Interesting. You're not fond of your other half? I've heard that is a problem among many matings. You should sever the tie, really. You'll be happier. Reconciling is also an option, though it would take feelings, and, correct me if I'm wrong, those have been tortured out of you.*"

Almost as one, they stepped closer, reducing the size of the circle. Two of them put their swords away. They did not intend to kill her.

"*Ah shit, you're trying to capture me. I was hoping for a clean kill.*" She whistled, a piercing sound that worked one time in ten.

"*We are under orders not to hurt you.*" The fighter who'd showed disgust stepped forward slowly. He must've been their leader. "*I do not want to break my orders.*"

"*That's comforting.*"

Clattering hooves echoed behind them. A man screamed, no doubt the one with the net, and the Bastard neighed as he ran around the corner, a sight for sore eyes. It took one moment for the horse to size up the problem, and then he shot forward like an arrow, running right at them.

"*Do you recognize him? He's one of yours. Was one, I should say.*" Shanti slashed at the fighter closest. Her strike was blocked. The fighter behind swung. She pivoted, the blade just missing, as her horse reared. His hooves kicked out, aiming for their leader.

Fast as hell, the leader dodged to the side. The Bastard neighed, coming back down before trying again.

"Grab her and let's go. Another of her brethren is coming!"

Stinging pain cut through Shanti's calf. A good strike. She kicked out, cracking a knee and bending it the wrong way. Her sword missed a face, but she continued with her body, knocking him with her forearm as it passed, and pulling it back to crack him on the temple with her sharp elbow. He fell like a stone.

More pain blossomed along her other leg, making her stumble. Someone pulled her hair, exposing her throat. Strong hands grabbed her throat as the Bastard turned. He kicked out, catching one of the fighters in the back. The fighter's spine snapped. The man screamed and fell to the ground.

Something hard knocked Shanti's head, dazing her. A fist rapped her arm. Metal sang on cobblestone, her sword falling from a suddenly limp hand. She needed to remember that move—that was a good one.

Rohnan yelled in the distance, an anguished sound of pure pain—emotional, thankfully, and not physical.

Another hard knock to the head and Shanti saw stars. Her limbs feeling like lead, she couldn't land punches. She flailed as she went weightless, carried in strong arms. Her ride started to run.

"Get the horses," her carrier said. *"We must hurry."*

"What of her brethren, One?" another of the fighters said.

"Take him out with the bow. Must I tell you every-thing?"

Shanti barely saw one of the fighters peel away. The Bastard neighed. The clattering of the hooves sounded off to the side, the horse running away. He must've seen the bow. He was crazy, not stupid.

Rohnan, however...

Vaguely, up ahead a little, she saw the fearful eyes of Leilius staring at her. A tiny flick of his knife and she knew what he was asking: *Should I try to save you?*

He must've known he would die trying. She shook her head, then exaggerated it so the movement seemed like a loll.

"Tac, is there anyone else?" One asked. The man was good, she'd give him that. Not easily fooled.

"Not with power."

That voice was familiar somehow, but she couldn't place it. Or maybe she just couldn't think anymore. Her head pounded and her body throbbed in pain. She'd received more than a couple of slices.

"Anyone that could follow us?" One asked, his pace not flagging through he was carrying a limp woman. She wasn't the lightest person she could think of. Muscle was heavy.

After a pause, Tac said, *"No. City folk, I think. They won't follow."*

Pounding hooves echoed against the walls before

the sound multiplied, one horse joined by another. The Bastard must've found Marc's horse.

Thinking of Marc, as her carrier slowed, putting her down only to quickly tie her up, Shanti saw a strange shape sticking out of a shadow. As she focused a little harder, she realized it was the side of a boot with worn tread.

Her body was pulled from the ground, her thoughts and vision both fuzzy. A familiar face stared at her, silent and serious. No fear showed in his expression. Instead, his eyebrows were drawn tightly over his eyes in determination and his hand clutched a knife.

Marc mouthed, "She said to follow—" He lightly jerked his head to the right.

Alexa blinked in confusion and looked around, her body mostly obscured by a large trash bin.

Shanti was hoisted up by the same strong hands. Another fighter jogged to them, a bow clutched by his side. *"I got her brethren, but only a flesh wound. The horse ran off. Should I stay and finish the job?"*

"You'd be captured by the Westwood man. No. Stay with us. We go."

Shanti grunted as she was handed off, then hoisted up again and draped over One's lap.

"Can I just ride?" she said, wheezing. *"Because I've been in this position before, and it is extremely uncom- fortable. Not to mention your pants smell like piss. Is it*

that short that you dribble down your front?"

Was she mistaken, or did One sigh? Clearly he hadn't signed up for the job he was currently doing. The jobs of killer and kidnapper demanded very different patience thresholds.

As the horse turned, she caught the scarred face of Tac, a name she hadn't known when he had been their prisoner. His gaze was rooted to something, in Marc's direction.

"What is it?" One demanded, turning his horse so he could follow the man's gaze.

"Who helped you escape?" Shanti said as a white-hot surge of pain pierced her heart. She struggled, trying to get off the horse. *"Did you kill Daniels, you disgusting vermin?"*

The man's eyes met hers. A spark of fire lit them, but he said nothing. Instead, he spat, and pulled himself onto his horse. *"Let's go. The captain must know Shanti is in danger, and soon he'll be on our tail. We don't want him to catch up with us."*

One's huff was probably accompanied by a sneer. He would think he was the best in the land, having been elevated to what was probably the best position in all of the Graygual. Shanti intended to give him a rude awakening before they killed her. Or worse, tried to breed her and made her kill herself.

CHAPTER TEN

"**H**URRY! WE HAVE to tell the captain!" Leilius hopped from one foot to the other. The Bloody Bastard stood behind them, stomping one of his hooves repeatedly.

Marc stared at Alexa for a moment. The attractive woman stared back with absolutely no recollection of saying, "If you do not follow her, she will die, and the world will blacken with death."

At least, he thought that was what she'd said. It was in her language, and he'd been somewhat terrified at the time that a group of people could kidnap S'am—he wasn't exactly thinking clearly.

Making a split-second decision, he jammed his knife into its holster. "We need to follow her. Rohnan is probably already headed back to the captain, so that will be covered. The Shadow and Shumas are both excellent trackers. Plus, Leilius picked up a rumor last night about a place in the south. They should have what they need. We have to get on their trail now, though."

"Why?" Xavier stepped closer, still out of breath

from running after S'am. He'd arrived as the Graygual were riding away.

Marc quickly told them what Alexa had said as he caught his horse. It wasn't saddled. Neither was the Bastard. Worse, there were two horses for five of them.

"We need more horses," Marc said, in a sudden panic. "We have to hurry!"

"Okay. Fine." Xavier glanced to the right. "The Ha-Ra Inn isn't far from here. Marc, you take whoever the Bastard will carry, and go. I'll take everyone else and steal some horses. Hopefully we won't be far behind you. Leave a trail for us to follow."

Marc nodded and eyed the Bastard. "Approach him one by one. Usually when S'am's in danger, he's more inclined to accept passengers. He won't let you control him, though. Just know that. He didn't get his name on a whim."

"We know." Leilius hurried over and moved to get on, clearly as eager to go as Marc was. The Bastard reached around and chomped at him, snatching at fabric.

"Someone else. C'mon, c'mon," Xavier said, pushing Maggie toward the horse. "Be mean with him."

Maggie scolded at the animal, showing no fear. She dodged a bite and reached his back. The Bastard went after her, kicking and biting, chasing her away.

"That's a big *no*, Maggie," Marc said, climbing on

his horse. "Big no."

"We'll just steal another horse," Xavier said, starting to jog away. Everyone but Alexa followed him. "They have plenty from the ones we sold today. Marc, leave that trail."

Alexa, brow rumpled, ignored the others as they ran into the night. Instead, she stalked toward the horse, head-on. The Bastard bristled and bared his teeth. "I'm not great at horse riding, but the fate of our people rests in *Chulan's* hands. It is my destiny to bridge the gap."

"I'm not sure what that means," Marc murmured. "But watch out for the—"

The horse chomped at her, his teeth clicking the air, just missing her shoulder. She pivoted and punched him in the face. He bit for her again before kicking out. She dodged and punched, landing a blow where he couldn't. Face fierce, she said, *"You will carry me, you filthy horse, and we will save the Chosen. That is your job in this world. If you do not do your job, I will kill you, roast you over a spit, and serve you up to my people. I will tell them they are eating cattle. Is that what you want, to be remembered as cattle? Tough cattle, at that."*

The horse neighed. Marc gulped. This girl might be harder than S'am, and that was saying something.

With one last glare, she nodded at the horse and crossed to his side. She jumped up, lithe and graceful, making it onto his back and grabbing his mane. Her next fierce glance was filled with impatience and stuck Marc's tongue to the roof of his mouth.

She might've been about the same age as him, and might not have been in as many battles, but her childhood was clearly very different to his. The hardness in her demeanor, and in her outlook, fit perfectly with the Shumas, and was shocking in a woman so young. He could not relate to her, not even a little.

It made him feel even sadder for their strife.

"Are you going to get moving anytime tonight, or should I leave you to stare?" she asked.

"Crap." Marc urged his horse forward.

"If I have *Sight,*" Alexa said as the Bastard lurched to a start, "I will fall off. Leave me if you must." The horse caught Marc's immediately, and then took the lead.

It sounded like her teeth were clenched. Marc wondered how long it would take the Bastard to put fear into her.

"I can't just leave you," Marc yelled, urging his horse faster. They clattered around a corner, both riders slipping way to the side and nearly falling. "The captain would *kill* me."

"Why do your people coddle women? *Great, miserable elders, what is this horse doing? Flak!*" The Bastard jumped over a hedge and picked up speed again. Marc's horse struggled faster, galloping through an empty street.

"We take care of our women. It's a nice thing to do. If we didn't, they'd poison us, or something else awful. Besides, you're in the army now. We don't leave our people behind."

A strange whine rang through the streets. It increased in pitch, a small jingling infusing the blare, like the metal workings of a crank. A moment later, behind them, another started. Then another.

"They're using the alarms," Marc said.

"Slow down, you bloody animal," Alexa screeched in her language, jostled as the Bastard took a corner way too fast. His hooves, not finding enough purchase on the cobblestone, skittered, making him stumble.

Marc's horse, of similar stock but lesser breeding, meaning it still had sense, slowed enough to keep its feet. Still Marc slid on the glossy back, barely keeping on. He really hoped Xavier remembered to get some extra saddles.

Around the next bend and they could see the gate. Half of it stood open, with a body lying facedown in front. Two people were bent over him, one looking like he was checking for a pulse. Another stood straight, holding a bow. Off to the side, people loitered, looking between the opened gate and the man on the ground. The siren wailed.

As Alexa and Marc ran at them, everyone looked up. The man with the bow started, and then raised his weapon. A moment later, he flinched and grimaced, lowering to the ground.

"No, Alexa!" Marc yelled. "Leave them be."

"He was going to shoot!"

"Whoa," Marc said, pulling on the horse's mane. He didn't know what else to use as reins. "Whoa!"

Marc's horse took the command gracefully, stopping gently.

"*Stop! Stop, you filthy animal. Whoa! Stop!*" The Bastard didn't even slow. He ran at the man with the bow and reared, kicking out with his front feet. Alexa yelled a series of phrases Marc had never heard before, and were probably not kind, holding on for dear life.

"We are going after the woman who was kidnapped," Marc called in a loud, clear voice. "The Graygual have taken the Wanderer. We are going to win her back."

"The Wanderer?" someone said. Everyone else was mute, too busy dodging, or watching others dodge, the mad horse with the dangling rider.

"More of us are coming. Leave the gates open. We have to go after her!" Marc put more urgency in his voice this time. "Alexa, let's go!"

"*Ride, you bloody bastard of a horse. Stop trying to kick him in the head and ride!*" She kicked the horse's sides and then slipped halfway off. He came down, allowing her one moment to climb back on, and then he was running again, hurtling out of the gate like a demon.

"I do hate that animal," Marc said, digging his heels into his horse and following. He hoped Xavier wouldn't have as much trouble getting through the gate.

They turned right, following the upturned ground from the fresh tread of fast-moving horses. In the moonlight, they could just see the group of Graygual ferrying Shanti away in the distance.

"Keep them in sight, but don't get too close," Marc said, not sure if she could hear him over the thundering of hooves.

His unspoken question was answered a moment later when she yelled back, "I'm not an idiot!"

Marc chanced a look at the ground behind them, seeing the trail cutting through the dried field. Xavier would have no problem following it if he came quickly. Which was lucky, because Marc didn't have anything to drop to leave a trail, unless he counted his clothes. He wasn't in the mood to ride the horse bareback while naked.

The Graygual were heading south, in the direction Leilius had surmised Xandre had set up camp. It was amazing the things Leilius could learn sneaking and listening in. S'am had trained him well.

"We're going to be intercepted," Alexa called back. She pointed to the city wall, curving around to the left.

"Who is it?" Marc asked, wishing he had a bow with him.

"They feel familiar."

Horses trotted out from the side, in no real rush. Surprise flitted through Marc as he recognized more of the Honor Guard.

Rachie, Gracas, and Ruisa saw them at about the same time, throwing up hands in salute. The hands dropped quickly, though.

"Slow for a moment," Marc said, veering slightly.

"We haven't time."

"Just a little."

Alexa cursed again as the Bastard neighed in annoyance.

"What are you doing here?" Rachie asked at the same time Gracas said, "We were just looking around."

"We weren't going to go in or anything," Rachie said over the end of Gracas' words. "We just got bored at camp so we snuck away."

"They've got S'am," Marc said in a rush. "We're following them."

"What?" Ruisa leaned forward in her saddle. Her horse picked up speed. "What did you say? Is that the Bastard?"

"The Graygual took S'am," Marc said, urging his horse faster. The others fell in, as he knew they would. "Alexa had a...premonition, or whatever, to follow.

Xavier and the others are getting horses. They'll be on their way shortly."

"How did they get her?" Rachie said.

"Inner Circle, we think. With that prisoner that got away. He must've disguised them so they could sneak up on S'am. There were a lot of them."

"Where's the captain?" Ruisa asked.

"Rohnan went back for him. We didn't wait." Marc looked ahead. The black specks hadn't become any smaller. They must've slowed too. Hopefully it meant S'am was putting up a fight.

"What do we do when we catch them?" Gracas asked.

"We're not going to catch them." Marc glanced behind them. Still no sign of Xavier. "We're going to follow them until the others catch up, and then…just keep following them, I guess. I don't know."

"That's a pretty stupid plan, Marc," Rachie said.

"Then don't come with us."

"Of course we're going with you." Rachie snorted. "But it doesn't stop your plan from being stupid."

"Where's Alena?" Marc asked.

"She didn't want to come. She said the risk of getting in trouble was too great to basically go look at a wall." Ruisa shook her head. "I bet she'll kick herself for not coming now."

"Not if we catch the Graygual without a plan," Rachie said. "She'll have dodged an arrow, then, because we're sure to die."

"We'll come up with a plan when Xavier gets here." Marc wiped his face in annoyance. "One thing at a time. Wait. Slow down more. They look like they are stopping. We don't want them to know we're following them. They might send someone back to kill us."

"How many do they have?" Gracas whispered as their horses slowed to walking pace. They drifted toward prickly bushes nesting between a couple of bare trees.

"Break up. Let's not cluster. It'll make it easier to see us." Marc hunched down for no real reason. "They have three really good fighters. I mean, they took S'am down, so they must be great. Then that one guy who blocks out the *Gift.*"

"Any they send back, I will kill," Alexa whispered. "They'll keep their *Gifted* with S'am. We'll only need to avoid the whole party."

"True." Gracas stroked his scraggly whiskers. "Or else they'll knock S'am out and send someone back."

Alexa tensed. She probably hadn't thought of that.

The group of Graygual had definitely stopped, but Marc couldn't see what they were doing. They were little more than a dark blob on a moonlit plain.

"I hate how hot it is here, even at night." Rachie pulled at his collar. "I'm all sticky."

"That beard makes you look ridiculous, not older," Ruisa said quietly, eyeing Gracas' face.

He frowned and dropped his hand. "Your face makes you look ridiculous, but do I say anything?"

"I can't help my face, but you can help that poor excuse for manliness on your chin," Ruisa shot back.

"Shut up," Marc seethed, staring at the blob. It seemed to be moving again. He glanced back, looking for Xavier, and was rewarded with another black shape coming alongside the gate.

"Okay, let's get moving slowly. Xavier is coming." Marc directed his horse away from the bushes. "I sure hope he brought a saddle."

"I sure hope he has a plan," Rachie murmured.

"YOU SHOULD HAVE left me where I was," Burson said for the fifth time, his tone grave. "We've now passed on to an even more perilous series of paths."

He sat in a chair with his hands untied, completely placid and no longer asking to leave the inn. Cayan stared down at him, his heart thumping and Shanti's mind invisible. Worse, he could feel her through the *Joining*, angst-ridden and resigned. It meant she thought she was headed to her death.

"Why didn't you tell me another of your kind was in the city?" Cayan demanded. "Why sit here in utter silence unless you were asking to leave?"

"If I told you, you both would have died in this city. I've told you this before. I cannot reveal everything I know; it could have disastrous consequences. In some instances, *you* need to make the choice. That is the only way of salvation."

Cayan flexed his fists, using all his willpower not to bash Burson where he sat.

"Where is she going?" Cayan asked.

"If I tell you, you'll die."

"Will my death save her life?"

"In essence, you will be trading yourself for her, yes."

"So be it. Tell me." Cayan stood over the man, feeling Sanders below them, getting the horses and army ready. Half of them would be riding intoxicated, but, experienced as they were, it wouldn't matter.

Burson raised a finger. A mad grin slid up his face. "If you figure it out for yourself, there is a chance you will both live."

"Burson, I am not above prying it out of you—"

"Captain!" Rohnan ran in. Blood ran down his arm and dripped from his fingers. "Boas is away to inform the army. Sanders is almost ready. We need to get moving."

Cayan bent down toward Burson, seething with anger. "Tell me where they've taken her, or I will beat it out of you."

"Leilius thought he had that information," Rohnan said, clenching and unclenching his bloody fist. He held a couple of sheets of paper in his good hand. "Or near enough. He wasn't positive, but he had pieced together all the rumors and gossip he'd heard. I took it from his room."

"I'm sure Shanti will be happy with Leilius' efforts," Burson said.

"Let's go." Cayan reached down and yanked Burson up by his collar. "You're coming too."

"That was always my fate, yes. Be it this way or another, I have my part to play."

"Do you need to wrap your arm, Rohnan?" Cayan asked as he left his room and hurried down the stairs.

"I will when I have a moment. We must hurry. Don't blame yourself for this—there is no way you could've known."

"Stay out of my head," Cayan growled, even as the crushing guilt threatened to overcome him. That wasn't going to help the situation. He needed to stay focused and push it away until she was safe.

"*What is happening?*" Budo ran out of the common room.

"*They've taken Shanti.*" Cayan paused and turned to him. "*Tell your Wanderer Network. Alert them. We need information on Xandre's—the Being Supreme's—*

whereabouts. Anything you can do to help might save her life."

"Of course. Yes. I can message you the location if I hear. But how will I get it to you?"

Cayan started away again. *"Get it to everyone. Tell them it is time to choose—the Wanderer and their freedom, or the Graygual and a cage. The time for hiding is over. Now it is time to fight."*

He pushed through the door and out into the street. As if on command, his horse was brought around by a stable hand, saddled and ready. Sanders rode out a moment later, turning back in his saddle and yelling at the others to hurry up.

"Xandre is amassing his armies as a distraction, it seems." Rohnan held out the pages.

Cayan took the pages and shook his head. "For most battle commanders, I'd say that is not possible. It makes Xandre extremely vulnerable if he is not with them, and leaves the land open for revolt. Sure, he might draw us there, but at what cost? He could not hope to capture Shanti that way. He's tried before and failed."

"He didn't hope to capture her that way, as we see."

"Clearly." Cayan studied a small square of map. The place Leilius had indicated was where Xandre resided. Had resided, in fact, for some months. Planning. Orchestrating all this until Shanti was close enough to grab. "He has always been way ahead of us. He planned for failure each time. If he didn't capture her along her route east, he'd do so in the Shadow Lands. That failing, he'd let the Hunter draw her. That failing, he'd fortify a few chosen cities to trap her in. That failing...this swampland holding a lone castle. One side is ocean, so probably a cliff, and the other uninhabitable land, certainly filled with both devised and natural dangers."

Cayan handed the map back and climbed on his horse, his mind whirling. "Burson, is that where they have taken her?"

"My telling you will result in—"

"Tell me!"

"It is, yes. Xandre will finally have his prize."

Cayan dug his heels into the sides of his horse. "He has *my* prize, and I intend to get her back."

CHAPTER ELEVEN

S HANTI WOKE UP with a pounding head and fuzzy vision. Hot, sticky air coated her skin as she lay in a hard bed covered with expensive silk. Stone walls closed her in, and no glass filled the small window.

After blinking and wiping her eyes, she sat up, her sight clearing, but it didn't do anything for her head.

A small wooden chair sat in the corner, rustic and battered to hell. Next to the bed stood a small stool holding a chamber pot, thankfully empty.

"Odd place to put that," Shanti said softly, trying out her voice. Though scratchy, it worked fine. Just like her limbs and digits.

She stood, fighting the immediate dizziness, which cleared relatively quickly. A cream drape, of sorts, covered her, airy and light. The clothes she'd been wearing were nowhere in sight, and the dirt she'd gained from being lugged from one place to the other had been cleaned.

"A jailer who cares. How lovely." She scowled at the situation. How stupid she'd been to end up...wherever she was. In all the time she'd been evading him, she still went and let down her guard in a recently occupied city. *Fool.*

At the window, she looked out on the blue of the sea, expansive and beautiful. If it hadn't been for the horrible weather, she'd feel like she was home.

Maybe she should actually thank him for the sheet-like clothing she was wearing. It was certainly cooler than her own would've been.

She gave the room another sweep, saw nothing out of place, and then tried the door. Surprise coursed through her as it pulled open. She stared down at the handle, mystified, as the man from last night stepped into view. One, they'd called him—both a name and a position, she'd bet.

"I expected it to be locked," she said, letting go of the cold metal. *"Nice digs."* She waved her finger around.

One's brow creased, ruining the blank stare he'd had a moment ago. *"Hot, though. Aren't you hot?"*

His gaze didn't waver.

"Good self-control. Most people would've looked down." She peeked out the door. Tac, the scarred man who was keeping her from reaching her power, waited in a chair outside, reading. He glanced up as she stepped out. *"Just you two, huh? Xandre isn't worried that I will snap his neck"*—she pointed at Tac—*"and then kill you?"*

One's face didn't change this time. *"The master requests your presence for a meal when you are hungry. Shall I lead you?"*

"My, my. What nice manners. A real gentleman. Except for the kidnapping, of course. And then the drugging me on the horse ride. What did you dose me with?"

"Something to keep you from trying to bite my legs or cock." One's eyes hardened. *"Are you ready to eat?"*

"Well, I had to do something, didn't I? You'd kidnapped me. I had to make you work for it." Shanti motioned him forward.

Tac stood, too.

"Are you dying to ask me how it feels when the shoe is on the other foot?" she asked Tac.

He stared straight ahead, giving no reply.

"Did you kill Daniels?" she asked. A shock of rage ran through her.

Tac didn't reply.

Holding her anger in check so it didn't dilute her senses, Shanti let it go for now and followed One down a wide set of stairs. Halfway down, her foot hit the step wrong. She tried to adjust, but her legs were like jelly. Tipping forward, she reached out for anything that would break her fall. She clutched One's large shoulders, her weight crashing into him a moment later. For one moment, she thought they would fall down the rest of the way, headfirst.

Instead, with a show of his strength, he braced to stop her fall before turning and offering her a steady hand. He didn't say a word, just helped set her back onto her feet and make sure she wouldn't tumble down a second time.

She took a deep breath, ignoring her clattering heart. She hadn't been this clumsy in a while, having been healthy, fed, rested, and looked after. It was not a welcome stroll down memory lane.

"That was your fault," she said. *"For drugging me."*

He stared at her for a moment, offered no comment, and then continued down the stairs, slower than they had done previously.

"You guys are the strong and silent types, huh?" she asked, picking her way more carefully. It was hard, her mind still lethargic. *"Or one of you is. The other is the scarred and silent type."*

As they continued, she filed away One's reactions. He did not so much as flinch when she hit him from behind. His reactions were cool and seemed almost trusting. His shoulders were heavily muscled, as was his back. Smaller than Cayan, but not as lean as Rohnan. Strength, fluidity, and speed, she'd bet, in perfect synchronicity. He'd be stronger than her, no doubt. Possibly faster, helped by his testosterone, but would he be as wily? She doubted it. It would be a tough fight. One she'd need to be healthy for. Or have the use of her

Gift.

"Ah. Here she is!" A short, bald man rose from a small chair in the corner of a spacious room—for a castle, at least. Some distance away, set against the far wall, was a large, heavily worked wooden chair. A red rug cut through the middle of the room, leading to the chair, as though for peasants to pay homage to the king.

"Yes, you have noticed the focal point of the room. Gaudy, isn't it?" The man, Xandre, the most ruthless tyrant the land had ever known, smiled and clasped his hands in front of him. He wore similar clothing to what she did, bare-footed.

"Is this language okay?" He pointed to his mouth. "You are mated, or soon to be mated, with the captain of the Westwood Lands, are you not? So you must be accustomed to this language by now. *Or should we speak in your native tongue? I didn't want to presume...*"

"A neutral language is fine." She stared into the blue eyes of a seemingly ordinary man. Slightly thick around the middle and narrow-shouldered, he was not accustomed to fighting. She'd never heard that he had the *Gift,* so it was a mystery how he could control men like One. More so the Inkna. Why hadn't anyone overthrown him?

"Would you like to sit?" he asked, holding his hand, palm up, toward a cushioned chair near where he'd been sitting. "Or we could go outside. There is a wonderful view. You will love it."

"Why am I here?" she asked, trying to get her bearings. This meeting was expected—meeting like *this* was not.

"Come." He motioned everyone out into the bright sunshine. Around the other side of the castle were seats and sunshades, looking out over the water. "Sit. Please. One, send for the meal. We'll have it here."

"Yes, master," One said in a near-perfect accent. He offered a slight bow and excused himself.

Before she could snap Xandre's neck, two Inkna in white shirts stepped into view.

"You see them, then." Xandre sat and crossed an ankle over his knee. "It is such a vulgar thing to bring up." He dropped into a farcical voice. "Just so you know, I have two master executioners ready to torture your brain if you try to kill me." Xandre shook his head and waved his hand. The Inkna disappeared from sight. "I hate them. I must be honest. I really abhor the whole group of people. But they are necessary."

"Why am I here, Xandre?"

He tsked. "I'm afraid I must insist on you calling me Being Supreme. Titles really make the man with these types of people."

"There is no way you think I'll call you Being Supreme. Let's not fool each other."

Xandre giggled, almost like a child. "True. I had

hoped. No matter."

Inner Circle members came in a stream, carrying trays of meats and cheeses. Bread and beverages were delivered last, set out in a decadent way.

"The cheese is going to melt out here," Shanti said, feeling the pang of hunger.

"Some melt inside as well, yes. It is a softer cheese, though. You'll love it."

"It gives me gas."

"Ah!" He laughed. "You are pulling my leg. It does not give you gas. I have that on good authority. You often eat cheese. And occasionally drink cow's milk, yes? Though only if there is nothing else, as often there isn't in some parts of the land. 'Filthy animals,' you call them, right? Or was that your horse? I forget."

Shanti made sure the surprise didn't show on her face. It was as Sanders had thought after Daniels' death—Xandre had someone within Cayan's faction relaying information to him. He had to.

She wondered why Rohnan hadn't been able to find out who. He'd been checking each person in the army at various times, looking for anyone who might not be honest. He'd turned up empty.

Tac took a seat removed from them and bent to his book. One took residence behind their chairs with his hands clasped behind his back. Everyone else cleared away, leaving her in a faux-intimate conversation with someone she hated more than anything else in the world.

"I'll ask again, Xandre, and if you don't answer, I'll try to kill you just for something to do. Why am I here?"

"So violent. So beautiful. You truly are a lovely creature, Shanti Cu-Hoi. Truly." Before she could grab his throat, just to see how hard she could squeeze before the Inkna or One reacted, he held up a hand. "You really would try to kill me and suffer the pain that would come. I did not think you were as mindless as my Inner Circle."

One shifted slightly.

Shanti cocked her head. "Huh. It seems you do have a *Gift* after all. Things make much more sense now." She smiled. "It is not mindless; it is lack of fear. Sometimes, to fill the gaps in annoying conversations, we simply want to choke someone. Isn't that right, One?"

"You will not turn him to your side," Xandre said pleasantly. His eyes darkened, giving him away.

Her smile burned brighter. Thanks to Burson, she knew how his talent worked. She knew any tiny action created flutters of paths that could lead to the same thing, or hundreds of different things. Looking around, she saw the fastidious control he employed. The trays were placed *just so*. The tables, the chairs—everything was laid out in perfect order. He went by titles, to distance people, and stayed away from the majority of his force, always moving, surrounded by his Inner Circle, a guard that didn't change.

"I bet you have a bunch of rules." She stood and walked toward the cliff. "You keep everything contained. You try not to allow chaos near you to cut down on the number of possible outcomes." She turned back to face them. Tightness had worked into Xandre's shoulders. "Do they know?" She nodded toward One.

"You are here because I could not pin you down. You are an amazing creature, who—"

"Stop with the flattery. It's annoying." She waved him away before wandering to Tac. On impulse, she grabbed his book—"Don't!" Xandre said—and threw it. The pages fluttered in a goodbye as it flew over the cliff.

Anger flared in Tac's eyes as he looked up. She remembered that rage, from somewhere down really deep. He seemed cool on the surface, but Sanders had gotten to him. Had pulled out the fire buried within.

She smiled down, but spoke to Xandre. "I am your worst nightmare. I don't do anything normally. Cayan will tell you. I choose paths that most people don't even think of. Wouldn't think of, because they are insane. You'll keep up for a while, but soon all the various outcomes will converge, and you'll have no idea what will happen next."

"Exactly. All the paths will converge into blackness. My question is..." Xandre, relaxed again, reached forward and grabbed a piece of bread. He smeared cheese on it and sat back. "Who will finally win?"

Shanti must've been back on the "known quantity" path when she made herself a plate and sat back gratefully. "That is a great question. At the moment, I am completely outnumbered. So I guess it depends on when you want to try to kill me."

"I won't be killing you."

"Oh? Then you'll loan me out to your men for sport? Isn't that what battle leaders in your position do?"

Xandre grimaced. "What must you think of me? How barbaric. Besides, you'd only kill them. Men lose all traces of thought when they give in to lust. Women, on the other hand, often hold a little back for just the right moment, and stick their knife in unsuspecting ribs."

"Had a narrow escape, did you?" Shanti tried the cheese, which was surprisingly delicious. "I sure hope this isn't drugged or poisoned."

"Again, what must you think of me? I spend nearly a lifetime getting you here, and you think I'll resort to tricks to kill you? No. I think if we communicate, openly, we can come to some discourse. Our problem is simply a confused past."

Shanti accidentally broke her cracker between her fingers. "Killing my people was a spot of confusion, was it?"

"The outcome was unfortunate, but I think if you see…"

"You've stopped talking because you've realized the likelihood of my getting extremely angry and trying to kill you is high, right?"

He spread cheese on another piece of toast.

"The thing is, you're afraid of pain," she said with her mouth full of cheese, just to annoy him. "You're afraid of me trying to choke the life out of you, even though One would stop me before I could, not to mention the Inkna. But you're still scared of the pain and fear that would come from me launching myself at you." Xandre's jaw clenched. A vein in this temple pulsed. She was getting to him. "One is not afraid, you can bet. I wonder why he listens to you?"

"Who would he listen to, if not me?" Xandre squinted and tilted his head. "There is *one* person who opposes me. Who has failed to succumb to my leadership. That is you. And here you are, imprisoned. You are at *my* mercy. He is at my mercy. The whole land is at my mercy. If he killed me, the Inkna would kill him and try to take over. They would, of course, die by your hand. Or someone else with mind power. I am the only thing holding all of this together, and I do it with brainpower no one in this land can match. *That* is why he listens to me. Why they all do. Why you will."

"Wow. Such a big ego in such a tiny body." Shanti bit into her bread, grinning into his angry stare. An unhinged stare. The cracks in his calm demeanor were showing.

"You will see reason," he said, and took a sip of his drink. He was visibly trying to calm down. "This will be helped, of course, by your loved ones coming for you. As you watch them die, you'll be much more willing to make a deal."

"Is it exhausting thinking so little of everyone else, or does it make you feel righteous?"

He put the drink down slowly. "Why did you not try to kill Tac and then One? I expected that."

"I thought about it, but if I had, then what?"

He stared at her, waiting.

"You really do think you're much smarter than everyone else. How annoying." She turned in her seat to look at One, who was watching her. "Is that not horribly annoying? I'd punch him in the gullet if I were you. Seriously."

One's face didn't change. The good little fighter.

"Maybe he is afraid of you," Shanti said, turning back. "Anyway, if I killed him—easy with Tac gone—I'd need to get out of here. My legs are weak, I'm in a sheet of some sort, I have no shoes, and no idea where I am. Two master executioners wouldn't keep me for long, but of course I assume you have more Inkna lurking around the place. They would bombard me with the *Gift,* and I'd run around, weaponless, no pants, trying to kill them. How long could I have possibly lasted if I made a mad attempt like that?"

"I don't quite know how to take you, Shanti Cu-Hoi. You are so different in person than you were described. I am intrigued and disgusted at the same time. I've never felt this way before."

"Well, don't get attached. My goal in life is to kill you. That's a pretty big shadow over our relationship." Shanti finished off the morsels on her plate and put it back. "Where are my weapons?"

"In a safe place. I realize they mean something to you."

"Yes. And my clothes?"

"They are being cleaned. I thought you'd be comfortable in that. Your people are no strangers to nudity, as are mine. We had a similar upbringing, you and I."

"Except I bet a tyrant didn't invade your village and kill your whole way of life, hmm? I bet we have that one difference."

"I think you'll find that we have more similarities than differences." He smiled benignly.

She punched him.

As her fist smacked against his mouth, she felt strong hands on her shoulders, ripping her away. She lifted her hands and let out a delighted laugh, even as

One tossed her onto the ground and stood between them. No pain came from the Inkna.

"I yield," she said, smiling over Xandre's split lower lip. "What happened there, Xandre? Did my impulse move faster than your *Gift*?"

Xandre's face had drained of color. He grabbed a cloth from the table and dabbed his lower lip, bringing it away to look at it. His eyes trained on the blood before red rushed into his cheeks. Anger.

Slowly, ever so slowly, he lowered the cloth. His eyes bored into Shanti. "You are playing a very dangerous game, girl."

"You see, that is where you're wrong. I have never been playing a game. I have been fighting for survival. Against you. We aren't friends, and we'll never be allies, Xandre. This will end one of two ways: I will kill you, or you will make someone kill me." She rose. One let her. "Are we done here?"

"Your friends are probably almost at the edge of the swamp by now, assuming they could follow you at all. I wonder who will die first…"

"Always with the superiority complex." Shanti shook her head, feeling reckless. "That is the problem with men like you—you are so busy thinking highly of yourself, you fail to really see the world around you."

She took a step toward One, needing to fight out some of her fear and anger. Needing to release. She also needed to see where her body was in terms of recovery from whatever they'd given her. It was a benefit that this loss, one she wouldn't have to guarantee if he was half as good as she suspected, would confirm in his mind that he was better. She doubted Xandre was the only one with a superiority complex.

"There is no point in trying," Xandre said. "He will beat you."

One's eyes glimmered, excitement flaring.

"Yes, he will. Don't tell him my first move, though. It'll spoil the fun."

CHAPTER TWELVE

"**H**OW IS THE CAPTAIN ever going to get through that maze?" Xavier asked, hunched near the castle wall and looking out over the swampland below.

Marc was staring at it too. They'd followed the Graygual along a path that seemed mostly benign until the light of day, and then realized they should've left hints or discarded items for the captain to follow. The area was a mess of tall reeds, deceptive grasses, and soggy land, the trail they'd followed last night easily blending into everything else.

Out of that sweltering bog rose the hill they were standing on, flattened at the top where the looming castle stood looking out over the sea. It was like the jutting rock had been put there by a divine hand, because no way did it appear natural. The location was perfect for defense. Too bad Xandre had the upper hand.

They'd gotten their horses up the hillside near dawn, after the Graygual were within the castle walls, and stashed them with the Graygual horses just outside the walls, which were crumbled and broken in more than one place. It would be easy to get back to them. Since most of the animals were from the same breeding lines, they blended in easily. Except for the Bastard. He wouldn't stay with the other horses. Alexa solved the problem by giving him a swat to the rump and sending him neighing back toward the swamps. If the Graygual recognized him, they'd remember him as the wild horse from the city and might assume he'd followed S'am. He'd be brought to heel or left out in the reeds, slogging through murky water.

"There are Inkna here." Alexa put her hand on the rough stone, one of the solid parts of an otherwise old and degrading wall surrounding the castle. It was afternoon, they'd rested as much as they could, and it was time for action. "A lot of them, and high-powered, from what I can tell. If the Inner Circle is gathered here then we're sunk. If the man who deadens *Gifts* doesn't do it, the Inkna will block my power. Then the Inner Circle will run us through with swords. None of us are any match for them. What good are we possibly going to do on our own?"

"This is why I've been harping on about a plan." Rachie shook his head.

"Are you sure her premonition said to follow?" Xavier asked, staring at Marc intensely.

It wouldn't do to say, "Mostly sure, yes." That might

not inspire the sort of confidence they needed.

"Yes. She said we had to follow, or S'am would die." Marc nodded decisively. Because really, they were there now. The choice was made.

"Okay." Xavier matched Marc's nod. "Then we need to figure this out. What are the chances Inkna are monitoring inside the castle?"

"Based on when the Hunter took over the West-wood Lands, the Inkna only monitored those they thought were a threat, right?" Ruisa scratched her cheek, clearly thinking.

"Alena would know," Gracas said.

"Alena's not here, you idiot." Rachie rolled his eyes.

"Didn't they mostly leave the women alone?" Ruisa looked around.

"I think so." Leilius was still staring down at the swamplands.

"So, as long as we don't raise suspicion, we'll be fi-ne." Xavier didn't look as confident as he sounded.

"What about the Inner Circle?" Alexa pressed.

"This is a castle." Leilius turned and looked along the wall. "An old castle. There might be secret rooms and doors and corridors in it. If nothing else, there'll be places to hide. Let's sneak in, kill the man who keeps her *Gift* deadened, get her, and get back out. If we have to kill an Inner Circle guard, we'll have to be sly about it."

"See? That's a plan." Rachie motioned toward Leilius. "It is the dumbest plan I've ever heard, but it is a plan."

"Got a better one?" Leilius scowled at him.

"Nope. Which is why we'll follow that one and hopefully not die." Rachie patted his sword, and then his knives. "I'm ready."

"Let's wait until nightfall." Marc stared down at the swamp, hoping to see an army making their way through. That was ridiculous thinking, of course, because there was no way the captain could have gotten the entire camp packed and underway in so short of time.

Another thought occurred to him. "Does the captain even know Xandre is here?"

"He should. I wrote it all down." Leilius looked up at the top of the wall. He slid his hands over the rough surface. "We dropped a couple of pieces of fabric, too. So he has that to follow."

"Like I told you, there is no way he'll see a couple of ripped pieces of your shirt hanging on the branch of a tree. Even if he does, why would he think they are yours?" Ruisa wiped her hand over her face. "I'm hungry."

"That's a problem, yes." Xavier lowered down to his butt. "We'll wait until nightfall, like Marc said. Then we'll work our way in and see what there is to see. The kitchens are bound to shut down at some time, and we can grab a bite then."

"I hope you're as good as you think you are," Alexa said to Leilius. Leilius' eyes widened and his face sagged under her scrutiny.

"He's better," Xavier said forcefully, his confidence returned ten-fold. "He was hand-trained by S'am."

Alexa eyed Xavier before her gaze roamed over his bristled stance and flexed muscles. Unperturbed, she shrugged, letting it go. "Why do you call her S'am?"

"Long story," Marc said. He sat at the base of the wall, his stomach doing flip-flops with what was to come. They were no match for the fighters inside those walls. Some of them would be as good as S'am, maybe better. They'd have stealth, eyes in the backs of their heads…

He looked at Alexa, willing her to suddenly tense up and rattle out more directions. Instead, her head swiveled until she was staring back at him. "What?"

Marc sighed and looked at his hands. He felt sick with what was to come. "Nothing. I guess I'll try to get some more sleep. I'll probably need it tonight."

AS DUSK APPROACHED, Cayan stared out at the land before them, a sweeping area of marsh that led up to a hill supporting a dilapidated castle, and in the distance a stretch of sea. The sound of waves crashing surged rhythmically. Cayan bet they'd be smashing against a cliff nearly impossible to scale, let alone get a boat alongside.

"Smart." He rested his boot on the springy ground, lightly applying pressure. A small amount of water circled his sole. "Very smart. He's chosen his location well."

"Too well." Sanders waited behind him, his face closed down in consternation. "He'll have rigged this place to kill, you can bet on it."

"Yes he will. What are the odds that he learned of Maggie's explosives?"

"Good, probably. He seems to know every other damn thing, including that we'd be in Belos. He had his men waiting around for her, waiting for an opportunity. He got one. He took it. Now we're in this shit hole."

"Yes, thank you, Sanders." Cayan glanced back at those who were with him. Especially Burson. "Do you know how to get through this?"

He shook his head solemnly. "I only know that one of us will die to do it. Don't ask me who. The face changes with the path."

"This stuff again. It was so nice when you were in another town," Sanders growled at Burson.

"I agree." Burson smiled at the sky, earning a dark look from Sanders.

"What is your best guess on the arrival of the rest of

our army?" Cayan asked Sanders.

"Tomorrow night, earliest."

"Boas may have alerted them, then taken whoever was ready," Sonson said, staring out at the swamp with a furrowed brow. "He thinks quickly in a bind and races toward danger when he can. He'll bring the animals, you can bet. We may have some help here by dawn."

"Help won't matter if we can't get through the swamp in any significant numbers." Sanders scuffed at the ground. "If we thread our way across now, I can probably pick up some tracks. Maybe the kids even left more shirt sleeves to help us. A lot will be guess work, though, if they went through larger pools. The enemy aren't fools. Sadly."

"I can get us through this." Sonson swiped at some tall reeds. "I'm no stranger to wetlands. And I can do it *without* losing anyone."

Burson shrugged. "Who's to say?"

"You, apparently." Sanders glanced at the sky. "Do we go now, or do we wait for daylight?"

Cayan stared at the castle, feeling pain and fire from Shanti. Not hopelessness, though. She'd had a fresh surge of determination not that long ago, amid some physical suffering. Knowing her, she had picked a fight when she wasn't strong enough to back it. That good news. Having her in a fighting spirit meant hope. She'd hold her own, at least for a while.

"Can we approach this from another side?" Cayan asked.

"I'm sure we could." Sanders looked away from the ocean. "But making our way there would take time, and we don't know if the path will be better or worse."

One thing they didn't have was time.

"Dawn," Cayan said, coming to a decision. "As soon as we have enough light, we'll pick our way through. Hopefully we'll have help by then." Something occurred to him. He turned back to Burson. "You said one would die crossing this swamp. Are any of the faces yours?"

"Yes. In which case, your probability of succeeding in Shanti's rescue falls dramatically. You'll be exposed to the largest collection of high-powered Inkna in the land." Burson stared up at the castle. "I wonder how the young people made it through. They must've received a guiding hand."

"Hopefully they will live long enough for us to ask them." Cayan shook his head and started back to the horses.

LEILIUS MOTIONED EVERYONE through the small hole in a crumbling part of the castle wall. The place was a mess of disrepair. If the captain could just make it through that swamp, he would be able to get in without any problem. There was no way the Graygual could defend all the entrances for long.

Silent and agile, every one of the Honor Guard passed by like ghosts in the night, not disturbing the rocks that lay scattered around. A dark shadow on the wall down the way stood quietly, looking out. Ruisa had been right—Inkna didn't often patrol their living quarters unless a known threat existed. With S'am no doubt hidden from their powers, they wouldn't be troubled. Hopefully.

A pockmarked wooden door separated them from inside the castle.

"Alexa, is anyone on the other side?" Xavier whispered.

She shook her head slowly before holding up a hand. The shake turned to a nod. "Just walked in," she said softly. "A man. Cunning. Probably a fighter."

Xavier leaned back and looked around. "Anyone know where we might be within the interior layout?"

"Does it look like I build castles for a living?" Rachie moved along the wall and disappeared around the bend.

"What's he doing?" Maggie asked.

"Probably looking around." Xavier stared at Alexa. "Any chance you can make one of those premonitions come?"

"No. I don't have any control, or any memory of them. I wouldn't even know I had them if someone hadn't told me."

Xavier blew out a breath as Rachie came back. "There's another door up the way. An Inkna is on the wall in front of it. He seems bored. Not paying very much attention."

"That might be too close for a group of us." Xavier motioned Rachie away again. "Scout out a little further."

"Yes, sir."

"He called you sir." Gracas nudged Xavier. "Big day, huh?"

"Would you focus?" Ruisa shoved Gracas out of the way. She stepped up to a rustic handle. "This door probably makes a lot of noise when you open it."

"The person inside is…leaving—gone. He's out." Alexa motioned her through. "Go."

"No." Xavier put his hand on Ruisa's shoulder. "Wait a moment. We can't rush with warriors of this caliber."

Leilius, standing on the edge of the group, felt his gut pulling him upward. "We should climb to the second floor," he said without thinking.

Xavier stepped back and looked up as Rachie rushed back toward them. Urgency covered his expression. "We have to go," he whispered furiously. "There's a Graygual coming. I don't like the way he moves."

In consternation, Xavier looked at the door, and then upward. His gaze fell on Leilius. "We'll split up.

You climb. Now. Get going. Gracas, Ruisa, and Maggie, you go too. The rest of us will go through the door. Marc, stay close to Alexa just in case she says something. Be prepared to muffle her voice."

Without another thought, Leilius was jogging down the way a little, eyeing the rough stone. He chose a place with divots and pockmarks and dug his fingers in. This would be a challenge, to say the least.

"Are you kidding?" Ruisa asked under her breath. Metal clinked and rusty hinges squeaked back the way they'd come. The others were going through the door. "Crap. That is going to draw attention."

She took to the wall like she was born to climb, gripping anything she could and digging in her toes to find purchase. Gracas started under Leilius, quickly losing grip and sliding back down. Maggie grabbed him and tried to push him back up before giving up and following after Ruisa. She didn't fare much better than Gracas.

"I have to find another way," Gracas said, hurrying down the wall.

"I'll go with him. No way am I getting up there." Maggie jogged after him.

"Wait—" Leilius saved his breath. The two were already out of sight.

A shout rang through the night in a familiar language, though he couldn't understand the words. It was back near the door.

"I didn't hear the door close, did you?" Ruisa asked through a strain-filled voice. She clung on, looking for grip.

"No," Leilius wheezed, pulling himself up to a window. It was open, no glass. Good news.

Another shout rang out. Footsteps sounded, fast and heavy. That couldn't be the advanced Graygual. Probably Inkna.

"Let's go, let's go!" Leilius pulled himself into the window and turned back for Ruisa. Expression intense and focused, she worked her way closer. The footsteps stopped for a moment. The hinges from the door squealed.

Leilius stuck out his hand. "Almost there."

Breathing heavily, Ruisa nodded slightly and kept working. One handhold at a time, clinging to the surface. Her foot slipped, dragging her weight down. She gritted her teeth, barely seen with the shadow across her face, but held.

Loud talking accompanied boot falls, coming closer. Walking.

"They're coming! Grab my hand." Leilius shook his hand in the air, reaching down for her.

She dug her foot into a divot and moved closer. Her arms shook with strain. Slowly, carefully, she reached for his hand.

The footsteps moved closer.

Leilius bent further and grabbed one of her hands as her other gave way. Her feet gave away. She slid down the stone, scratching her face. All her weight tugged at Leilius, threatening to drag him through the window.

His turn to grit his teeth, he held on with everything he had. She swung her free hand up and grabbed his wrist. He pulled as she did, shortening the distance between them. *Thank God she's strong.*

Leilius leaned back, his heart hammering, a body coming into view. Black uniform but slightly jerky movements; it had to be an Inkna. Giving it everything he had, hoping the Inkna wasn't patrolling with his Gift, Leilius hauled a squirming Ruisa into the window and fell backward. She pushed off the window ledge, falling on top of him.

They were up a moment later, turning around and looking out through the window at the Inkna passing below. The Inkna looked away right and veered toward a hole in the defense wall. He bent, glancing around it, before straightening. As he turned, Ruisa fell away and jerked Leilius with her.

"You shouldn't move!" Leilius whispered, so low he could barely hear himself. He couldn't read her expression, but she shook her head.

Leilius waited, not daring to repeat himself. No pain seared their minds. The heavy footfalls kept going, slowly. Checking things out.

He heaved a big sigh, clutching his chest where his heart was still trying to get out of his ribcage.

"Hey." Ruisa tugged on his sleeve. "We need to get out of here."

Looking around for the first time, Leilius realized that everything was extremely orderly. The bed, a four-poster affair, was made with precision. The furniture was placed in an organized way, with not even the chair angled slightly. A stack of black uniforms sat atop a small chair, perfectly folded.

Ruisa bent, looking closer at those uniforms. "A red circle on the breast, completely filled in. I don't think that's Inkna."

"No. We don't want to be in this room when the owner of those uniforms goes to bed."

Ruisa rushed to the door and bent to the keyhole. After looking through for a moment, she straightened up and grabbed the handle. She turned and pulled. The door didn't budge. "Oh no."

"What is it?" Leilius met her there, staring down at her hand.

She looked at him with somber eyes. "It's locked. We're trapped."

CHAPTER THIRTEEN

"HURRY!" Alexa motioned wildly for Marc to get away from the door. It was still standing wide open. "There's someone coming!"

Before Marc could protest, Xavier ripped him away from it and thrust him at a shadow in the corner of a large kitchen. Xavier ran across the room, folding into another shadow just as a Graygual stalked in carrying two trays.

He noticed the door and slowed, his brow crumpling. After dropping his trays on the large wooden table, the Graygual moved slowly toward the opened door. A second Graygual entered, his trays holding the remnants of what appeared to be a large supper.

"What's the problem?" one of the Graygual asked, hesitating near the table.

"Did you open this door?" The other pointed at the door, standing next to it.

"No..."

The Inkna they'd been running from outside poked his head through the doorway, clearly having the same question on his mind as the Graygual.

"What are you doing spying?" the Graygual near the door said angrily. *"Get out of here, you mind raper."*

"All that training to be a cook." The Inkna sneered. *"You are so low your belly scrapes the floor."*

"The master allows us in his presence while your kind are put outside like dogs." The Graygual flung his hand at the Inkna. *"Get out, dog. Go back where you belong."*

The Inkna shouted something Marc didn't understand before taking a step back. The Graygual slammed the door in his face, bristling with rage.

"Filthy," the other Graygual said, disgust in his voice. *"It's too bad they have their uses."*

"C'mon." The first Graygual headed for the interior door. *"Let's finish up."*

Marc let out a breath he hadn't realized he was holding. Adrenaline coursed through his body. He'd thought they'd get caught. They *should* have been caught. Marc had no idea the Graygual and the Inkna hated and mistrusted each other so much, but it was a damn good thing they did. Alexa held out a hand in the *stop* gesture.

The Graygual entered again, carrying more trays. Not paying attention to anything but their task at hand, they stacked up the dirty dishes. This time, only one left, and the other busied himself organizing a tub for washing up. He wasn't going anywhere.

Xavier stared at Alexa for a moment. She pointed at the Graygual, and then drew her finger across her neck. Xavier nodded once, slowly, clearly not realizing that trying to kill this sort of Graygual was a death wish for anyone but the captain and Shanti.

Slowly, carefully, Xavier extracted a knife, utterly silent, thank the heavens. Alexa followed suit. Then Rachie.

They were all either extremely dumb, or utterly insane. There was no other explanation. If they didn't get killed, they'd alert the whole castle that there were enemies in their midst.

Besides, what if everything went according to plan? Which *never* happened. Then what? Did these nitwits assume no one would notice the absence of a *cook*? By breakfast time, the whole place would be hunting down their food.

Marc waved his hands to get Xavier's attention, and when he did, shook his head and mouthed, "No." Big no. N-O.

Xavier scowled, sinking into a ready crouch.

"When the sun is at its zenith, chaos will keep the hero alive."

The whole room froze. The Graygual turned toward Alexa's hiding place, confusion on his face. Marc and Xavier shared a quick look, and both surged forward at the same time.

The Graygual reacted, one moment washing dishes, the next standing in a relaxed sort of crouch with his sword in his hand. It meant very bad things.

"Don't play with him. Kill as quickly as possible," Xavier said, moving with speed the captain would be proud of.

Play with him? Xavier obviously didn't have a firm grasp on reality.

Rachie came from the side, his sword in hand. The Graygual met Rachie's lunge easily and countered, slicing a line down Rachie's arm. Rachie bit his lip and retreated as Xavier barreled into the Graygual, Sanders-style. His bigger body took the man to the ground, trapping the Graygual's sword under them. Xavier jabbed his knife into the Graygual before being body flipped off. He knocked against the table. A tray wobbled and then fell, clanging on the ground.

Marc dashed in and struck twice before flinging himself away, knowing that if he stuck around, that Graygual would carve letters into him. Xavier was back again, tackling the bleeding Graygual and jamming his knife into his neck. Xavier rolled away as the Graygual jerked, the strength leaving him as fast as the gushing blood.

"That's the last of the trays—" The second Graygual cut off as he entered the room, hesitating as his gaze fell on the downed body, a move that took away his only

chance at survival. Alexa was on him in an instant, thrusting her sword through his middle. She yanked it back and then stabbed him through again.

He looked down at the sword tip sticking out of his front as he sank to his knees. Alexa pulled the blade out of his back. He fell forward onto his face.

"Who's going to make breakfast?" Marc asked, out of breath. "Because if people don't get their breakfast, they're going to be pissed, and guess who they'll go looking for." Marc waved his bloody knife over the two guys lying facedown. "Yeah. These guys, that's who."

"Ouch." Rachie inspected his arm.

"What did she say?" Xavier pointed at Alexa.

"She said that when the sun is at its zenith—noon—chaos will keep the hero alive." Marc looked at all the dirty dishes. "We need to get these squared away, because if someone comes looking for a midnight snack and sees all this mess, guess who they're going to go looking for?" Marc raised his eyebrows at the others. He waved his knife over the dead guys again. "Exactly. These guys."

"Cut off some of their fabric. I need to wrap my arm." Rachie tapped Xavier, who was vaguely looking at the wall.

"So we need to create chaos to keep the hero alive…" Xavier looked at Marc. "Who's the hero?"

"She didn't say. But we won't live until tomorrow if

we don't sort out the dishes and the dead bodies." Marc waved his knife above the dead guys again, this time more dramatically.

"It doesn't matter who the hero is. It doesn't change our job." Alexa bent for one of the Graygual.

"Finally someone listens." Marc grabbed the Graygual's top half as Alexa lifted the bottom and they moved him toward a corner. "Or what about under the last shelf in the pantry?"

Alexa rolled her eyes. "We need to drop them outside the wall where no one patrols. A missing person is better than a dead body."

"How the hell are we going to do that?" Marc demanded.

"Look both ways, cross really quickly, drag them through a hole and behind the wall, run back. Why are you in this group?"

"Xavier. Help me wrap my arm." Rachie prodded Xavier again.

"Why isn't anyone coming to check out the noise?" Marc wondered as Alexa opened the door slowly and stuck her head out. She threw it open the rest of the way and quickly lifted the body again.

"They were yelling at the Inkna a moment ago," Alexa said before they hurried the body out and disposed of it. Back in the kitchen between drops, she continued, "Clearly people here are either used to outbursts and noise, or we are in the bowels of the castle and can't be heard."

"S'am didn't mention that you're kind of a know-it-all," Marc mumbled as they got rid of the second body.

Back in the kitchen and with the door closed, Marc rolled up his sleeves. "I'll wash. Who's drying?"

"Are you serious?" Xavier tied off the fabric on Rachie's arm and stacked the empty plates quietly. He set them in the corner out of sight. "We're not doing the damn dishes."

"Oh." Marc shook his head at himself. "Right, yeah. Of course."

"Now what?" Rachie asked, taking a lump of ham off one of the trays.

"Eat, then we'll hide the trays with the plates and try to find the others. We need to tell them to lie low until the morning." Xavier grabbed a half-eaten piece of bread. "If I wasn't so hungry I'd think this was gross."

"If I wasn't so terrified that those guys were probably the weaker of the fighters in this house, I'd have a bigger appetite." Marc grabbed a piece of ham.

"If I wasn't so amazed that it took three Westwood men to do the job of one Shumas woman, I'd scoff." Alexa grabbed a piece of bread. "No. I'm still going to scoff."

"You just walked up behind him. Real clever," Rachie said through a mouthful.

"Yes. It was. Which is why I'm not wounded." Alexa blinked in such a way that said Rachie was an idiot.

"Quiet down." Xavier started filling a sack with food. "Hurry up and eat and let's go. We need to find the others."

SHANTI STARED ACROSS the small table at One. They were, once again, at the sitting area overlooking the great nothingness where darkness covered the raging sea below. Tac sat off to the side, a new book in hand, staring at the stars. It was like he was asleep while sitting up, his brain completely shut off. Shanti was sure Inkna lurked somewhere just out of sight, making sure she behaved, though given the earlier display by One, she doubted they'd think they were needed. One had beaten her bloody, taking to her without mercy until Xandre had called him off.

Or, at least, that was what he had made it look like.

The truth was, he'd taken it easy on her in a way Xandre wouldn't understand. He hadn't hit her any-where he might cause permanent damage. He could've ripped her arm out of its socket at one point, or tweaked it painfully at the very least, but he'd backed off, with a blow to her stomach instead. All her injuries were to fleshy areas that would bruise spectacularly, but heal easily.

"Let's get down to the heart of it. Is Xandre hiding somewhere, listening to everything we say? Otherwise, why haven't you locked me in my room?" she asked One, focusing on his facial expressions and his body language. Unfortunately, the man didn't seem to have many tics to give away his thoughts.

"He is not hiding, no," Tac said, staring upward. "He is in his chamber. You shocked him today. Your unpredictability is something he rarely encounters. He's probably planning what to do with you. As for your room, I wanted to sit out here. What's the difference?"

One's eyes widened, proving Shanti's earlier theory false. Apparently, shock got through his self-control just fine. He stared at Tac for a moment. "This is not a conversation you are a part of."

Tac smiled, sending a chill down Shanti's spine. "I am a part of all conversations." He lowered his head, leveling a hard stare at One. "Xandre makes you relevant. You're smart enough to realize that. Without him, you're nothing but a highly trained mercenary."

"A mercenary that could easily teach you to watch your tongue." One's lip quirked into a snarl.

"Maybe. But without me, the Inkna can easily teach *you* to watch your tongue. You need me, whether you want to admit it or not."

"The Inkna have their place. A place they stayed in before we scraped you out of that destroyed village and raised you above the rest of the land. I had my position before you knew the might of the Graygual, don't forget that."

"Vain." Tac shook his head and looked back at the stars, his smile still curling his lips. "So very vain. You have helped create an empire which the Inkna financially run. The real threat is the Chosen, not you. The Shumas. The Shadow. Other people fluent in mental power, who can also fight. *That* is who they really fear. Not Xandre. Certainly not you. How long do you think it will take them to realize that they are a target because of their affiliation with Graygual? That they'd have more power as allies with the Chosen? Hell, they could take down a tyrant, make a deal with the captain, and exist in peace. You think they aren't disgusted that their women are used for breeding? That their sons are either killed if they don't have power, or are put through excruciating training if they do?"

Tac blew out a breath. "I bet they've already figured it out. And I bet Xandre knows that. Why else hasn't he killed Shanti? He needs her. He is a genius with a power that mostly steers him along the winning path, but there comes a point when there are simply too many pieces to control. Too much strife to ignore. With great oppression comes great courage, and he will become the target if he doesn't gain control." Tac glanced at Shanti. "And here we are. At the cusp of the next thing."

"You don't sound like a loyal player in this game," One said in a low voice filled with warning.

Tac waved the thought away and went back to staring at the sky. "I'll die before this is all through. Should've died already. With my family. I don't care what happens. Xandre feeds me, provides me with books I haven't read, and gives me an easy life so long as I protect him from the Inkna. Until I'm sent to the Underland, I'll do what I'm told. Doesn't mean I don't have a thinking brain on my shoulders. My eyes are open; I just don't care what they see anymore."

"Wow. This is depressing." Shanti picked up a berry from the solitary dessert tray and popped it into her mouth. The larger trays and the used plates had already been taken to the kitchens. "So, One, what will you do if the Inkna overthrow Xandre?"

"That won't happen." One was still staring at Tac.

"Just for kicks, what if it did?"

"I'd die," he answered without inflection. Tac nodded.

"I doubt the Inkna who are listening love that their great plans have been figured out and discussed." Shanti glanced over her shoulder, but didn't see anything. Not that she expected an Inkna to pop his head around the corner and throw her a thumbs-up or anything.

"Nope." Tac rested his book on his lap.

"Xandre will hear of his," One said, still staring

down the other man. A muscle pulsed in his jaw, the effect of clenching and unclenching. It seemed One was trying to control his temper. Interesting.

"So, One…" Shanti schooled her tone, light and un-affected. "Why did you take it easy on me earlier?"

One's head snapped toward her. His eyes flicked toward the Inkna location.

Another secret. Also interesting. There were layers to Xandre's camp. Shanti wondered if he knew that.

"You were not at your full strength. What would be the point in making sure you never would be again? That would interfere with the master's plans."

"Diplomatic," Tac said quietly.

One's hands curled into fists.

"I get the feeling you two don't talk much." Shanti crossed an ankle over her knee, and winced. Her leg still hurt from when One had expertly kicked it several times in the same spot. He was fast, strong, and had perfect form. *Perfect* form. He'd earned his position, Shanti could tell. It would take everything she had to beat him.

"We speak when spoken to," One said evenly. "The master does not like a lot of chatter. It interrupts his thinking. Usually *this one* follows those rules."

"The master is not here." Tac shrugged.

"He will hear about this," One said again.

"Will he?" Tac smiled. "You're not the only one capable of loose lips. At least I'm not pulling punches."

One cocked his head, as though he were cracking his neck. "I did not pull punches."

"He most certainly did not pull punches, no." Shanti massaged her ribs when a flicker of movement caught her eye. Wondering if Xandre was sneaking close enough to be able to listen after all, she focused in on the patch of darkness near the stone wall of the castle. A hand moved, barely definable, like a wave.

A shock of adrenaline coursed through Shanti as Gracas leaned a little into the light. *What are they doing here?*

Cayan wasn't with him. She could feel him off somewhere in the distance, probably separated by that swamp.

Another shape leaned forward until moonlight showered her head. Maggie!

Shanti jerked her head away, looking out over the sea. Fear coursed through her. If those two were here, ones that hadn't even been in the city, she would bet more were. If any of them were found, they'd be killed on the spot. Or worse, they'd be tortured to get Shanti to do what Xandre wanted.

The last thing she wanted to be responsible for was the death of those growing boys and girls. Even Maggie, fully an adult, wouldn't be in this mess if Shanti hadn't come along.

Guilt rushed in, as it always did when she realized she'd put someone she cared for in danger.

Shuffling behind her caught her attention. The Inkna stepped out. Did they feel the new additions?

Reacting quickly, she surged up and grabbed the base of One's chair. He didn't react, watching with an intrigued sparkle in his eyes, curious as to what she'd do.

She would beat the hell out of him, that was what she'd do.

Using all her strength, she overturned his chair. He fell onto his back and rolled gracefully, up on his feet a moment later. He winked at her. She couldn't help a smile. They were both born to fight, and if this had been a sparring session, she'd go after him with glee. But there were lives on the line.

She spun and kicked, smashing her foot into the side of Tac's face. He flew, turning over his chair and spilling onto the ground. One rushed her, but it was too late. The damage had been done.

Her *Gift* flooded into her, more powerful than both of the hidden Inkna guards combined. Electricity fizzled through her body as she *struck,* slicing through their offenses easily and stabbing her power directly into their brains. They stopped, pain freezing their muscles.

A fist came for her face, but she dodged easily. She *sliced* and *pounded* the Inkna, battering their attempts at another offense. They weren't putting up a huge struggle.

A moment later, she knew why.

One staggered, his kick sloppy. She met his shin with her knee, blocking. He squinted and shook his head as a blast hit Shanti's mind.

The Inkna were trying to take down both of them, and they'd surely blame it on her.

"Guess Tac was right," she said, peppering One with punches. She smashed her forearm across his face and then whirled around him, throwing him into a head-lock. Before she could execute it, he reached back and caught her shoulders. Bending with force, he threw her over him. She landed on her back, the wind knocked out of her.

He was on her a moment later, covering her body with his to pin her down, hammering a fist into her ribs. He smashed another fist in before grunting, probably taking another Inkna assault.

She bucked to get her knees under him and then flung him off. Quickly hopping up to her feet, she backed away for an extra couple seconds, and *smashed* into the Inkna offense, battering their power away again. This time she didn't let up. She created a white-hot blast of power, confined to a spear, and *pierced* into the meaty tissue of their minds. Their bodies crumpled as a stack of solid muscle crashed into her, taking her to the ground again.

She bit his shoulder and tried to get her arms around his neck to cut off his air supply. He countered, ripping her arms away and grappling.

At a glance, she saw Maggie and Gracas staring at her with wide eyes, swords in their hands.

She spared a moment of struggle to wave them away urgently. It was all One needed. He snatched her limbs and wrapped her up in his immovable body—not as strong as Cayan, but certainly stronger than she was. With his weight over her and her limbs pinned, she could do nothing but kill him with her *Gift,* or stare up at his impassive face and wait for an opportunity.

A moment passed and the same reasoning as before rolled through her mind—*then what?* There were still a lot of Graygual, and probably even more Inkna, and her Honor Guard trapped in the area with her. One's death wouldn't do much in the grand scheme of things, and as it stood, he had helped her. It might've been slight, but it was eyebrow raising.

"You killed two Inkna," he said in her language.

"You are really heavy."

"Were they trying to kill you?"

"I think they were trying to kill us both, which was stupid, since they should've been focusing all their attentions on me. I get the feeling they haven't been in battle before?"

"They were at the Shadow Lands, but not one on one, no." One's eyes bored into hers. *"I had heard you were strong in the power. I did not realize you were that strong."*

"They didn't either. Back to you being really heavy. Are you going to make a move? At the very least, can you shift a little? I realize you might not be in charge of certain parts of your body, but they are digging into me."

"I am not aroused."

"Well, your hips certainly are. Or are they always that hard?" Shanti struggled to get more breath, letting her *Gift* spread out as far as she could. At the edges of her range, she met the glorious tingles of Cayan's mind. Their *Joined* power fizzled up her center, giving off that spicy feeling she loved. He was not conscious, though. Probably asleep, which was good. She couldn't feel many with him, which meant it would be easy for Xandre to send out a group and wipe them out. He needed more time, because a small distance east of the castle, in what was probably a camp, lay a vast collection of power. She felt it rouse, spikes of the *Gift* reaching and searching her way.

"They are bone. Of course they are always that hard." One's expression turned quizzical.

"Not much for joking, huh?" A slash of power coursed through her mind. She slammed down her shields. One winced. *"I'm powerful, but I can't ward off*

the stockpile of Inkna you have close by. They are just now realizing one of their—"

One was off her in a flash. Not bothering to secure her, he bent to Tac and shook. *"Wake up, you fool."* One was back to using the Graygual tongue.

"It's amazing how many people know multiple languages. A real melting pot dealing with Xandre, huh?" Shanti battered away a mental probe and returned an attack. She looked at the place Maggie and Gracas had been, relieved to see them gone. Quickly scouring the castle, she located the others, either sneaking through the castle, sneaking around outside, or inside one of the upstairs rooms.

What were Leilius and Ruisa looking for in the rooms? Whatever it was, Shanti hoped it would help.

A sharp stab of pain assaulted her, making her stagger. She reached out blindly, fighting the scouring agony as it dripped down her body.

"Wake up!" One said.

Shanti heard a slap of skin, One hitting Tac, before another thrust of pain brought her to her knees. Invisible needles jabbed her eyes. Acid dripped down her skin. Fire boiled her blood.

"Not good," Shanti said, clenching her teeth. Her forearms hit a hard surface. She fell forward as scorching points stabbed her body. It felt like she was being burned alive.

"Shanti Cu-Hoi." Strong arms came around her as soft footfalls hurried toward them. *"Wake him up,"* One directed as Shanti rose into the sky. *"Is there somewhere I can take you, Shanti? What can shield you from mind pain?"*

Clearly the Inkna were focusing only on her. How nice of them to give her all of their attention.

She dug her fingers into skin and curled within herself, putting all her strength into her shield. After that, she drifted away from the pain, wondering if Tac would wake up before the Inkna killed her.

CHAPTER FOURTEEN

"*Don't let them kill her!*" someone bellowed from within the hall.

Leilius froze by the door as footfalls thundered down the hall. "I wonder who he's talking about?"

Boots scuffed on the stone outside and caught Leilius' attention. He rushed to the window in time to see Maggie and Gracas rush by, swords in hand. A few moments later, four Graygual ran after them, but without weapons in their hands.

"Crap, the Graygual are on to us. We have to get out of here and help hide everyone." Leilius licked his lips and stared down the sheer face of the wall. He could get back down, probably, but Ruisa had barely been able to climb upward. It would take her a long time to hunt for hand- and footholds, and she was probably still tired.

He glanced around the room. Rope would sure help them out right then.

Ruisa stood by a large trunk, pushing up the lid as she stared in Leilius' direction.

"What are you doing? Get away from there." Leilius

waved her away.

Ruisa looked down at the contents. "Everything is so incredibly organized."

"Which means the packer will probably know if one thing is out of place."

"He wouldn't know it was us, though." She picked out a gold chain and studied a sort of amulet dangling from the end. "Pretty."

"Who else would it be? C'mon, we have to figure out how to get out of here."

"Pick the lock."

Shouting rang through the night. A hoarse scream curled Leilius' toes. Thankfully, it sounded like a man. He just hoped it wasn't someone they had come with.

He looked around the room wildly. "With what?"

"You're the spy—figure it out." Ruisa picked out something else and studied it.

"Cut that out!" Leilius wiped the sweat off his forehead, his mind racing.

"*What set them off?*" someone asked in a venomous tone.

"*She killed two of theirs. They reacted when—*"

The voices drifted away. Leilius put his ear to the door, trying to hear anything else, but could only get the hum of voices. "Sounds like someone attacked S'am. Or else one of the girls that came with us. I can't be sure."

"You can understand Graygual?" Ruisa asked, holding up yet another thing that she shouldn't have been touching.

"I have an ear for languages and put a lot of time into that one after the Shadow Lands. Rohnan has been teaching me. I can only understand it, though. My accent is horrible and the words don't come easily when I try to speak it. Rohnan says that is normal—"

"Okay, okay, I get it." Ruisa made a *let's go* motion. "Keep working on that lock."

"I haven't *started* working on the lock." Leilius wiped his moist palms on his pants. "Is there anything in that trunk that'll help me pick a lock?"

The sound of objects moving made Leilius grit his teeth. There was absolutely no way Ruisa would be able to put everything back the way she found it. She held something out, still looking downward. "Try this."

He grabbed it out of her hand, finding a pack of lockpicks.

"Oh, here." Ruisa handed out something else. "Looks like a key."

"How are you finding these things?" Leilius glanced over her shoulder at the shadowy box. He couldn't make heads or tails of anything.

"I'm an orphan. I've rifled through a lot of other people's personal items in the dead of night so they wouldn't know."

"Does privacy mean nothing to you?" Leilius mumbled, taking the heavy key. "I doubt these doors have spare keys."

He fit the key in the lock and turned. The lock disengaged. "Oh shit, it worked." He braced by the door for a moment as his heart picked up speed; he knew he was about to run into danger again. Somehow, being locked in a room was less daunting than having no cover in a castle filled with a lot of men. The stakes might not have been higher, but the room for error certainly was.

"Put that stuff away. We're—" Leilius started as Ruisa materialized by his side. "You probably should've been trained to spy."

"I was. I just said I was an orphan, remember?"

"It's as if you think that by being an orphan, you don't have to live by the rules.

"Kind of a big jump in logic, that." She paused. "What are you waiting for."

"The right time."

"It's quiet. *Now* is the right time." Ruisa moved him to the side and took the handle, thankfully having more courage to continue their task than he did.

The door opened on silent hinges, ghosting the crack in the door larger. Ruisa slowly stuck out her head with her knife held low. Her shoulders disappeared in the crack next, then her body was gone.

Here we go.

Taking a deep breath, Leilius slowly exhaled as he slipped out of the door and closed it behind him. After locking it, he slipped the key into his pocket and took in the scene. Doorways lined the hallway, with an empty chair sitting in front of the room at the end. Sparsely placed torches burned on the walls, blackening the stone and casting an eerie glow within the space.

"They attacked One."

A blast of surprise rocked through Leilius. *Someone was coming!*

He hurried across the hall and down the way, running to a large tapestry on an extended portion of wall. He slipped into the shadow next to it and froze. A slight shuffle came from Ruisa down the hallway as she hopefully found a good hiding place.

"Filthy rats," someone else said. Two Graygual turned the corner, walking slowly. Both sets of eyes scanned in front of them before settling on the chair at the end.

"That's what she calls Inkna, too. Rats. She hates them."

"She hates us."

"One tried to help her. The master said that would help earn her trust. Maybe loosen her up. If we had her people, we wouldn't need the Inkna. We could just do away with them."

The one on the right sniffed. *"What's the difference?*

We trade one mind raper with another. We need to exterminate the whole breed. It isn't right. Anyone with mental fuckery needs to die."

The other one put out a hand to slow the first. He glanced around before lowering his voice. *"That's just the thing. The only reason her people, or the Shadow, are giving us any trouble is because the master messed with their homes. They don't want any part of all this. If they killed the Inkna, they'd be content just to live in a good land and mind their own business."*

"You're full of snaif." Leilius hadn't heard that last word before. He wondered if S'am knew of it. She loved collecting bad words—he needed to remember it for her. *"They might not have wanted to get involved in the beginning, but now they are. They are a hard, stubborn type of people. The master isn't going to turn her, no matter how nice that stuck-up trash is to her."*

The first sucked air through his teeth. His gaze hit the door Leilius had recently exited. *"You'd better watch what you say about One."*

"Why? You trying to kiss his—" Leilius didn't get the last word.

The other put a hand on the first and pulled, getting them walking again. His gaze was still on that door. *"I'm not trying anything with that—"* Leilius shook his head in frustration as the man's words jumbled together. *"But he can kill you. Me. Any one of us. How many times does he have to prove it? You don't want to be on his list, or you might go out and never come back. He'll make up a reason for how you died, and the master will never question. He's got the master's favor."*

"That's only because of his position. If we unseat him, he'll *go out and never come back."*

"It's because One is as smart as he is cunning, you fool. The master doesn't have friends and he doesn't sympathize. He killed the former Three, and they grew up in neighboring villages. Don't get on One's bad side if you value your neck, that's all I'm saying."

They stopped further down. "You're weak." He opened a door, which wasn't locked. "You don't have what it takes to rise within the Inner Circle. You'll always be dangling out on the edges, hoping for an easy ride." The Graygual shot a scathing look back at the door of the room Leilius had exited before disappearing.

The first shook his head and continued on down the way, muttering to himself. His hand came up, like an unconscious movement, and grazed a knife at his belt. A moment later he'd disappeared through another unlocked door.

The hallway fell silent. Leilius exhaled softly. A hand found his shoulder, scaring him out of his skin.

Ruisa grinned from behind a tapestry, peeking out at him. "Didn't hear me coming?" she whispered, rubbing it in.

"I was taking a moment."

Her expression melted into seriousness and her glance drifted beyond him. "What were they saying?"

Leilius shook his head, his gaze finding that door. "The Inner Circle sounds like a snake pit. And you rummaged through a trunk belonging to the smartest, scariest member among them. If I didn't have bad luck, I'd have no luck at all."

She rolled her eyes. "I put everything back. So now what?"

"We need to find the others and figure out what to do next. Those guys didn't sound panicked, so S'am must be okay, but there are more Inkna here than she can handle."

"The captain is coming and we have the root to suppress mind power. The Inkna aren't the problem. The Graygual are the problem. Remember how that one outside of the Mugdock land moved? He was insanely fast."

Leilius shuddered. He didn't need reminding about the Inner Circle. "There are more of them than she can handle, too. I don't know why we followed at all. The captain has to sort this out, not us."

"Complaining isn't solving the problem. C'mon." Ruisa pulled at his arm and started forward. She got five steps, however, into full view, before a shadow sailed across the far wall.

Leilius shoved her toward a groove in a darkened patch before slinking back into his shadow of choice. Her new hiding place wasn't great, but it was better than the tapestry, at least, where her toes had peeked out the bottom.

Her glare was equal parts confusion and irritation, pointing at him through the silence. There wasn't so much as a rustle of fabric to announce the gliding figure making his way down the hallway. His footfalls made no sound, though he was a tall, well-built man. Movements lithe and graceful, he walked perfectly balanced, as though he always had a sword in his hand. His gaze flashed up and down the corridor. For a moment, it rooted to the empty chair at the end. He passed Ruisa without noticing her, and then Leilius; the breeze made by his wake was a mostly clean smell, with only a hint of perspiration.

With a last look around, the Graygual stopped in front of the door Leilius had exited. Shivers ran down Leilius' spine as a key was produced and fitted into the lock. Another look and the Graygual turned. The lock disengaged.

A strong, scar-ridden hand flattened against the door, ready to push it open. He paused, which was vastly different from other men freezing. Freezing implied a tenseness, but there was nothing tense about this man. In fact, he was a terrifying type of fluid despite his whole body going still, as if he were ready to spring forward with a kill shot at any moment.

Slowly, still strangely silent, as though he were not really in this world, the Graygual turned.

Fire ants crawled and bit Leilius' flesh. The desire to scream and run was so strong that he stated to quiver.

The Graygual's eyes, barely seen in the dim light of a nearby torch, scanned the wall opposite his door. His hand dropped, sliding down the wood until soft fingers fell across metal. He sniffed, and continued to look over the walls and floor around him. In a moment, that hard, intelligent gaze landed on the tapestry. It dropped quickly, scanning the bottom, and then around the sides. Flowing over it before moving on, next those eyes were pointed directly at Leilius.

CHAPTER FIFTEEN

"WAIT!" ALEXA THREW out a hand and caught Xavier, stopping his forward progress. Marc bumped into the back of her before following their lead. "There's someone on the floor with Leilius."

They each drifted to the sides on the first floor near the stairs, having ample options to hide behind the furniture littering the area. Rachie and Marc took advantage immediately, getting out of sight while the others altered their plans yet again. This was probably the fourth path they'd taken to get to the two Honor Guard members upstairs. Each attempt before led into a still and silent sentry, staring straight ahead with a stern face.

"It's one of the Graygual," Alexa whispered, veering to the side with her hand on Xavier's shoulder, directing him.

He went with her like she'd molded him out of putty, glancing down at her hand and then into her face with an intensity unrelated to their desperate situation.

"Xavier," Marc whispered. He stepped into the open

long enough to flick Xavier on the neck. "Pay attention, you idiot! Now is not the time to drool."

Xavier blinked before his brow crumpled into a glower. "I was waiting to hear what she said."

Sure he was, the dope.

"He seems suspicious. Leilius is near him. I think." Alexa shook her head. "It could be him; I'm not positive. A girl—Ruisa, I think—is down the way. Leilius is about to poop himself in fear. Something is happening."

Alexa turned to Xavier. "We have to help," she whispered furiously. "It's only one of them and there are a six of us. We can take him."

Xavier glanced back at Marc, and a brief flash of uncertainty crossed his features. He was probably thinking there were only five worth mentioning— actually, four and a half, because Leilius wasn't great either. Determination stole over, though. If Leilius and Ruisa were up there with one of the Graygual, they had to try and help.

Marc started forward at the same time Rachie did, not needing to be told to get moving. They hurried up the stairs quietly, Marc by far the loudest in the ground.

Alexa's hand swung back and fell on Marc's chest. She stopped, forcing him to stop with her. The others slowed, looking back in confusion. Shadow and flickering light falling across her features from the sporadic torches, she met Marc's eyes and slowly shook her head.

"Stay back. He'll hear you."

Without another word, they kept going. Without him.

Fear crept into his middle as he was left standing on the deserted stairs. He looked around, realizing the lack of anywhere to hide. If someone came after them, which was bound to happen sooner or later, they'd find a lanky guy with a poor understanding of weaponry standing in hostile enemy territory like an idiot. They'd run him through for sure.

Coming to a quick decision, Marc hurried back down the stairs and hid behind a heavy couch with sagging cushions. There he waited, letting the heavy silence settle around him.

The minutes slowly ticked by, with no indication of what was going on upstairs. If they'd started fighting, he couldn't hear from his location.

"You're in quite a pickle, Xandre."

Marc's head snapped around at the sound of S'am's voice. She walked into the spacious room next to a short, balding man. Three Graygual and the scarred man they'd once taken prisoner trailed them. A dirty and torn piece of fabric flowed around her with a gaping hole in the side.

"Please, pinch that together, will you?" The short man, who must've been Xandre, waved his finger at the tear.

"Your Inkna are attacking your Inner Circle. It doesn't sound like you have a firm handle on your minions." S'am smiled in that taunting way she did when she was trying to inspire violence.

"This slice of chaos was expected, as I have told you. I have introduced someone who makes a habit of jeopardizing herself. Had you not taken out Tac, things would've progressed smoothly. You are lucky I know how to stop them."

Shanti tsked. *"Finger pointing only creates enemies, Xandre. Especially such childlike finger pointing. I'm lucky you knew how to stop them? Inkna can't fight, and their range has limits. How to stop them is pretty logical. I wonder that your people didn't know how. You created a defensive force that can't think on their own. How are you still alive?"*

"Take her to her room and lock her in. I need time to reflect." Xandre massaged his temples and slowed.

With a smug expression, Shanti continued on until her grin melted away. Her eyes snapped toward Marc's hiding place. He ducked away and winced, realizing too late how often Leilius had told him not to move.

"Wait," Shanti said suddenly.

A pregnant pause filled the room, and movement ground to a halt.

"What kind of partnership did you have in mind?" she asked.

Marc couldn't help rising just a little bit, glancing over the arm of the chair to see Shanti walking back toward Xandre. He was staring at her quizzically.

"I want to know my options so I can sleep on it." Shanti stopped with her side to Marc and hands on her hips.

"You would help rule, of course," Xandre said hesitantly.

S'am's fingers waggled. *"You know very well I don't want this land ruled. Was that a test?"*

"Interesting. A new path has just opened up to me. One with much success. You hate when your loved ones are in danger, yes?" A small smile spread across Xandre's face.

S'am's fingers waggled again, almost like she was waving. *"You know I hate when my loved ones are in danger. You thrive off that, not to mention that you've already threatened me with it. Do you have memory problems? Should I be concerned you won't remember this conversation?"*

"I knew it, yes. But I did not see the way clearly."

Fingers waggled. *"If you stay like that,* you'll *be seen. Easily,"* she said.

Xandre shook his head. *"What?"*

Dawning smacked into Marc as her message finally became clear. She wanted him to run.

He looked at the stairs, the only place he could go

and not be seen by her group. Of course, other dangers waited up there.

"People will see right through you, Xandre," S'am said. *"Your lack of control will be viewed as weakness. And let's be honest, the Inkna use you as much as you use them. They've asked for an alliance with me before, way before I had a pot to piss in. Now my pot is huge. They are not loyal to you. You should run. Soon."*

Marc paused in his crouch, ready to run but now holding off.

"I do not run, Shanti Cu-Hoi. That is your area of expertise. And see what happened when you stopped? You ended up here."

"Now you should."

Marc quickly crawled forward to the next large piece of furniture.

"This conversation is starting to elude you, I think," Xandre said in puzzlement. *"An effect of the Inkna attack, perhaps? I know where the Inkna stand. It was I who contracted them, was it not? They will always sell themselves to the highest bidder. Which is why you are so invaluable to me."*

Marc crawled to the next piece of furniture before making it to the stairs. He scooted up and flattened himself just around the first bend, breathing heavily in the soft silence.

"Delusions of grandeur are so much fun, aren't they?"

S'am said. Marc heaved a sigh at the absence of running feet toward him. *"You can have virtually anything you want with an overactive imagination. It's bringing it to reality that is troublesome. Then people start rumors about how crazy you are..."*

"I am not the one with all these personalities. It must be why your future is a revolving door. So many paths weaving in and out of each other, all with grossly different outcomes."

"I think the word you meant to say was exciting. *It's exciting being around me. I'm a party."*

"Get her out of here. I've had enough."

A thrill arrested Marc. They were coming!

He hastened up the stairs and sincerely hoped that the way was clear. Of course, he was never that lucky.

LEILIUS COULD SWEAR that a worry wrinkle infused the stony face of the Graygual. He couldn't see clearly, but something about the man's demeanor screamed, "Eh?"

For a moment, nobody moved. Despite the desire to throw up his hands and say, "You got me!" Leilius kept everything relaxed and immobile. Thankfully, Ruisa was doing the same, because no sound came from down the hall.

The Graygual's hand moved back up, and he pushed open his door. Despite its weight, the wood swung quickly and banged against the wall. Leilius almost jumped at the sound, and that would definitely have given him away.

The Graygual stepped into the middle of the hall-way. His eyes darted in Ruisa's direction before moving back toward Leilius' hiding spot. The wrinkle reemerged between his eyebrows—this time Leilius was sure of it. The torches, spaced as they were, did funny things to the lighting, though. It made Leilius' hiding place effective. But it was only a matter of time before the Graygual jabbed forward with his sword to settle the matter once and for all.

Metal clicked and a door swung open. A man stepped out in a loose, flowing sack of fabric. Leilius recognized him as the Graygual from earlier who absolutely hated the man standing almost in front of Leilius...which may or may not simply be called One.

The Graygual's expression darkened, and he looked like he was expecting trouble. One didn't so much as flick a finger.

"*There was a bang,*" the sack-wearing Graygual said.

"*And so you stepped out in a sack to meet the ene-my?*" One replied.

"*I don't see an enemy. I see you. Unless you are try-ing to imply...*"

One's fingers twitched this time, and his hand drift-ed toward the throwing knife in his belt. "*We have a prisoner in this castle. A prisoner that we have heard brings strangers flocking to her aid in times of trouble. Her people worship her. You've seen it in the cities and towns. They will come to save her. Maybe tonight. I ask again—you are sauntering out to greet a disturbing sound in a sack and without a weapon?"*

The Graygual sneered. *"I could take her worshippers down naked. I have a weapon."*

The Graygual's movements were so fast that Leilius couldn't help jumping that time. A knife came out of nowhere and flashed in his hand. Another blink and the Graygual was in a balanced pose, ready to throw. Leilius hadn't even thought to grab his own weapon, something that should've been second nature!

One wasn't so slow of thought, however. Almost lazily, he brought his hand up and turned at the same time. By the time he was facing the other Graygual, a knife was flying through the air. It sailed past the head of the other Graygual, nicking his ear. The other man's eyes widened and he jerked as his fingers, letting go of his own knife. It sailed right for One's chest.

With fluid movements born of a lifetime of practice, One angled his body just enough for the knife to glide past. He turned again and another knife was flying, one Leilius hadn't even noticed him grab. It nicked the other side of the Graygual's head before sticking into the wall behind him.

"You had just one weapon?" One said in a rough voice devoid of humor. It sounded like a threat.

Someone else stepped out of their room, fully dressed and with a sword in hand. Yet another, as well, just as prepared. Leilius had landed himself in the Graygual sleeping quarters. Fabulous.

"What is happening?" someone asked.

"Six was getting ahead of himself," One said, his eyes rooted to the undressed Graygual. *"Making threats he couldn't back up and didn't think through."*

"Not threats," Six said defiantly. *"I was simply showing you that I had a weapon."*

"You threw a weapon at a fellow Circle member, intending to kill him. That is punishable by death, or have you forgotten what happened to the former Three?" One turned his back on Six and the others long enough to retrieve Six's knife. He passed right by Ruisa, twice, but didn't look in her direction. He was clearly distracted, though his movements were controlled.

"I knew that weapon wouldn't kill you," Six said. Leilius thought he heard a tiny quiver of uncertainty in his voice.

"Did you, now? Do you often throw knives at someone's heart in jest?"

Six licked his lips nervously. *"You are not just someone. I knew you would be fast enough to dodge it. Otherwise, why would I throw my only knife?"*

"Why? Because you thought you only needed one, obviously. You are lazy. You have no real skill. I knew how you would try to prove your point. The question I have, however, is what would've happened if you had struck me? What would you have told the master?"

Six shifted from side to side. *"I told you. I wasn't trying to kill you. It was in jest."*

"Yes, I see."

Leilius knew what would happen one second before it did. One threw the knife up, caught it by the blade, and threw in an easy, fluid motion that only S'am had ever made look so graceful and refined.

Six hadn't guessed One's resolve. He twisted but didn't get out of the way in time. The knife sliced a thick gash in his arm, almost stuck but not quite. Blood immediately soaked through the cream fabric.

Six barely flinched, but his eyes were filled with understanding. *"So soon before a battle, that counts as a death strike,"* he said in an accusatory voice. *"That is against our laws for such a trivial jest."*

"Seven, get my knives," One said, now facing Six. *"We'll agree to disagree on your supposed jest, Six. However, that throw was not a death strike. The knife didn't stick. It's nothing but a flesh wound. If you can't fight through the minimal pain of a gash, you shouldn't be in our Inner Circle anyway. That is our law."*

Six's face drained of color. *"This is not a trivial*

gash." His eyes flicked toward the wound, blood now dripping down his arm. There was no way he'd be as fast and strong with a wound of that size, and everyone in that hall knew it. Shanti had excellent fighters in her company, who could take members of the Inner Circle at their healthiest. Six was done for.

Seven retrieved One's knives and walked past Six without so much as a glance. He handed the knives over and stood mutely to the side, looking straight ahead. One put them away, finally ripping his stare away from Six. He glanced toward Leilius, but didn't linger. Instead, he tucked himself into his room. The lock engaged. He clearly didn't trust his fellow fighters.

"*I told you not to mess with him,*" Seven said. "*You're going to need to find a duty that doesn't put you in the front line.*"

"*I'm going to take this to the master,*" Six said angrily. "*One has gotten out of hand. He's abusing his power.*"

"*He is One,*" Seven said quietly, shaking his head. He walked back to his room. "*The master gave him that power. I wouldn't advise bothering the master. His punishments are worse than that wound.*"

"*Surely he'll see my point,*" Six said to the other retreating Graygual.

"*Go to bed.*" Seven closed his door without a backward glance.

The other Graygual, after a pitying look, did the

same.

Six looked down at his arm for a moment. For the first time, pain seeped into his expression. He covered the wound with his hand and sent a hard glare at One's door. His look moved to the stairs at the other end of the corridor. After a moment of indecision, though, he finally sagged and turned into his room. Defeated.

Leilius sagged too, and nearly followed that up by slumping to the floor. Ruisa bent forward. The light caught her ashen face and wary eyes.

A large shadow roamed across the wall.

Not again.

Ruisa pulled back as half of a face moved out from behind the bend. Thankfully, it was a face Leilius knew well.

The rest of Xavier's head followed a moment later, until his whole body was edging down the side of the wall. Alexa came right behind him, and Leilius was so thankful that he wanted to cry like a baby. She was the only one who could help them against those Graygual. The rest of them didn't stand a chance.

Xavier's lips moved, but Leilius couldn't hear what he said. That meant One wouldn't be able to either.

Leilius took off down the hall with stiff limbs and a desperate need to get back outside. Hanging around Graygual would eventually mean death. "Go, go!" Leilius motioned them back the way they'd come.

Xavier pushed forward, jostled. A white-faced Marc stepped around him, his eyes wild. "Go!" Marc pointed toward Leilius.

"Not this way," Ruisa whispered, jogging toward them. "This is the wrong level to be on, trust me."

"They're coming," Marc said through clenched teeth. He had the presence of mind to be quiet.

"Who's coming?" Xavier asked, glancing back at the stairs.

"S'am, Graygual, and that prisoner who killed Daniels! She said to run. So *run!*"

"Shit." Leilius' stomach rolled as he thought about what they were running toward. "I think the ones up here are worse than the ones who are coming."

"I don't see ones up here. I see ones *back there.*" Marc hooked a frantic thumb over his shoulder. "She said run. *Run!*"

"Let's go." Xavier started to jog.

"This is a terrible idea," Ruisa said, following.

"Step lighter, Marc!" Rachie whispered.

They jogged through the corridor, fabric rustling, breath heaving, and feet pattering.

"Faster." Leilius pushed those in front of him.

Loud voices echoed through the walls. S'am's voice, coming up the stairwell.

Heart in his throat, Leilius reached the end of the corridor and nearly threw up. There was a large arched door, bigger than the bedrooms. It was locked. They were trapped.

"No. Oh no, no," he said.

S'am's voice got louder. She was right around the bend, Leilius could tell.

Taking a chance, he turned toward the door with the chair beside it. The Graygual had looked at that door when they'd mentioned the prisoner. It had to be hers. *Had* to be.

The handle turned and the door pushed inward. He almost fell through as the rest crowded in after him, until Marc shouldered Xavier out of the way and took great care in shutting it.

Breathing hard, they all stared at each other.

Alexa spoke first. "What if they check the room before they let her in?"

Eyes widened. Xavier brought out his sword. "Then we'll see if our combined might can take them down again."

"Again?" Leilius asked.

"Why are you being so loud?" came a familiar voice. It was One's.

"What did he say?" Xavier asked.

"Shhh!" Leilius waved Xavier away and pressed his ear against the door.

"I am alive. How marvelous, don't you think?" S'am laughed, her voice getting louder all the time.

"What are you hiding?" One asked.

"You know, I don't like you as much when you're surrounded by your brethren. You're an ass. If you'll excuse me, I need my beauty sleep."

"I want to check your room. I don't trust this change in your demeanor."

"Hide!" Leilius said, shoving at people. "One has taken an interest."

"One what?" Xavier asked as Ruisa slid under the bed. Marc looked out the window and shook his head.

"I want you to—" S'am's words had no meaning for Leilius, which meant they were probably slang words of the crass variety that Rohnan wouldn't say.

The handle rattled and Leilius backed away. He drew his sword, knowing they couldn't all fit under the bed or climb out the window. The door pushed open and S'am's body filled the doorway. Her gaze flew around the room before she shoved Leilius to the right. He fell on top of Rachie, who was sitting on the other side of a chair, not well hidden.

She turned back, still in the doorway, but angled. *"Do I have to worry about your men craving a woman's body?"*

"I doubt you ever worry about such things, not with your skill set." It almost sounded like humor. S'am didn't answer. One continued, *"I will lock the door."*

"Don't expect me to believe your men are without a

skeleton key."

"The master and I alone have skeleton keys, but if anyone tries to get in another way, I will kill them if you don't do if for me."

"Fair enough." She nodded before shutting the door. The lock turned over with a loud click.

No one spoke as she stood with her finger to her lips. After a while she shook her head and moved away. In barely a whisper, she said, "You lot are a bunch of idiots. Now we're all trapped in here together."

CHAPTER SIXTEEN

THE NEXT DAY, Cayan stared out over the swamp as the early morning rays speckled the tall reeds. Everything appeared gray and murky in the twilight, just now giving shape to the looming castle high above. In the distance, waves crashed against the cliffs.

"We've got incoming, sir. Sonson was right. We've got help." Sanders walked up beside him and braced his hands on his hips. "What a shit hole. I am not looking forward to walking through that."

"I've been thinking a lot about what happens after all this," Cayan said softly, focusing on the pull of Shanti. He couldn't feel her power, but her closeness existed in their *Joining,* always next to his heart.

"We settle down, finally, and have a nice, relaxed ale together, sir."

"I might not get to that castle. If I do, I might not get Shanti out again."

"Ah." Sanders clasped his arms behind his back and rolled back onto his heels for a moment. "It's that part of the battle, is it? The time where we discuss mortality and everything is called into question."

"Happens every battle."

"So it does." Sanders fell silent for a moment, watching the castle come into sharper focus as the first rays of the sun drifted over the horizon. "That woman has already given them hell, you know yourself. That ol' Being Supreme has no idea of the kind of trouble he brought into his world. No idea. There is no amount of preparation that can get a man ready for the likes of Shanti."

"If we don't make it in, she won't make it out."

"She still would. She'd probably jump off the cliff and swim all the way up to Clintos. I wouldn't put it past her. And she's got that crazy Honor Guard in there. You said yourself that Maggie and Gracas were tucked up outside the castle somewhere. They are a strange band of misfits, but no one else works as well with Shanti. Not even her own people. Those boys and girls are just as harebrained and unpredictable as she is. Together they'd drive anyone insane."

Rohnan moved up beside them, but didn't say a word. He must've known the anger that would be unleashed if he did. There was a reason Cayan kept the dips in his confidence to himself—a leader needed to be the beacon of hope for his army. Cayan was the strength. The backbone. It was his job to be sure of the outcome. In the merit of what they did.

He'd never had so much on the line. His future was locked away in that castle in more ways than one. The land's future was as well. Everything rested on his actions.

He eyed the way in front of him, thinking of what Burson had said. They'd lose one. Maybe more. Before all this was over, maybe a lot more.

"How many have arrived?" he asked.

Sanders glanced behind him. "Another dozen, all with power. The cats and beasts are here, too, though I'm not sure how they'll get through the swamp. Portolmous said the Shadow Lord was quickly getting everyone else under way. He thinks they'll be here by midday, maybe later."

"They got the whole camp on the move that fast?"

"Not alone. A large group of city folk traveled out to help. They brought food, fresh horses... The Wanderer Network is in full effect. Shanti gathered everyone behind her, like Burson always said she would, and now they're responding to your leadership. All we have left to do is get the girl."

Cayan stared at that castle, as though merely looking would unlock the way to it. "The *Gift* won't help either party unless Burson or their man is downed. That leaves the surprises of the swamp and arrow fire when we get closer. They'll be able to hit us before we can get to solid ground. Even a terrible shot would stick us like pincushions, and they will undoubtedly be great. This looks like a suicide mission."

"It has been a suicide mission since *Chulan* was five years old and Xandre sent one of his higher officers to burn out our villages," Rohnan said quietly, his staff held within his unbandaged arm. "The elders would say that it has been a suicide mission since before she was born. Had it been anyone else—you, me—we wouldn't have made it this far. We wouldn't be standing here. The number of times she should have failed are numerous. Yet here she is. Here we are. It is time to trust in our victory. Give her a sign that we are coming, and then lead the way. Somehow, she will bring us in."

"Well, look who showed up." Sanders looked around Cayan at Rohnan. "I don't think I've ever heard that much fire and conviction in his voice." Sanders looked at the castle again. "But damned if I don't want to storm the gates."

"Then let's storm the gates." Confidence rushing back in, Cayan turned toward the gathering of excellent and cunning warriors, their faces stern masks of determination. Two cats slunk forward and rubbed their heads and then necks along his legs. The third, Shanti's, cried, standing on his own. One of the beasts roared, a sound that shimmied up Cayan's bones. Its mate joined, loud and vicious. The warriors braced, ready.

Somewhere within the expanse of the swamp, the neigh of a solitary horse answered their call.

SHANTI RUSHED TO the window and looked out, forgetting that she faced the sea. It stretched out to the sides, filling her world. "Did you hear that?" she asked, trying to look as much to the side as she could.

"What?" Marc skulked up behind her and looked out over her shoulder.

"I thought I heard the beasts."

"The captain should be here by now, but I doubt the beasts would have made it that fast."

Wishful thinking, probably, Shanti thought, as she stared out at the water. It was about time to get going. She needed to create a diversion so the Honor Guard could get out of her room and cause chaos of some sort. Alexa hadn't had another vision, but Marc was certain of her last.

"Okay, we need to—"

"What's that?" Marc pointed out of the window, almost battering her in the face with his arm.

"What?" Shanti tried to follow his finger. Her eyes got lost in the brilliant blue as the sun showered the sea with light.

"There are shapes out there." Marc squinted. "Are those ships?"

Searching, Shanti shook her head in confusion. "I can't see anything."

"Let's get going," Xavier said. He stood by the door with a determined expression nearly covering the tightness of his eyes. He wasn't looking forward to the next few hours.

Shanti left Marc staring out the window. She gave Xavier a warm hug before turning to Rachie.

"No, thank you." Rachie put up his hand to stop her. "While being hugged by a very pretty woman is a great thing, you being nice means death. I'd prefer a kick if you do anything."

Shanti struck out, catching him on the leg and knocking him to the ground. Leilius shook his head at her next, his eyes solemn.

"I agree with them," Ruisa said, shaking her head.

"Me too," Marc said, finally turning away from the window.

"Since when did you hug people?" Alexa asked, perplexed.

"Now I feel like an asshole for accepting it." Xavier hardened his face. "I wish you could do the courage thing. Those Graygual are fast."

Shanti looked each of them in the eyes. "I am fast."

"You were never trying to kill us."

"They won't be trying to kill you. They have no minds of their own. They will capture you and take you to Xandre. Xandre will then try to use you against me, probably by torturing you. They won't kill you."

"You aren't good at pre-battle speeches, S'am," Marc whined.

"My point is, they will be more careful with you. You have to pull back when you aren't trying to kill—especially when all your training has been with killing in mind. Use that to your advantage." She looked down at another loose bit of fabric. "It'll be awfully hard to hide a black leg brace with black-handled knives under light cream fabric."

"I can help." Ruisa grabbed the discarded sack of Shanti's from the day before. "We can wrap your breasts and put the knives in between. You can just say you were tried of swinging in the wind."

"I didn't need that mental image, Ruisa." Rachie scrubbed at his eyes.

"I thought you liked looking at, thinking about, and playing with breasts?" Ruisa grinned as Shanti stripped. All the boys turned away without being asked.

"Not hers!" Rachie shook his head.

"Midday, right?" Marc trudged back to the window. "We're supposed to cause havoc at midday?"

"You're the one who heard her. Shouldn't you know?" Xavier joined Marc.

Anticipation ran through Shanti, followed quickly by a jolt of adrenaline. Battle was on the horizon, she could feel it.

"Yeah. I just wanted to make sure, I guess," Marc mumbled, slouching a little. "How are we going to get out of this room?"

"They'll either come for me, or they'll unlock the door and let me come out myself." Shanti lifted her arms for Ruisa to wrap the fabric around her. Leilius had given her his throwing knives, since he wasn't good with them anyway, despite having the largest collection of knives strapped to his person out of all of them. The fact lifted Alexa's brows in surprise.

"These knives won't be easy to grab," Ruisa said, her voice heavy with concentration. "You'll have to dig for them a little."

"What is that?" Xavier pointed into the distance.

"They look kind of like ships to me," Marc said.

"Hard-to-get-at knives are better than no knives," Shanti said.

Rachie followed Xavier and stared out. "I can't see anything."

"After I leave," S'am continued, "the Graygual will probably spread around the castle. You should be free to sneak out and spread yourselves around the castle too. Find Maggie and Gracas first, but then get into positions where you can throw knives at the Graygual's backs. They will be as good as me."

"At least we have a lot of practice in being up

against impossible odds." Xavier sounded uncharacter-istically glum. He clearly thought their chances of survival were low. It was time for desperate measures.

As soon as her makeshift robe was back in position, Shanti moved up behind him and punched him in the kidney. He grunted and bent, staggering out of the way. Marc and Rachie spun around with wary eyes.

"No more of that." Shanti skewered them all with a hard stare. "They are faster. They are better. But you have the element of surprise. You have more knowledge. They don't even know you're here. Stick something sharp in them before they *do* know, and then run like hell. A dying man doesn't run very fast. Even these dying men. Got it? I didn't train you to give up when you were needed most, did I?"

Everyone shook their heads.

Shanti struck out, hitting Xavier in the chest and kicking Rachie in the thigh.

"No, S'am!" Marc said quickly, backing up. He was always first to remember the training when she started doling out punches.

"No, S'am," Ruisa quickly repeated as Alexa said, "*No, Chosen.*"

"Okay, then." Shanti positioned herself in the middle of the room, as Cayan might've done, and braced her hands on her hips. Their backs straightened, as they'd been taught in the army. Then she dropped her stance and moved among them, as she'd done since they'd known her. It was this that had created the tight bond. The unit. *This* was how they became the Honor Guard. "This is just like the Shadow Lands. The principles are the same."

They all said, "Yes, S'am," at the same time.

"You've been across this land, in countless battles, seeing horrific things, and still you are here, in the belly of the enemy. You made it here without the captain. You made it here without the army at your back. You started just like this—removed. With me. We have each other, we'll work off each other, and we'll cut Xandre's throat together."

"Yes, S'am," they said, a little too loudly.

Shanti glanced at the door. It wouldn't do for anyone sitting on the chair outside to hear a chorus of voices coming from her room.

She nodded but then couldn't think of any way to end what was probably her first great pre-battle speech, so she punched Marc for good measure.

"Why?" he asked as he huffed out a breath and leaned against the wall.

She looked out of the window, trying to see the phantom ships. Only endless blue filled her gaze. The sky was brighter now. Someone would come for her soon.

As if someone had heard her thoughts, a knock

sounded. Her adrenaline spiked and she touched her chest, familiarizing herself with the positioning of the knives, and nodded to the others. They scattered to the edges of the room, curling into shadows or sliding under the bed.

Shanti yanked the bedcovers onto the floor before opening the door. One stood there, straight and tall. His eyes flicked, darting into the room behind her, and paused. A crease formed between his brows before he met her eyes again, disapproving. Or maybe disappointed; she couldn't tell. Judging her for the mess, definitely.

"You are wanted," One said flatly.

"In a great mood this morning, I see. And here I thought you'd be devoid of personality. How silly of me." She stepped out the door, leaving it open. He didn't move as she passed, waiting.

"Right. The stickler for everything just so." Shanti sauntered back and grabbed the door handle, closing it behind her.

"Lock it," he said, his gaze assessing. He handed over the key.

She frowned, because while he always seemed to assess her, this time there was a hint of suspicion in his tone.

A quick surge of fear that One knew about the Honor Guard ran through her. Why else would he insist that she lock the door behind her? Even he would be hard-pressed to fight all of them right then. Clearly he was saving the capture for another time, in which case, they'd need to make a stand now.

Heart in her throat, fingers itching to grab her knives, she schooled her tone into one of calm unaffectedness. *"What's the point? I thought you had control over your people?"*

"You are too smart to ask that question."

"The faith you have in me nearly brings me to tears." She blinked and fanned her face. After a moment she affected a scowl, needing more information before she took action. The man wasn't doing much in the way of facial expressions, sadly. *"But really, it's fine. If someone wanders in, I'll have an excuse to kill them."*

His jaw clenched. *"Soon the master will have me punish you for not obeying. You do not want that."*

Shanti laughed. She couldn't help it. *"I look forward to your attempted punishments. We'll see if I am as easy to cull as your normal charges. I suspect I am not."*

Fire sparked in his eyes. His jaw clenched again. *"You are unsettling the balance in this castle. Places and positions are being called into question. The ambitious are growing in number and desperation. I lock my door for a reason. You will, too."*

"Tac, do you also lock your door?" she asked, looking at the man sitting in the chair. He was trying to keep her alive, not kill those in her room. It spoke volumes about

Xandre's shaky leadership style.

"*Of course,*" Tac said before licking his finger and turning a page. "*I wasn't too keen on the idea of the Inkna trying to kill me in my sleep.*"

"*At least I'm keeping with the popular crowd,*" Shanti said sarcastically as she forced herself to quash the fear of discovery. "*Pity. I was hoping my room would be clean by the time I got back.*" She turned the key in the lock and sincerely hoped the Honor Guard thought to make a rope out of bedclothes so they could get out. There was nothing for it, though. She couldn't very well shove the key under the door.

One held out his hand, palm up.

"*I'm not one for handholding. Thanks, though,*" Shanti said as Tac stood.

"*Key.*"

"*If you'd just given me pockets, I wouldn't need yours.*" She handed the key over.

"*I see you bound your breasts.*" One nodded her forward and kept pace, his eyes scanning. As they passed a large tapestry down the way, he focused his attention on a little alcove next to it.

"*It's not polite to look at a woman's breasts.*"

"*Be that as it may, are you planning to cause trouble today?*"

"*Yes.*"

His jaw clenched again.

"What would you do if you were held captive?" Shanti asked, genuinely curious. *"Would you do nothing?"*

"So far, yes."

Shanti looked over in surprise as they entered the stairwell. Behind them, mild surprise flitted across Tac's face, and then disappeared.

"Ah, Shanti Cu-Hoi," Xandre said as they reached the bottom of the stairs, cutting out Shanti's desire to pepper One with questions. Not that he would answer... *"Please, join me for breakfast. We are in a new place today. I think you'll love the entertainment I have planned."*

Something heavy and hot lodged in her chest at the satisfied little smirk on Xandre's face. Graygual flocked around him, eyes burning, ready to fight. With dread, she followed them around the castle, this time not going to the area overlooking the ocean, but climbing to a wider part of intact wall where another table and chairs looked out over the swamp. Some breakfast items lined trays with plates next to them. Three spyglasses lay to one side.

A sweat broke out on Shanti's forehead. She knew what this was. Knew what she'd be watching.

"Have a seat." Xandre indicated a chair in front of the table with a bowl for washing up in front of it. *"I'd hate for you to miss the show."*

Shanti sat down slowly and took the quickly proffered spyglass. Unable to help herself, she looked through it, tracing the swamp. It didn't take long to find the collection of people, less than two dozen, picking their way through the watery land. Judging by their slow pace and how far they were in, they'd could have already been at it an hour or two.

"They are just getting to the first obstacles," Xandre said, sounding giddy. He sat as far from her as possible, angled so he could see both her and the swamp.

Shanti traced the way in front of them, seeing nothing that looked like any more than natural hazards, something that particular team of people could easily traverse. Taking down the spyglass, she noticed bows positioned along the wall. Even if Cayan made it, he'd be easy pickings for the archers.

She barely stopped herself from looking behind her, wondering how the Honor Guard would sneak up on this group without being seen. It would be a miracle. Which was exactly what Cayan would need.

CHAPTER SEVENTEEN

"T HIS ISN'T GOOD, right?" Rachie tried the handle. "We're going to have to go out through the window."

Alexa stood with her back against the wall next to the door, her eyes closed. Leilius watched her, wondering if she was going to give them some helpful advice. Xavier was watching her too, probably for the same reason.

"They really do look like ships. Four of them," Marc said from the window.

"Who cares?" Ruisa asked, joining him. "A few ships making a run for it are not going to help us get out of this room."

"Neither is standing there, staring at Alexa. Clearly we're going to have to climb out of this window."

Ruisa glanced back at Leilius. "Not without a rope."

Leilius examined the sheets. "Anyone really good at knots?"

Marc flinched away from the window. He held his finger to his mouth before edging closer again. "Someone just passed by for the second time since I've been standing here. They are patrolling."

"Inkna or Graygual?" Rachie looked through the keyhole before straightening up and looking back.

"Graygual. Same one. I haven't seen any Inkna."

"The Inkna are gathered together." Alexa opened her hazel eyes and stared at Xavier. "Why haven't they felt us?"

"They wouldn't be looking in the castle."

Her brow furrowed. "Why wouldn't they?"

"Because they don't think there is anyone in here. You guys, we need to get out of here and get in position before the captain shows up. Or worse, some curious Graygual tries to sneak in here." Leilius looked down and saw that the coast was clear. *For now.*

"Marc, keep watch here," Xavier said, taking control. "We need to be sure of how often that Graygual walks by, and if anyone else is making rounds. Leilius, strip that bed and let's fashion a rope as best we can. No one is climbing down a wall like that."

"Falling down, more like," Rachie muttered, helping with the sheets.

"I can't believe he didn't notice his stuff had been rummaged through," Leilius said as he worked.

"Watch the ground, not the sea, Marc," Xavier said.

"I have a thing called peripheral vision. I can do two things at once." Marc huffed.

"I told you, I put everything back." Ruisa crossed her arms, bending to the fireplace. What she was looking for, Leilius didn't know.

"What are you talking about?" Xavier asked.

Leilius told him how Ruisa went through One's trunk last night.

"That was stupid, given your description of how he folded and placed his clothes," Xavier responded.

"I found the key, didn't I?" she asked as she felt along the brick.

"Let's be thankful he didn't look in the trunk, then." Xavier ripped a strip off a sheet. "Because there is no way you put everything back, perfectly, in the dark. Something was off, and it sounds like he's the type who'd know it."

"Are you expecting this debate to go anywhere?" Ruisa pinched a protrusion. She scowled down at it and tried to wiggle it.

"What are you doing?" Leilius asked, pausing in his work.

"Shhh." Marc ducked back from the window. He shook his head, and a moment later, whispered, "He's coming often."

"I'd thought the Inner Circle was six people, or something." Rachie was staring down at Leilius' pants.

"Clearly he added more when he decided to bring S'am into his life." Leilius backed away from the intense stare. "What are you looking at—"

Rachie's hand shot out. Leilius flinched, thinking the other guy was trying to grab his junk. Instead, a tug on his pocket and Rachie was holding the key to One's door. "Why didn't you tell us you had a key?"

"It's to One's door. We're not in One's room…"

"Pick the lock with it." Rachie started off toward the door.

"You can't pick a lock with the wrong key. I didn't bring the stuff we found that might've helped. And yes, I'm kicking myself for it, okay? Let's not dwell."

"Sure, dwell on my going in the trunk, though nothing came of it, but don't dwell on your leaving behind something that could actually *help*." Ruisa shook her head as she peered inside the fireplace.

"What are you looking for?" Alexa asked.

"Shhh!" Marc flinched away from the window again. "He looked up here this time," he whispered.

"A secret door or something," Ruisa said quietly, now almost inside the fireplace.

"This group is like a gypsy show," Alexa muttered.

"Mutter those types of things in your own language if you insist on saying them out loud." Xavier tied together two strips of fabric and pulled, his muscles flexing. The fabric ripped apart.

"Have to braid it," Marc said, analyzing.

Leilius tried to grab the key away from Rachie.

"Give it back. We might need it."

"We do need it." Rachie fit the key in the lock. "See?"

"Just because it fits in there, that doesn't mean it actually turns—" The lock clicked over. Everyone froze, except Rachie. A big grin spread across his face.

"This changes things," Marc said from the window.

Xavier dropped the fabric and started for the door. "Ghost key. Makes sense that One would have it."

"He said he had a skeleton key." Leilius hung his head. "I'm an idiot."

"Which means it's *another* thing he'll miss," Marc said.

Ruisa rolled her eyes dramatically. "You're welcome, by the way. For saving all your asses."

"Nothing has been saved yet." Xavier focused in on Alexa. "Are we clear?"

"Yes. I can't feel anyone on this floor." She pushed him aside and joined Rachie at the door. "Let's go and get in position. Remember, I need to stay as far away from mental power as possible."

They opened the door and filed through, silent and stealthy. At the end of the hall, they went down the steps, letting Alexa lead the way. Once on ground level, she motioned them right and through two more rooms. Finally, they emerged on the cliff side.

"Hey," someone whispered.

Leilius ripped out his knife and stepped away from the others so he could run or fight—he wasn't sure which yet.

On the other side of a sitting area, Gracas popped up for a brief moment, then sat back down.

Relief flooding Leilius at seeing them again, he raced over with the others, finding the two displaced Honor Guard crouching with dirty faces and mussed hair.

"Where have you been?" Gracas asked, his eyes still scanning.

"Trapped in S'am's room. You?" Xavier helped them up.

"Hiding. Do you guys have anything to eat?" Maggie asked, licking her lips.

"Good point." Xavier nodded, looking at Alexa again. "We should work around to the kitchen. We'll have you scout the way, then take up our positions."

"What positions?" Maggie asked.

Xavier motioned them on, explaining everything they'd learned in such a short time. Moving around the sea side of the castle, they found empty walkways and halls.

"The captain must be working closer," Xavier surmised. They filed through a dimly lit corridor with no windows. He lowered his voice to a barely heard whisper. "They are probably readying to greet him when he gets here."

"And we're supposed to attack from the rear as that happens?" Maggie asked evenly.

They paused for Alexa to hold up her hand. A moment later, they darted into an empty kitchen. The heels of loaves of bread and a brick of cheese had been left out on the large table. Sliced meat sat off to the side.

"I wonder if they noticed the absence of the kitchen people," Marc asked.

"There aren't that many of them. They had to, right?" Leilius scratched his nose and waited for Gracas and Maggie to grab first. They were clearly the hungriest.

"Then why not sound an alarm?" Xavier shook his head and wandered toward the back door. Alexa had already taken up position near the other entrance.

"A lot of things about this place aren't making sense," Alexa murmured. "It seems like there is something else going on that we're not seeing."

"Whatever it is, we have a job to do. Hurry." Leilius took a turn and grabbed enough to satisfy him. He stuffed a little more into his pockets before nodding to Xavier. "I'm going to work my way around and find S'am's group. I can get close without being seen. It's what she trained me for."

Xavier stared at him gravely. "If you get caught…"

"S'am has faith in us. In me. She only has faith in

people who are excellent. I won't get caught."

Marc turned with wide eyes, his jaw set and his back straight. Rachie and Gracas straightened up too, fierce determination lighting his eyes.

"It's true," Alexa murmured from the doorway. "If she has taken all this time with you, there is a reason. She gave me a chance. We all have to make good."

With a deep breath, Leilius shook everyone's hands. He looked at each face, memorizing their features. It might be the last time he saw any of them. After a silent farewell, he drifted out of the door and skulked his way along the corridor. It was time to be there for S'am like she'd always been there for him.

"STOP!" SANDERS HELD up his hand.

Beside him, Boas showed him a furrowed brow. "What?"

Sanders crouched to look closer at a shallow pool, reeds and grasses sticking up, undisturbed. Within their depths, though, a metallic object lurked. Something that didn't belong there. He disturbed the water carefully with the tip of his finger and watched the small waves ebb and flow around it.

"There is something in here." He stood and surveyed the land around them before glancing at the sky. The sun was climbing faster than they were traveling.

They had to move quicker. Sanders didn't want to spend the night sleeping in damp conditions.

"How can you see with the glimmer on the water?" Portolmous asked behind them.

"I have something here." Boas took a step back from another shallow pool. "It doesn't look as though the vegetation has been disturbed at all. It was laid well."

"What is it?" the captain asked.

"I don't know, but I don't want to find out." Sanders moved to the side. His foot squelched into mud and sank. He pulled it out with effort and chose another spot before it sank again.

"What the—" Boas put his arms out and looked down. "Sinking mud. Back up! Back up! This is the wrong way!"

"What's sinking mud?" Sanders asked as the ground sucked in his feet. He yanked at a foot, but just sank a little deeper. "What's happening?"

"We had it in the Shadow Lands. Don't struggle— you'll go down faster." Boas yelled something in his language. Those behind him grabbed his shoulders and dragged him backward.

The mud engulfed Sanders' shins, pulling him downward. He stayed still as panic gripped him, the need to thrash and rip his legs out consuming his desire. The descent slowed, but didn't stop. The mud grabbed at his knees.

"Any time you're ready," he said, fighting the panic.

Hands grabbed his shoulders. He was dragged backward, a person on each arm. The mud resisted, not wanting to release him. Finally, his feet made a suctioned *pop* when he was finally pulled free and fell heavily onto his butt.

"Clever," Portolmous said, standing over Sanders, who was trying to get a grip. Men he could fight. Even better, faster, and stronger men than he was. But the ground? No. That shit was out of his league.

"Let's try this way." Boas pointed to the right. "There is a narrow path of firm ground."

"If the metallic items didn't catch us, the ground would while we looked at them," the captain said thoughtfully. "Being more careful is not an option. There is a time limit, regardless of there being anyone waiting at the other end or not. This defense was planned with precision."

"I agree." Portolmous glanced at Burson. He probably had the same impulse Sanders did—to ask which person would die with each new way they chose. Was it always the same person, or did it change? Did any of the routes result in more death?

"Not that way," Sanders said, eyeing the path Boas chose. "It looks like the obvious choice, which means it'll have nasty traps. We should go this way." Sanders pointed at a watery route with little dryness.

"There is no telling how deep some of those pools are. The water is too murky." Portolmous shook his head.

More people looked at Burson this time. No one asked the question.

"Left," the captain said. He looked at the castle, then at the sky. "Let's remember, they use horses in and out of here. We might get a little wet."

"Why not do both?" Portolmous said.

"No." Burson shook his head. "Not both. Not here, at any rate. Not now."

"That solves that." Sanders started left, going too slowly. All this was too slow. "Drag me out if I scream."

Boas laughed, catching up. "Enjoyed the mud, did you?"

Unable to see the bottom of the small pool, Sanders cursed as water rose up his leg. When it reached the bottom of his balls, he cocked his head, but forced himself to keep going. Something brushed against his ankle. He paused for a second and his head snapped toward Boas. "Did you feel that?"

"A creature in the depths?" Boas asked.

"Not the phrasing I'd use in this situation. I'd be more comfortable calling it *something*. As in, did *something* just brush by your damn foot?"

"Something big, yes." Boas kept going.

"You have balls of steel."

"You wouldn't last too long in the Shadow Land."

"No shit. I hated that place."

Someone behind them sucked in a breath. Another person gasped.

"Ouch," someone muttered.

"What happened?" the captain asked as Sanders' balls dipped into warm water. He grimaced.

"Something bit me. Let's hope it doesn't respond to—*flak*."

Sanders turned back at the sound of thrashing. Sayas dipped and then started hopping. Clearly it was his leg that was bitten. Kallon reached out to him.

"We need to move faster," Kallon said, his voice calm.

"How can you stay calm with a creature trying to bite your feet off!" Sanders put on speed.

"Now you use the term creature?" Boas fell in beside him, leaning forward through the waist deep water.

"It's eating people. My fears are confirmed."

"Is it bad?" the captain asked, also calm.

Did none of these people have fears of terrible things that lurked at the bottom of ponds, or was Sanders the only one traumatized by childhood explorations gone wrong?

Sayas' answer was in his language, which probably meant that it was certainly not good.

The land started to slope upward toward a drier

patch. Sanders looked at his stomach where the water was starting to recede.

"It feels as though…" Boas looked down. "I might've stepped in something—" He was ripped under the water.

"What the fuck?" Sanders paused when a hand grabbed his knee. "Shit. Stay back."

He reached under the surface and felt hair. Further down and he found shoulders. Sanders hooked his hands under Boas' arms and pulled. He didn't come all the way, though; somehow he was anchored.

"Come behind me," he yelled back, ripping out his knife. "Boas is caught in something."

The warm water enveloped Sanders' head as he ducked under. Using Boas' body, he pulled himself downward until he found the hole in the ground. Still further down, trying not to flinch when something grazed his body and kept swimming, he felt down to Boas' feet. A rope was tethered to his ankle.

He grabbed hold and swiped his knife across, severing it. Boas swam upward, dragging Sanders with him. His head broke the water and he took a gasping breath before being dragged to the side where he could touch bottom. Boas stood right beside him, steadied by the captain, heaving.

"Anything broken?" the captain asked.

"Pride only. I pissed myself." Boas scrubbed his fingers through his wet hair.

"Oh, great. I swam through your piss." Sanders walked the rest of the way out, feeling his way with greater care. "I'm not sure I'm going to volunteer to go first anymore."

"This is not the most fun I've ever had, either." Boas walked onto the small island and surveyed the way ahead. "Is this the right way, or the wrong?"

Sayas made it and immediately stooped to his foot. Jagged teeth marks cut a crescent shape in his ankle. Blood seeped down his skin.

"I have a wrap," Portolmous said.

Sanders let them doctor as he moved on, scouting the way. They were a quarter of the way but the sun was already high in the sky. He blocked the sun with his hand and looked at the castle. Was it him, or were there figures looking out over the wall?

There were probably figures looking out, waiting for the right moment.

"Xandre didn't get all his power without having the intelligence to back it up," Boas said, coming up beside him.

"We're not going to make it before sundown."

"We're not going to make it at all."

The truth of that statement settled in Sanders' stomach. He shifted to look back at Burson. "You never mentioned we'd all die out here. Was that because it hadn't occurred to you, or we've strayed?"

Burson turned his face up to the sky in a smile. As he did so, Sanders caught movement behind him. The cats, who had so far followed at a distance, slogging through like the humans, had now turned away east. The beasts, on heavy chains, were pulling at their leads, trying to head in the same direction.

"Can't be," said the captain incredulously.

A horse neighed and bucked, clawing at the air with his front feet. He was cutting his way to them across the swamp, taking a zigzagging path. He neighed again and bobbed his head. The cats sped up, working toward him more quickly. The beasts roared and ripped their heads, yanking their leads free. They trotted in that direction.

"That is the strangest horse I've ever seen in all my life," Boas said, blocking the sun with his hand. "I would not believe this is happening if I wasn't seeing it with my own eyes."

"He's like a big dog," Sonson said thoughtfully. "He's smart enough to get in, and then come back to help. How he is gathering the other animals, I have no idea."

"He's an ornery bastard who'll never say die." The captain started to follow the same path. "He's Shanti's horse, through and through. Let's go. Our miracle has arrived."

CHAPTER EIGHTEEN

"*WHAT'S HAPPENING?*" XANDRE stood and walked to the wall. A member of the Inner Circle moved a short distance away. One shifted in his seat, but didn't stand. He had clearly been ordered to guard Shanti, hence his close proximity.

She looked up at the sky. The sun was nearing its zenith. Rising the spyglass, she saw that Cayan was quickly winding his way closer, his team weaving along a crooked path, following that mad bastard of a horse.

A grin tweaked her lips. That animal was worth his weight in gold. The Graygual should've guarded him to the last.

"*They have brought all the animals with them.*" Xandre spread his hands on the wall, staring out. "*So be it. Ready the defenses. Bring me a master executioner.*"

The Inner Circle member bowed and darted away.

Xandre turned slowly until his back was to the wall, looking down at Shanti. He gazed for a long time, a strange gleam coming to his eyes. A familiar gleam. He was accessing his *Sight*. She'd seen that look in Burson's eyes plenty of times.

"*This was always a possible outcome, of course,*" he said. "*I confess, I didn't think it would come to pass. The probability was so slim. A* horse *leading them to the wall? Ridiculous.*" Sadness took over his expression. "*It has created a great many other events that are not favorable for what I'm trying to do here. So I am forced to reconcile the matter. It grieves me to no end, I assure you.*"

"*All that flowery speech just to say you're going to try and kill me? Being in the Inner Circle must be such a mood killer.*" She crossed an ankle over her knee, blanking her mind. She wasn't certain how his *Gift* worked, but she was pretty sure that if she created plans, the paths would be laid out for him to see, like a map. She needed to react within an instant if she was going to beat him.

Beating the Inner Circle afterward, however…

"*I do not want to do this, you see. It feels like killing a piece of the past. While you would have made things a little easier, I don't actually* need *you. Navigating the power in this land is easy. Brutality, spreading fear, and the occasional nice gesture keeps people in line. It works so well. And will continue working well as I live out my days in luxury. I just need to maintain things. Having my army in place is sufficient for that.*"

"*Are you trying to convince me, or yourself?*"

Xandre gave her a placating smile as the Master Executioner climbed the steps, his white coat practically glaring in the bright sun. He stood off to the side and clasped his hands together. Sweat stood out on his face from the heat.

"You were always a moving target, as it were. Tracking you, infiltrating your camp, trying to capture you. So entertaining. I loved it." His smile grew. *"And finally I won, and here you are. At my disposal. Truly a fitting end to a long game of cat and mouse."*

"Please tell me that's the end of your speech. I'm about to fall asleep."

"I know about the missing members of the Inner Circle."

"Mhm." Shanti focused on her blank mind, since she had no idea what he was talking about.

"You have extraordinary abilities. Ones that go beyond fighting and mental warfare."

"You're talking about my personality, aren't you? Yes, I'm a real charmer. Everyone says so."

"I wonder. Why wasn't I informed last night? A grudge, perhaps. You were left to do the job some in my faction have previously attempted and failed." He turned to the master executioner. An Inner Circle member closed in, making the master executioner glance behind him, suddenly wary. *"I've warned you…"*

"Me?" Shanti asked, confused. She didn't know what

was happening.

The Graygual moved, his arm swinging forward. A bloody sword tip poked out of the Inkna's middle. Surprise lit his face. He reached around his back as his legs became unsteady.

"The Inkna breed deceit and lies," Xandre said, watching the man sink to the ground. The Graygual put his foot on the Inkna's shoulder and pushed while pulling his sword free. The Inkna writhed on the ground as the Graygual wiped his blade.

"Am I the only one who didn't see that coming?" Shanti asked, looking at One.

His lips were a thin line, but he showed no surprise. Although that kind of thing probably happened all the time around Xandre. He'd surely stopped being shocked some time ago.

"One less Inkna for Sanders to kill. He won't thank you for that." Shanti tsked, her stomach fluttering. The sun was overhead now. Cayan was so close. In range of arrows. It was about to kick off, whatever *it* was.

She hoped *it* wasn't her death.

"Mental power is an unfair advantage. Unpredictable." Xandre stood in front of Shanti. The hairs rose on her arms with how he was looking at her. Expectant. *"That was always the part of you that disgusted me. Ever since I heard about what you'd done to my warrior. Unhappily, I've armed myself with the same power. I had*

to, didn't I? To confront you and yours. But it never sat right. Useful, but despicable."

"Big words for someone who not only has a Gift *of his own, but who also employs the Inkna power to subdue an entire land."*

His smile was childlike. *"Cheat to win, as they say."*

"You're a walking contradiction. I bet you have no friends."

A bead of sweat dripped down her back. The desire to surge up and snap his neck was so strong that she could barely think straight. One sat loose and still beside her, though. He'd expect it, and he'd be ready. She had to stall and see what came next, to let Xandre keep the lead until a better situation presented itself.

"I would've let you keep your mate," he said sadly. *"Would've let you try to breed."*

"Ew. That's not how people talk."

"Alas." His words trailed away and he waited.

"I'm not going to try and kill you," she said.

"Suddenly you show restraint. I won't tell One…" Xandre's gaze dipped to her chest, finishing his statement with the look. He wouldn't tell One about the knives hidden in her binding. He'd surely sense the possibility that she'd try to kill him with them.

"What a guy, huh? Real magnanimous." Shanti folded her hands in her lap.

Xandre glanced at One before walking to the stairs.

Tac stood, book still in hand, and followed.

"You're going to go hide?" Shanti called after Xandre.

He laughed. *"Of course not. There is a possibility, however minuscule, that you will live. You'd then find and kill me. I am going to escape."*

Panic swept through her. She couldn't let him get away again. She couldn't come so close, *again,* and lose him. This had to end. All of this.

Without thinking, she was up, chasing after him. One was there in an instant, grabbing at her arm. Two other Inner Circle closed off her way, swords drawn.

Along the wall, men in black ran to take up their bows, the force of the Inner Circle bigger than she'd expected. Where had they come from? She hadn't sensed them last night, hadn't seen them around the castle or coming and going from their rooms.

She dug in her binding and snatched out the knives. Whirling, she threw one. It lodged in the side of one of their necks. He lurched forward anyway, his sword strike wild. It sliced across One's side, who had been wrestling with her and hadn't seen it coming. He staggered away.

The other Graygual slashed at her and then struck, precise and powerful. She dodged and moved before flinging another knife. The one in front batted at it with his sword. Down the wall, a Graygual loosed his arrow downward, toward the swamp. Another followed.

"You are beaten," the Graygual said. He slashed at her, but she expected it and was already moving. He slashed again, just missing.

"And you are careless." She reached down and scooped up the knife lodged in the other Graygual's neck as One checked his side.

Another sword strike. It cut the fabric on her side, glancing her skin. Pain welled up, easily ignored. She dodged another as One straightened up. He'd engage at any moment. Her time was coming to an end.

She glanced up, seeing the archers loose more arrows. There was no help coming. The Honor Guard hadn't made it.

Desperate, she readied for another knife throw, her last, probably, when someone dodged out from the side. A knife struck and the Graygual jumped and spun, swinging his sword. Leilius flung his arms up and hopped back, bowing his body. The tip of the sword sliced through his stomach. He cried out but lunged forward again, pain and desperation on his face. His body slammed into the Graygual, taking him to the ground. Leilius jabbed his knife repeatedly, stabbing the Graygual in the side.

Choking back fear for Leilius, Shanti kicked the Graygual in the side of the head. Leilius continued to pummel, but was slowing. Hurt.

"Elders, please see him safe." Knowing she couldn't

check on him yet or they'd both die, she snatched up the dying Graygual's sword and spun. A sword fell toward her head. She dove out of the way and rolled, hopping up a moment later. One braced and surged forward, his sword work perfect.

It was time for him to meet an equal, maybe for the first time.

She blocked a thrust and started on the attack, knowing his training and offsetting it with her experience fighting it. He kicked out and she met the impact, shin to shin. She lunged and then pulled back. Metal rang as their swords clashed. His sword sliced through the air but met nothingness as she moved away. She kicked, hitting him in the thigh, and quickly dodged his thrust.

A knife flowered in his other hand. She threw her own knife but he jerked away, evading, his following throw going wide too. A grin tickled his lips, then a full smile.

She feigned a sword strike, and he feigned blocking it. Her next thrust was met with a hard counter, his power and strength wobbling her wrist. She couldn't get the blade up in time to block his next strike, so she crumpled and rolled out from under it.

In the past she would've surged up and continued on, it becoming a game of endurance, of which she had plenty. That was before she trained with Sanders.

This time, she surged *forward,* hitting his knees with her shoulder. He undoubtedly thought of stabbing downward, aiming for the center of her back, but that would make him sacrifice ever walking again. His body reacted as any fighter's would.

He twisted and angled himself, going with her momentum in a way that allowed his knees to bend. It knocked him off kilter, and he crashed to the ground with her on top of him. She barely glimpsed the wall during her fall. A Graygual lay on the ground with a knife in his back. Rachie was running toward her, bow in hand. She hoped he'd seen to the other Graygual first so Cayan could get through.

A fist slammed into her ribs. She grunted and crawled up One's body, pure rock beneath her. She couldn't let him unleash that strength, a strategy she had to employ with Cayan every time they fought. She was well versed.

She brought her knee up, hitting the sweet spot. His balls crunched and the wind pushed out of his mouth. He'd have a few seconds before his brain registered the pain, but the shock made even the hardest man pause—she'd tested the theory many times. With the dead time, she snatched the sword and rolled, raking it across his body and scrambling to her feet. She gripped the blade and stabbed down, but he was already moving. The blade sparked as it scraped against stone. One hopped up, his teeth gritted.

"*Ouch, huh?*" Shanti said with a grin as Rachie stopped and nocked an arrow. "*By the way, I brought friends.*"

"*I know,*" he said. The effort to straighten and ignore the pain was obvious. A little awe-inspiring, too, if she was being honest. "*They were in my room last night. In the hallway, I am certain. They killed staff. It was sloppy—I knew it wasn't you. They were in your room, yes?*"

Shanti gaped for a moment. One quickly stepped to the side, shielding himself with her. An arrow zipped by. Rachie's curse reached them.

"*Xandre...*" She was having trouble finding words to make sense of this.

"*I was curious if he would figure it out. You stump him. It is a nice change. He's human, after all. Being in his presence, seeing what I've seen—his planning always comes to fruition. He always narrowly misses death. Part of me wondered if he was a god. I will admit, this has...changed my perspective on some things.*"

He dodged again, never close enough for her to engage, but unexpected enough to enrage Rachie. "Stop moving so fast! S'am, get out of the way!"

"I thought you were supposed to be a good shot," Leilius said, his voice weak.

A wave of relief flowed through Shanti. Getting her

mind back in the moment, she said, *"Let me guess—you're going to join with me and take him down."* She lifted her eyebrows.

His lopsided smile was genuine and clearly a foreign expression. *"And be killed when I turn my back? No. My people have wronged yours. I had a hand in that, though distantly. We will always be at war, you and I, regardless of our opinions of each other."*

Shanti dodged to the side, leaving an opening for Rachie. Which Rachie clearly wasn't expecting, and missed entirely as One shadowed her.

"I will avoid killing such a piece of art as you, if it can be helped," One said. He offered her a slight bow, then he was running, his arm over his side and his gait uneven. It seemed his side hurt as much as his groin.

Rachie loosed an arrow. It grazed One's leg, making him stagger. He ran on before taking the next set of stairs and disappearing.

No time to think about that strange exchange, Shanti dashed to Leilius, parting the fabric on his shirt and looking at a nasty gash that was bleeding profusely. "Rachie, get something to put on this. His blood loss might be life-threatening."

"I'll be okay," Leilius said, though he made no move to get up.

Shanti stepped to the wall and looked over. Cayan was climbing the small hill toward a broken part of the wall. His group trailed behind him, hurrying. One person was being carried over another's shoulder, with arms dangling down. She couldn't see who it was.

"Let's go," she yelled to Rachie with a last look along the wall. Black-clad bodies lay on the ground. Down the way someone was running toward her—it looked like a woman.

An explosion sounded in the distance. Shanti snatched up a looking glass and stared out. Near the beginning of the swamp a horde of people gathered, many she recognized, some she didn't. It was the rest of her camp and what looked like city people, all there to help.

Another explosion sounded, but not in the swamp. It was behind the horde.

She jerked her glass up in time to see a wall of Graygual running at them from the rear. That damn Xandre had planned for even this.

"Burson might have the same *Gift*," she said through clenched teeth. "But he doesn't have the handle on it that Xandre does."

"What do we do, S'am?" Rachie asked, kneeling by Leilius.

"Nothing. Our camp have both fighters and the *Gift*. They'll be fine. We, however…" It was Ruisa running toward them. "Carry Leilius down. He can't stay here."

"I can probably walk, S'am—"

"S'am," Ruisa said as she drew up, out of breath. "There are more of them, pulling in from the west. Xandre is marching in an army, it seems like. Xavier is over that way with Alexa. He wants to know what to do."

"Xandre must've gone out that way. *Flak!*" Shanti waited for Rachie to hoist up a wincing Leilius. "Let's connect with Cayan before we move on. Go tell Xavier and Alexa to pull it in."

"He knew about us being in his room," Leilius said as Ruisa turned. "Told you."

She hesitated for one moment, irritation crossing her face, before she was running again.

"Not the time, idiot," Rachie said.

They made it down the stairs and hurried toward where Cayan was crawling onto the walkway. When he straightened, his face was grim and eyes sorrowful. She swallowed down a lump in her throat, feeling the support radiate around him.

"Who?" she asked, cold overcoming her for a moment as she looked at the others bringing through a limp body. "*Who?*"

CHAPTER NINETEEN

"SAYAS AND PAHONA," Cayan said as Rohnan crawled up behind him, his face bleak. "Portolmous has an arrow in his stomach. He needs help, but he's hanging on."

The breath exited Shanti's body in a whoosh. Pain laced through her. She nodded mutely. There would be time to grieve later. There was still surviving to do.

One of the cats gracefully jumped onto the walkway. He sought Shanti, rubbing his head and neck on her legs.

"Anyone bring extra clothes?" she asked, doing a quick survey of those in front of her while still forcing down the pain inside her.

No one said anything. Sanders crawled through next with a grim Kallon.

"Let's kill these bastards, once and for all," Sanders barked. "Where is he?"

"Did you know," Burson said conversationally, "that two *Seer Gifts* can cancel each other out if the wielder knows how? We can smother each other. Of course, this then starts a mental fight, leaving you vulnerable at times…"

"Which *Gift,* the *Sight* or the other one?" Shanti asked. "Because if it's the *Sight,* you'll be out of your league with Xandre."

"Where'd he go?" Cayan asked.

"That answer might surprise you." Burson smiled at the sky.

"I'm going to throw you over the cliff if you keep it up," Sanders growled. "Would that surprise *you?*"

"Not really."

An explosion made Shanti duck. Another and then two more went off in rapid fire. They were huge, deep blasts, out toward the sea. A moment later they caught sight of Marc sprinting along the walkway. "Help! Help!"

"What's happening?" Shanti asked, rushing toward him.

"Shall I cut out the other *Gift?*" Burson asked amid the panic.

"They're coming. They're coming!" Marc dodged to the side as Kallon ran his way. Sanders was beside him a moment later, blocking Shanti's attempt.

Two Graygual ran around the bend, swords in hand. Their hard eyes widened when they came in sight of the blocked entryway. They staggered to a stop and about-faced.

Kallon was on them immediately, slicing through one of their middles. Sanders tackled the other, his sword dropped, a knife in hand. He grabbed hold of the Graygual's hair and ripped his blade across the man's throat. Blood sprayed everywhere. Sanders wiped his blade as Kallon finished the other.

"Way better than our attempts," Marc said, out of breath.

Another series of blasts ripped through the air. The sound of something hitting the castle around the bend had them all ducking. Stone flew out to the side. The ground shook.

"Ships. I told you." Marc braced his hands on his knees and panted. "Ships came. They are firing on Xandre's vessel."

"Xandre's vessel?" Shanti ran that way, heart in her throat. "How?"

Around the bend, where the sea was visible, another series of blasts had her rethinking her plan of taking a shortcut through the castle.

She kept going around, and as soon as she could, she got to the cliff and looked over. She recognized the ship immediately. Jooston the seafarer. He'd taken them to the Shadow Lands. Around him were three other ships, all pointed at the cliffs and castle with cannons extended.

"How did he know to come?" she said, half in a

daze.

"I told your Wanderer Network to embrace freedom. I told them where we were going. They are answering." Cayan got on his belly and stuck his head farther over the side.

Another series of blasts erupted from the black barrels, many angled upward, some not so much. Cannonballs slapped the cliff face, breaking away chunks and shaking the ground. Others made it over, pounding into the castle.

"There is a rope and pulley system down the side," Cayan said, pushing back to his hands and knees, then standing. "I can't see it, but there is surely a platform and waiting ship down there somewhere. He must have a way for getting around the surging tide."

"Of course he does. He had plenty of time to stare at it and analyze all the ways to go about it." Shanti clenched her fists as a large chunk of the ground broke away. She looked up at the castle and the walkway. Stone toppled up ahead. "We can't go that way. Stone will rain down on us."

"If Xandre gets back up, he'll go out the west, under cover from his troops. That's our play." Cayan started jogging. "Time to take on an army."

"Like you weren't expecting that?" Sanders asked, quickly following.

"I was asking about whether I should attempt to cut

out the power blocking you from using your *Gifts*?" Burson said patiently. He jogged with the rest of them, no weapons at his disposal. "It will unleash the Inkna, however. There will be no protection."

"Do it," Shanti said. "We can fight and use our *Gifts* at the same time. That is, if you are *sure* you can outmatch him."

"Odds are slightly in your favor."

"That's confidence inspiring," Sanders growled.

"Do it," Shanti repeated.

As they came around the bend, they found Xavier and the rest of them. Their eyes showed relief upon seeing Shanti. Xavier pointed back the way they'd come as more blasts sounded. "Big army, S'am. Compared to us, I mean. And a lot of Inkna."

"Any chance of explosives, Maggie?" Cayan asked as they ran by.

"No, sir. I have nothing to make them with."

"We need to prepare for them having them." Shanti winced as she stepped on something sharp. The sandals Xandre provided would hinder her in battle. "I need to find some proper clothes, Cayan."

"I'll get some, S'am," Ruisa called. "I know where there are some. I have a key."

Another blast sounded behind them now, the castle still taking heavy fire.

"Are you crazy?" Rachie said from within the group

of fighters. "You'll get stone rained down on you."

"It's in the back half. I'll be quick." Ruisa ran without further argument, not waiting for approval.

"I see the Honor Guard has gone back to the way you do things," Cayan said as he slowed, his eyes scanning. Shanti knew he was waiting for Ruisa to get back, rather than being careful as he progressed.

"He does not understand his *Gift* very well," Burson said quietly, his brow furrowed in concentration. "Or else he has an ulterior motive."

Like ripping off a bandage, their *Gifts* blossomed and spread, covering the area in a fog. The minds of the Inkna popped up, plentiful and suddenly confused. Many were nervous, too, probably sensing the battle to come.

The minds around her merged into one, centered around Cayan and her *Gifts*. Within the *Joining*, electricity sizzled. Power boiled, hot and wild.

"Strike them," Cayan said, still slowed on the path. His muscles flexed, his desire to surge ahead showing in his demeanor.

Shanti rained down spires of power, striking hastily made shields, splintering them. The weaker minds cracked open, now vulnerable to attacks. Before they could erect another shield, the Shadow *battered* them, ripping into the Inkna minds and scrambling what they found. The Shumas lent Shanti more power, making her next strike more potent. It tore through soft brain matter. Inkna crumpled, their intellects dying like a snuffed candle.

"The stronger Inkna are forging a mental collective," Sonson said, his sword in hand.

"Here, S'am." Ruisa sprinted out of the castle with wild eyes, ducking as a cannonball hit the other side. "I had to go through the middle to get to the stairway. The whole sea side is a mess."

Shanti stared at her clothes and her sword for a beat, surprised. "Where did you find these?"

"In your room. They were in One's trunk last night. When I didn't see them in there a moment ago, I checked your room really quickly. They were on your made bed. Someone had straightened up your room."

"He wants you on equal footing," Cayan said, staring at the way ahead. "I didn't think the Graygual cherished a fair fight."

"Or were that obsessive about a clean room," Sanders muttered.

"He's the first I've found." Shanti shook her head. "But then, he's the smartest I've found, too. Maybe he hasn't completely succumbed to the brainwashing."

"That won't save him." Cayan flexed from head to toe.

"He knows that. Let's go." Shanti pushed forward, immediately joined by everyone else. Cayan retook the lead, his worry for her ingrained and not easily quelled.

A surge of power washed over them, singeing their consciousness. Many staggered with the pain, but no one fell, not even the Honor Guard. Sanders dug into a pocket as he ran, and produced the root that would wipe out the effect of the *Gift*.

"Who wants it?" he asked.

All the non-*Gifted* reached for it immediately.

"Why does this taste like crap?" Xavier coughed.

"Actual crap, too." Rachie retched.

"It got wet in the swamp. Let's hope we don't get sick." Sanders' face screwed up in disgust as he chewed.

"That would've been nice to know *before* I took it," Ruisa muttered.

"Keep that handy in case Burson loses his grip," Cayan said. A great wave of power burst out from him, rolling over the grounds and smashing into the Inkna. Shanti could feel them quail under the strength, backed by her and her Shumas. More minds blinked out as they succumbed.

A roar of male voices rose up, just around the bend.

"That'll be their army." Cayan didn't slow. He ran around the corner and drew his sword.

The stone wall lay in bits in one section, crumbled from forced entry long ago. The ground leading up to that gap in the defense was bare, devoid of obstacle or army. Beyond, however, waiting on the far side of the gap, was a sea of Graygual, easily more than double Shanti's small force. Perhaps triple. They waited in the trees, spanning down the hillside with their swords drawn.

Cayan slowed, looking down at the sea of faces. Another wave of power exploded out, ramming into the Inkna. Their counterattack railed into Shanti's company, weak by comparison. Shanti hit back with a mental might that Xandre had not been able to duplicate. Not even close.

"Burson, I can't feel the Graygual," she said, *searching*. Waiting for Cayan to formulate a plan.

"They are protected. Their man is releasing his hold on the Inkna in order to better protect the Graygual. I can't pry him free."

"So he's in the area."

"Running, yes. Working down that hillside."

"They are trying to funnel us down through that stone fence," Cayan said, scanning the walls. "The Hunter would never have been so careless with his battle plans."

"What does the Hunter have to do with anything?" Shanti asked, confused.

"He was better than this. Either there is a surprise to come, or they have squandered one of their battle geniuses."

"They probably didn't put much thought into this,"

Burson said, wiping his palms on his pants. Sweat stood out on his forehead and his face showed nervousness. "We've taken the least likely paths today. Paths that should not have been possible. I'm sure he discounted them, not having worked with the Chosen before. You two were prophesied for a reason."

"Pepper them with arrows as we run in," Sonson said.

"Clear the way for me. I want Xandre." Shanti's grip tightened on her sword. Rohnan stepped up beside her, wanting his share. The other Shumas shifted, and the feeling of vengeance welled up.

"Honor Guard, take to the walls," Cayan said brusquely. "You'll be our cover. The rest of us take the Graygual, cutting a path through the center toward Xandre."

The Honor Guard received bows if they didn't already have them, and jogged toward the stairs at the far side of the space, except for Alexa. She gave Shanti a baleful look crusted with defiance. *They are not my people. You are my people. I wish to go with you.*

I know this, Shanti said, her heart going out to the girl. The need to get going pushed on her. *But you are most valuable where we might hear your Gift. That is your job among our people. So you will need to stay close to Marc in a place where you can be heard.*

You will have the same amount of Honor, Kallon

said, resting his hand on Alexa's shoulder. *"We appreciate your sacrifice."*

"Let the beasts loose," Cayan said. "What of the horses?"

"I know where they are!" Xavier called from the stairs.

"Get them. Hurry."

"The Graygual weren't the only ones ill prepared," Sonson said, shifting from side to side.

"He is getting away," Burson said, more agitated. "If we don't hurry, we will all be lost."

"Don't need the extra pressure, old man." Sanders stretched his neck. "But horses will tip the scales."

An attack seared their brains, the Inkna continuing with their assault, but from farther away. It could only mean they were leaving with Xandre.

Urgency boiled through Shanti. She bounced from foot to foot. A short time later, Xavier rode into the space. The Honor Guard horses came easily. Behind them, agitated and clearly unhappy, were some of the Graygual stock, finely bred animals with fierce eyes and stamping feet.

"There were only a few left. The Bastard helped." Xavier looked back warily to where the Bastard stamped a foot. He bit at one of the Graygual horses, who neighed and trotted forward a few feet.

"These probably belonged to the dead," Shanti said,

running at her horse. "Thank you for being an insane bastard everyone is afraid of," she said as she jumped on.

"Mount up. Let's go!" Cayan jumped onto a saddle-less horse.

"I hope I don't fall off," Shanti muttered as everyone else climbed on a horse. Many of the Shumas kept to their feet, since there weren't enough horses and they were the worst riders.

"Honor Guard, are you ready?" Cayan called.

"We're ready, sir. We've got you covered." Xavier nocked an arrow, as did the others.

Snarling, the beasts were led forward, the hair on their bodies standing on end. Saliva dripped from their open mouths, exposing their large canines. The cats slunk toward the edges of the wall, always looking for cover.

"Go!" Cayan called.

Boas slapped the male beast on the butt. It snapped back at him, but a moment later, lurched forward. Its mate followed, her snarl rolling out in front of her. The cats ran through a gate a moment later, their graceful lope taking them quickly out of sight.

Shanti lifted her heels. Before she could tap them to the Bastard's sides, he jolted forward, from standstill to sprint faster than Shanti could adjust. She clutched his mane with one hand and nearly dropped her sword from the other. They ran through the wall and down the hill, Cayan's horse hard-pressed to catch them. In front of them spread a sea of black among the trees, covering the hillside. Shanti could feel the Inkna moving away in the distance as one. She had a long way to go to catch them.

CHAPTER TWENTY

THE BEASTS BARRELED into the line of Graygual as Shanti *slashed* the minds of the Inkna. Two more dropped off, their focus splintered with their plight. Shadow *tore* into them next, with Cayan rolling his intense power down the entire hillside.

One of the beasts swiped its claws across a Graygual face before clamping its jaws around the throat of another. It shook its head, tearing the head off and letting it fall to the ground. Blood splattered as the other beast rose up on its hind legs and slashed through Graygual bodies.

"Helpful, those beasts," Shanti said to herself through gritted teeth as the Bastard bore down on three Graygual running at her.

The Graygual cover of power wobbled for a moment, exposing the vulnerable minds around her. Shanti seized the opportunity and *struck,* sending a sharp point of power into their brains. The Shumas and Shadow did the same. Graygual dropped, loose-limbed. Their minds disappeared a moment later, covered again. Cayan's power boomed out, too late.

Shanti struck downward, cutting into a shoulder. She swung to the other side, chopping a face. The Bastard rose up and kicked out, bashing faces and making Graygual flail back. He worked in farther, surrounded now as the cover wobbled again.

This time Cayan was ready. As the Shumas and Shadows rained down their *Gifts,* dropping Graygual like dolls, Cayan's immense *Gift BOOMED,* slamming into the unprotected forces and driving them to their knees. When the cover wobbled back into place, it was too late.

"Hah!" Shanti said, digging her heels into the Bastard. He ran forward, trampling Graygual who hadn't regained their footing. Then he hopped and bounced, stepping on heads and crushing them like melons. Brains splattered the muddy ground.

"Run, you bloody animal," Shanti hollered. "Run!"

It wasn't until Cayan's horse streaked by, following orders, that the Bastard did as he was told. Shanti slashed and cut as she went, getting anyone who was standing up, but more concerned with making her way to Xandre. The Inkna still moved, slower now. Struggling. Another wave of attack came from the Shadow a moment before the cover on the Graygual wobbled again. Electricity sizzled with her power, piercing the Graygual minds. Cayan's power thundered forward, flattening those in front of them.

Shanti saw him. On horseback.

Xandre.

His Inner Circle packed in tightly, including One. She could recognize his size and movements compared to the others. He was more confident. More graceful. More lethal.

As she watched, desperation taking over her at the distance between them, Xandre's horse reared. He held on as the horses around him also stopped or reared too.

"What's happening?" she heard Cayan ask.

Xandre's horse faltered, like it was being attacked. It sank to its knees, dumping Xandre on the ground. A moment later, Shanti saw why. The cats had stayed to the edges of the battle and cut off the running horses, spooking them before finally attacking.

"I'll never doubt you again, Cayan," Shanti said in a wispy voice, her heart now in her throat, her whole being focused on the balding man struggling upward.

The mental cover juddered, but before Shanti could strike, the Graygual were back under protection. The horses, however, were not.

Shanti *wrenched* their minds, making them buck. Some stumbled. Graygual fell from saddles.

A glance behind saw many of the Shumas keeping pace. The Shadow and Westwood were further behind, taking out any Graygual that had made it through the

last smashing of power. They were still unprotected—
Tac was focusing solely on his small group.

Xandre took a moment to stare at a large cat with
crimson-stained teeth snarling at him. One stepped in
front of him immediately. The two other cats stood to
either side, blocking any forward progress. All three of
them slowly drifted forward.

"Hurry," Shanti said to the Bastard, wanting the kill
for herself. The horse cut through the distance quickly,
a little ahead of Cayan. She pulled his mane to slow him
enough to be able to jump off. Her legs hit the ground at
a bad angle, and she rolled before hopping up.

Anticipation zinging through her blood, she
straightened out and stared down the Inner Circle, now
fanning out to face her. She walked forward slowly,
taking their measure as the horses ran off wildly. Her
gaze hit each face, as she waited to see if any of them
would rush at her.

Until she hit a face she didn't expect, but recognized.

"Tomous, no," she said.

Standing behind them, next to Tac, with his arm in
a cast, was a traitor she'd *never* expected.

"I am sorry, Chosen," Tomous said, taking a step
backward. He must've seen the white-hot flash of rage
boil through her. "For Daniels. I liked him, but…" He
glanced at Xandre. "I had no choice."

Rage infused Cayan, hot and violent. He glanced at Tomous, death in his eyes. The look didn't linger. It went back to One, who he had been studying. Sizing him up.

"You're the one who has been telling Xandre our plans," Shanti said, betrayal hot and raw. She'd trusted him. Comforted him. Rohnan had talked him through his guilt, clearing him of being a traitor, thinking Tomous had felt bad for not helping Daniels. Not protecting him.

Turned out, he was feeling guilty for holding the knife that killed him.

"His guilt had been so raw," Rohnan said, as if reading her mind. "So consuming…"

"Say no more," Burson commanded in a rough tone. He slid off his horse and limped into the area. Crimson sparkled on his side in the late afternoon sun. "Let that matter drop."

"So you're saying, don't kill that sniveling little traitor right now?" Shanti asked, stepping forward and clenching the hilt of her sword. The Inner Circle braced themselves. One glanced between her and the cats. Pressure descended on the scene like a blanket.

"You never fail to surprise me," Xandre said, turning to her with an incredulous expression. His voice was calm and confident despite the numbers against him. It made her nervous about whatever else he might have planned. So far, he'd evaded every threat to his life. "It is so exciting around you."

"She surprises us all." Burson took a few steps forward. He was in pain, she could tell. "Do you recognize the feel of my mind? Or can you not do that with only the *Sight*?"

Xandre's brow furrowed. He stared at Burson mutely.

Burson smiled manically. He glanced at the sky. "Yes, you recognize me. I am the dead man you saw once. The dead man the Hunter captured. You knew I would get saved, didn't you? I bet you did. But you didn't care, because every path of mine ended in death." Burson ticked the sky with his finger. "You are shortsighted. Your quest for power and control has blinded you to the continued pursuit of knowledge. You did not learn about the holes in the fabric that certain individuals can create. No matter how assured you are of one path, when the Chosen moves, the destination always warps. Always. Instead of being excited about experiencing it, you should've dreaded the coming of the Chosen. And now look. The least likely outcome is coming to pass. I couldn't have planned it better. Which is why I didn't plan at all."

"Who are you?"

"Someone who witnessed the destruction of a way of life because of you. Someone who said no to your

O V E R T A K E N

beguiling words early on. Someone who swore to see you dead."

"I was assured I was the only one in this age with the *Sight*," Xandre said. "I wonder why I wasn't informed of you."

"Because you killed the person that could've sussed me out. You developed your abilities before I did. But rest assured, there are others. Just as Shanti has learned of other powerful *Gifts*, and I have learned of other *Masking Gifts*, there are twos of every power level and type, a male and a female. At least, that's what I've reasoned. Procreation, you see. Nature likes to further her creations."

"Kill him," Xandre said softly.

"Nope." Sonson stepped toward Burson with his sword out.

"My death will not come from your hand." Burson turned toward Cayan. "I told Tomous to kill Daniels. I convinced him to act as traitor. So many of your people died because of me. I refused to tell you why you should let me go in Belos, even though I could have, because I knew you'd then capture me. That you'd blame Shanti's capture on yourself. That you would sacrifice yourself to get to her. I manipulated you from the beginning. If I'd been upfront the whole time, I'm sure I would've—"

"Sanders, back down," Cayan said in a tone that had everyone's backs snapping straight. One's gaze shifted from Shanti to Cayan, his eyes slightly widening, as though seeing Cayan for the first time. "None of this is news. Listening to him has always been a risk."

"And there, you see?" Burson smiled at Xandre. "You saw yourself that that should've worked, did you not? That Sanders, overcome with rage, would snap my neck? It is only intriguing until it is intensely frustrating, I can tell you."

"Why Daniels, though?" Sanders asked. "Why the traitor?"

"Sometimes we revel in the upper hand so much, in the power of it, that we feel immortal." Burson hunched, his arm covering his side. "It makes us singularly focused, which makes us weak. Xandre has been fixated on Shanti, and thus has been blinded to much else. He damaged her early life, and through Tomous, has been watching her rebuild in fascination, letting his own existence flounder. It is a very interesting saga that I would've loved to record."

"Enough talking," Cayan said suddenly. "This ends now."

Two Inner Circle members launched toward him, their swords drawn. One came at Shanti, his eyes excited but wary, his stance and movements graceful despite his wound.

"Take over for Cayan," Shanti directed, advancing on One. "Above all, don't let Xandre get away!"

One's sword slashed toward her, a move repeated from the last time she'd faced him. Unlike their previous encounter, though, she had her own sword and clothes. She had proper boots. She blocked his thrust and counterattacked. He moved away. She kicked out, catching him in the thigh. He took it and struck. His blade hit off hers.

One of the cats screamed, its version of a battle cry. A beast ran into the area, charging an Inner Circle fighter.

"You have unique soldiers," One said as he circled. Out of the corner of her eye, Shanti saw Xandre bolt.

"No!" She attacked One, but for every strike he was right there, blocking and ready with a counter. She slashed down at him, then kicked, then slashed again, fast and brutal. He moved around her, defending. Not letting her too close. Trying to let her tire herself out.

"That won't work," she said, watching as Kallon worked with the female beast to take out the Inner Circle fighter. Several Graygual from the charge pushed in on them, somehow having survived the attack and once again protected by Tac, who was jogging off toward Xandre with Tomous chasing. The Inkna lay in heaps, dead or dying.

He was getting away!

"Cayan, hurry," she said.

"I can't get away just yet," he said through gritted

teeth.

"I am figuring out what will *work. And, I admit, enjoying myself immensely."* One crashed down his blade hard, making her put more strength into blocking. She altered her style, moving faster and letting the blows fall away so as to use less effort. *"Interesting. And effective."*

"I don't need commentary." Shanti lunged, backed up quickly to block a counterattack, moved in again, and then kicked. She caught his knee. He staggered but regrouped before she could send in a kill strike. "Cayan!"

"Sanders, take him." Cayan darted away from the remaining Inner Circle member. Sanders filled his place immediately, blood sprayed across his uniform.

"Go, love," Cayan said, moving in beside her. He eyed his new enemy.

One hesitated, backing up a step and glancing around him. The Graygual were still pressing, but the Shumas, Shadow, and beasts were handling them. The better fighters, like Kallon, Rohnan, and Sanders, were taking down the Inner Circle one by one.

One's eyes hit Shanti again. *"If our lives had been different, I would've strived to make you happy. You are an incredible woman."*

"I have a mate already. And if you think I'm *good, get ready for more power."* Without another word, she took off running like death was chasing her. Rohnan

was behind her a moment later.

Her feet squelched and water splashed as the lands turned wetter. Up ahead, running within the increasingly sparse trees, were Xandre and his two minions. She put on a desperate burst of speed. She didn't care if this ended in death for her; she would kill that tyrant.

Her foot hit a hole and jolted her body. She staggered and fell to her knees. Something prickled her and heat seared her leg. That was probably bad.

"We almost have him, Chosen," Rohnan said, helping her up.

They pushed on, faster than the others despite Shanti's leg starting to go numb.

Up ahead, Xandre faltered and then fell. He turned, quick as a snake, and jabbed behind him, hitting Tomous. Tomous staggered and fell to one knee, dropping his head and lowering his sword, thwarted by Xandre's *sight*. Tac slowed, his bow lowered for the time being.

A moment later Shanti was there, closing in, Rohnan at her side.

Tac rushed to step in front of Xandre, lifting his nocked bow, sighting on her middle.

"You won't get through both of us," Shanti said with her sword put away and her knife in hand. "You're not fast enough."

"I'm not supposed to get through both of you. Just

you." Tac blew out a breath. "I never wanted to be in this position."

"Do it," Xandre urged. "Do it. I gave you your vengeance. Do this."

Tomous struggled up, his side wet with blood from a puncture in his ribs. He lifted his sword to slash at Xandre, but before his hand could fall, Xandre was at him. With viciousness Shanti didn't expect, he stuck Tomous in the side of the neck and ripped the knife across. Blood gushed out and down his skin.

Xandre shoved the man away and turned his rage-filled eyes on Shanti. "You will go down with me!" He laughed, a cackle that rose the hairs on her body. The numbness crept up, now at her hips and working down her other leg. Poison. Had to be.

"Kill her, brother!"

Tac turned his arrow point to Rohnan, who advanced, staff whirling. Tac let go of the string as Shanti stumbled around him, half dragging her leg behind. She batted Xandre's thrust away, still slow despite his viciousness. Another knife came out of nowhere and raced toward her chest.

"Nice move. Did One teach you that?" She grabbed his wrist with one hand and slammed her other forearm into his. His arm bone snapped, a sickly sound.

He screamed. His other knife came up for her. She caught it, ripped it from his grip, and stabbed him in the eye, her heart pounding. He spasmed. His body tensed as he died.

She ripped the knife out and stabbed his other eye, just to be sure. Nice and deep. Then slit his throat, just in case. Then, as his dead weight pulled her to the ground, she stuck the blade in his heart, just in case the strange tales of undead were true. She couldn't be too careful where Xandre was concerned.

Tears dripping down her face for fulfilling her duty, barely able to breathe, whether from the deed or the poison, she slumped onto him, still pressing the knife down into his chest.

"What is wrong with you?" Tac said into her ear. She felt his hand on her shoulder, but couldn't feel much of anything else. Air rattled out of her lungs.

"Rohnan?" she asked desperately, trying to look around through her blackening vision.

"Only a flesh wound. I knocked him out, though. I had to. Oh no. You're hurt. I need to get you help." Tac lifted her up into his arms. She couldn't even lift the knife to struggle.

She was jostled, as though he was running. "I am sorry," he said into her ear. Over and over. "I am sorry for my part. But it was my destiny. I am part of the prophecy. Burson placed me. Told me how to act when close to Xandre so his power didn't oust me. Relayed how I should enlist Tomous. Burson said only those scarred the deepest could help you in the final act. Tomous was trying to help. All he did—he was trying to help. He wanted to kill Xandre as much as I did. Please. Oh God, what is wrong with you? What's happening? We have to keep you alive!"

"Why didn't you just let me kill him the other night?" Shanti asked, slurring badly. Numbness had consumed her. Cold crept through her chest.

She didn't care. Right then, she did not care. She'd fulfilled her destiny. Somehow she had made it to the end of her path and claimed vengeance for her people. The intense weight had lifted from her shoulders. She was free.

"Because the Inkna would've killed you immediately afterward. I knew you had help. I felt those other minds in your room and around the castle. I kept them hidden from the Inkna. But your living is the only way the land will heal. That's what the prophecies say. You need to stay—"

Blackness consumed her.

CHAPTER TWENTY-ONE

"W HAT HAPPENED?" MARC asked, jumping off his horse, panting with fatigue. The rest of the Honor Guard dismounted too, drawing their swords.

They hadn't planned to venture into the fighting, but a half-heard prophecy by Alexa had them all run into the melee, capturing riderless horses, and trying to make it through the battle to get to S'am's side.

The man called Tac stopped with S'am in his arms. His face was ashen. "Help! There's something wrong with her." He held her out toward Marc.

It was Xavier who quickly stepped up and took her. "What's the matter with her?"

"I don't know. She limped and was slurring..." Tac shook his head.

"Set her down," Marc instructed, rolling up his sleeves. "Hurry! And watch that guy. Up until a moment ago he was the enemy. You should never trust a turncoat."

Xavier and the others did as instructed. Without

hesitation, Marc looked in her eyes, observed the dilation of her pupils, and continued over her exposed skin. Not seeing anything, he kept on, not blushing when he had to partially expose her body—he'd come a long way since he'd first seen her. On her leg, just above her boot, the skin had turned a worrying deep red. Veins leading away from the puncture were darker than normal.

"Poison." Marc looked up for Ruisa. "You need to help her. You're better at this than me."

She bent to S'am quickly, looking at the wound. The sound of footfalls made Marc glance up, his hand going to his knife. Dread pierced him as he recognized one of the Inner Circle coming their way.

"Quick!" He surged to his feet, knife forgotten, and now fumbling for his sword. "Help!"

The Honor Guard made a circle around S'am. The Inner Circle member, who was already limping, stumbled and fell to his knees. He glanced up with bleary eyes, looking directly at Alexa. A knife came out of nowhere, and before any of them knew it, she was sinking to the ground, her hands clutched around a blade in her stomach.

"No!" Xavier ran forward as the Inner Circle fighter was getting to his feet. Another knife appeared in his hand like magic. It was in Xavier's leg a moment later.

"Holy shit," Rachie said, bracing. Marc knew exactly

what he was thinking—while, as a group, the Honor Guard might've taken some of the Inner Circle, this one was beyond them.

The man took two limping steps, winced, and then threw himself onto the back of one of the horses. He looked back where the captain ran toward them, limping as well.

"Stop with the mental power, little girl, or I will kill you this time," he said in S'am's language. The man glanced down at S'am, and sadness crossed his face. He turned the horse like it was an extension of himself and said over his shoulder, *"That poison is* Teanna root. *Hopefully you know someone who can create an antidote."*

He spurred the horse and rode as the captain neared. The captain hefted a knife, sighted, and threw, all in one smooth motion. The knife fell short as the horse weaved through some unseen obstacle course.

"Did he say Teanna root?" Ruisa asked, looking up.

Marc ripped off a sleeve and pressed it around Alexa's knife wound. "Yes. Do you know it?"

"She hasn't much time. It acts quickly. Get a fire going and boil some water. I'll go look for the antidote."

"Where are you going to look?" Marc asked as Xavier took hold of the knife handle sticking out of his leg and yanked. Pain overtook his features, but he only grunted.

"I'll head back toward the castle, where there are hopefully less traps. It's a plant. Pretty common in the wetlands. They probably used Teanna root in case one of their own got hit and needed to counteract it quickly."

The captain bent and picked S'am up. He strode quickly to the nearest horse. "Ruisa, go. Quickly. Rachie and Gracas, get Alexa and Xavier back to the castle."

"Yes, sir," everyone chorused.

"Is Xandre dead?" The captain handed S'am off to Rachie so he could get on the horse, then put out his hands to receive her.

"She killed him," Tac said solemnly. "I had to give Rohnan a flesh wound and then knock him out. Burson's orders. He's back over there." Tac pointed. "But she was... Well, she needs to live. Burson was very clear that she needed to live in order for the land to heal."

"What about me, sir?" Marc asked, still applying pressure to Alexa's wound.

"First, check to make sure Xandre is really dead. Check on Rohnan. Then you'll need to make haste back to the castle. There'll be a lot of doctoring to do. You'll be needed."

"Yes, sir."

"You're in charge of him, as well." Cayan motioned at Tac. "Making sure he gets back to the castle. If he tries to run, kill him." The captain spurred on the horse as Rachie and Gracas helped the wounded.

Marc looked at Tac, his face and arms scarred and his demeanor rough. How Marc would keep him in line, or kill him, was beyond him. Bluffing came to mind.

"All right. Fine. You, with me." Marc scowled and motioned Tac on.

"Pick up your sword, idiot," Rachie said as Alexa was handed up to him.

Good idea. Marc snatched his sword off the ground and repeated the command, this time by gesturing with his sword. "Hurry up. I have to clean up your mess."

"I was told—" Tac began.

"Spare me or I'll stick you with the pointy end." Marc waved his sword again. He didn't miss Gracas rolling his eyes.

CHAPTER TWENTY-TWO

AYAN SAT IN a chair beside Shanti's cot, his elbows perched on his knees, head in his palms. It was midnight, or thereabouts. Ruisa had found her plant quickly and seen to Shanti. She reckoned Shanti would come out of it, that she would live. The hardest part was waiting.

She had that right.

He listened to the still of the night outside of his tent for a moment, thinking over the aftermath of the battle. Marc had worked miracles, as he often did, reviving Rohnan, then working his way around to everyone else. From their small group, there were wounded, but only two other fatalities, both Shadow.

Sanders had made the trip back across the swamp to the other faction of people, leading those who were able. Thankfully, he'd remembered the way, and everyone made it across safely. He'd arrived too late to help, however. The Shadow Lord had everything under control with Lucius carrying out her orders. Where the Graygual and Inkna were trying to trap the collected armies against the swamp, they turned out to be the ones who were trapped as another horde of city folk turned up. They'd had pitchforks, rusty swords, and one woman brought her cast iron pan, all trying to do their part to help the Wanderer. They swept through the Graygual and Inkna alike.

Cayan looked at Shanti again—her pale face was deathly. He sighed and put his head back into his hands.

"Captain?" someone called softly from outside the tent.

Cayan stood and cultivated a confident expression before he stuck his head out of the flap. Lucius waited for him, his face drawn. Beyond him, making a circle around the tent, were the Shumas and many of the Shadow, waiting. Hoping.

"Yes?" Cayan asked.

"There is not a trace of the Inner Circle member that got away."

Cayan figured as much. That man had been more than exceptional. Better than anyone, besides Shanti, that Cayan had fought. That man wouldn't be found if he didn't want to be, Cayan had no doubt. "The others?"

"An Inner Circle member was captured alive, but he swallowed his own tongue." Lucius shook his head. "I had no idea that was actually possible, but he managed."

"The Graygual army?"

"We've captured a few of those, too. So far they are still alive, though Tac managed to kill a couple when we weren't looking."

"What is the story with him?"

Lucius looked at the tent. "He asks about Shanti constantly. Burson, who keeps muttering that he should be dead by now, verified that he enlisted Tac's help. Also Tomous." Lucius braced his hands on his hips and looked away. "Tac said that Tomous was broken up about Daniels. He tried to explain to Daniels what was happening, and why, but Daniels insisted you be spoken to first. Tac and Tomous were specifically told, by Burson, that if that happened, the plan wouldn't work."

"So instead of tying him up, or knocking him out, they killed him?" The words tasted foul in Cayan's mouth.

"They couldn't have him telling you, I guess." Lucius shook his head again, then spat. "It is a wonder Burson is still alive, I'll admit. He was the puppet master in all of this. A lot of people died."

Cayan rubbed his face, suddenly bone-weary. "I mourn every loss, but it isn't lost on me that a lot *more* would've died if we hadn't received his help along the way. Xandre would've gotten away, for one. It was the Wanderer network that sent the seafarer to our aid. He said that before he left port, people up and down the coast had started fighting back with vigor."

"I thought they already were, sir?"

"In certain cities, yes, where the Graygual host was light. Now everyone is rising up, I hear. But they wait to hear from the woman that made it all possible. That stood up to a tyrant, against all odds." Cayan looked back at the tent. "They are waiting for Shanti, and she is in a deep sleep."

"She'll come out of it, captain."

Cayan glanced to the side, where Kallon and Rohnan sat together with many of their people. While Shanti slept, they refused to, keeping vigil.

"She will not leave us now," Rohnan said, sounding hopeful. "She fulfilled her duty, and now she will commune with the elders in the deep sleep. When they send her back to her mortal body, it will be into the new world she has created. It will be with their blessing, forgiving her for all the sorrow she had to cause in order to bring this around."

"I didn't realize he was so religious, but now I'm glad of it." Lucius ran his fingers through his hair. "What are the next steps, sir? So I can plan."

"As soon as the seafarer has the docks and lowering system fixed," Cayan said to Lucius, finally looking away, "we'll transfer the wounded and whoever else will fit onto his ships. He'll take us up to Clintos. Sanders can lead the rest out of the swamps and travel to meet us."

"Should we not take them to a port a little closer?"

"Seafarer says that Clintos is a fortified city. They have eradicated all the Graygual, and anyone who isn't siding with Shanti or the Shadow. It's the safest place. With it being only a couple more days, max, it's worth the risk."

Cayan paused, willing the courage for more bad news. "What of the wounded in the Honor Guard?"

Lucius' eyes went downcast. "Leilius and Alexa are barely hanging on. Marc is taking a lot of care with them. The Shadow healers that Esme sent in are helping with the others. Boas appears to be out of danger. He's already joking about the scar he'll have on his cheek."

Cayan blew out a breath, sadness pulling at him. He nodded, not able to ask about any more. If he wallowed in the loss, it would drown him. Instead, he turned back to the tent and resumed his seat, waiting.

CHAPTER TWENTY-THREE

S HANTI CAME TO consciousness slowly. The smell of the sea calmed her, reminding her of home. She fluttered her eyes open and found herself in a humble room with a rocking chair in the corner and another chair pulled up next to the bed. The shades were drawn over the window, but behind them sunlight was trying to force its way in.

She wiggled her toes and fingers. It was a good sign that she could. Next she shifted within the light and airy sheets. Her muscles groaned in protest.

Voices sounded outside the door, low and urgent. Shanti let her *Gift* unfurl, pushing through the room, then expanding across the city. The spicy feeling of her *Joining* with Cayan simmered up, warm and delicious. She felt the answering throb of his power, feeling hers and wanting to play.

The voices outside stopped. The door swung open, showing a drawn and pale Cayan with desperate relief coating his face. Shanti saw him take a deep breath and let it out slowly.

"You had me worried," he said.

"You, a man, admitting to being worried? Wow. You must've been out of your skin."

His lips tweaked up into a smile. The tightness around his eyes, and within his shoulders, eased. "You weren't getting any better."

"Was it poison?"

He entered the room stiffly and took a seat by the bed. Rohnan stepped in after him, calm yet appearing exhausted, with dark circles under his eyes. Kallon followed, entering the room enough to scoot along the wall and take up residence. He, too, had deep purple bags.

"Yes. Some sort of root." Cayan didn't seem to notice the others. His eyes were roaming her face. "One of the Inner Circle Graygual told Ruisa what it was as he was escaping."

"One."

"One of the Inner Circle Graygual, yes."

"No, I mean, it was One. The man I had you take over fighting?" Shanti watched dawning light his eyes. She nodded. "You let him get away, huh?"

Fire kindled Cayan's look. "If he'd stayed and fought, like the higher-leveled Graygual usually do, I would've killed him."

"Which is probably why he ran." Shanti twisted and flexed, making sure everything was working properly.

She glanced under the sheet and smiled. "No sickbed nightgown in his hospital, huh?"

Cayan grinned. "Despite Marc's insistence, no. It has not been so long that I have forgotten how you'd prefer to be treated."

"Why wear a sheet in a bed covered in sheets?" Kallon asked. "It makes no sense. Your people are very prudish."

"At least we're back to trivial matters." Cayan stretched and rubbed his neck. His gaze came right back to her face. "You were out for three days."

"And where am I now?"

"Clintos. We arrived late last night. This is the finest inn in the city. And though I've tried to pay several times, the innkeeper won't let me. For you, anyway. The Wanderer will be taken care of wherever she goes. Or so he says."

"I see. I really could've used that when I was first running from Xandre." A heavy weight settled on her chest. She let her head fall to the side where Rohnan sat in the corner, rocking placidly. "I killed him." She looked at Kallon and found pride. "I killed Xandre. The Being Supreme. I did it. I fulfilled my duty."

Tears came to her eyes. Rohnan's eyes glossed over, too. Cayan took her hand.

She couldn't believe it. All her life, she never thought she'd actually see this day. Even when hope glimmered, she thought that she'd die to succeed. And here she was, with the man she loved by her side, with her loved ones in the room with her, alive.

Unfortunately, it came at a cost. "How many did we lose?" she asked Rohnan. She couldn't celebrate the victory without mourning the lost.

Rohnan's face fell. Kallon's hardened. "Two from our group," Rohnan said. "And five more from the larger battle on the other side of the swamp. We burned them in a pyre after the battle, and carry their ashes with us. We'll release them among the trees of the Westwood Lands, I think. In our new home. The Shadow will be doing the same."

Shanti stared for a minute with her heart in her throat. Her eyes burned again, for a different reason. "You've chosen that as your home? You won't be going back?"

"We've chosen you as our home, Shanti." Rohnan smiled with the name change. She was no longer the Chosen. That duty had been fulfilled. Nor the Wanderer. Since finding Cayan, she was no longer lost. "We have sent for the children. Seafarer and his crew will take trusted men and secure them. The seas are safer than land, still. It'll take longer, but we'll compensate them well. If they'll take it."

Shanti smiled with Rohnan talking about compensation, since he had not one gold piece to his name that didn't come from Cayan. She bet those words even came from Cayan. She said nothing, though. She'd saved a land, but it would've been futile if she didn't also save the children.

"Sanders? The Honor Guard?"

Shanti noticed Cayan's eyes dim. He patted her hand. "When you're better we'll see everyone. Rest."

"I've rested for three days." She threw back the cover and swung her legs to the edge of the bed. Her head swam. She shrugged off Cayan's hand and stood, reaching for the bedpost to keep herself upright.

"Now I see why Marc and the doctor are always so annoyed when trying to heal you." Cayan stood to steady her, jealousy on a low burn. He didn't like her being nude with other men around. It was nice that he was trying not to show it.

"You guys can sleep. I see you haven't had much. Sleep, and when you wake, we'll go home to put the lost to rest among the trees." Shanti paused when she found two piles of clothing. One was a frilly dress as ugly as it was bright, and one was a pantsuit of a pale blue, an overly feminine rendition of Cayan's army's uniform.

"The Shadow Lord is of the mind that you should play the part of the victorious Wanderer," Cayan said, his eyes twinkling again. "They left it up to you to choose."

"No." Shanti pushed them both away. "I want what

I always wear. They can take it, or get a punch in the mouth."

Cayan laughed and nodded at Rohnan, who went to the corner and came back with clothes she could move in. She gratefully strapped on her weapons and felt the pinch of hunger.

"Sleep. All of you. I'll be fine—" She paused. "What of Tac?"

Cayan stiffened and told her about Burson's involvement with him, and his final words on Tomous. "He's being held right now. He is not protecting his mind from Rohnan or anyone else."

"He's waiting for you to kill him," Rohnan said solemnly. "He desires it. He's suffered for a long time, in the presence of the man responsible for killing his loved ones."

"Do we grant him peace, or do we help him to recover?" Shanti asked.

"I gave him a knife," Kallon said. "He can grant his own peace, or he can harden up and keep going. Like we have."

"Don't come looking to the Shumas for sympathy." Shanti sighed and gave Cayan a kiss. "I'll see you tomorrow."

Everyone started. "Where will you go?" Rohnan asked, concern radiating from him.

"By the way you all look, tomorrow might be too

soon." Shanti walked out the door before they could protest.

Her first destination was one she wasn't looking forward to. She tracked Marc down the hall of the—very clean—inn and to a room at the back. No one walked in the halls, and she didn't hear any laughter or shouts filtering up from the common area. She could not remember ever being in an inn that quiet.

Of course, she'd never been in an inn where the bannister looked brand new and the floors didn't have a scrape on them...

She knocked softly and waited until the door opened, revealing a face as tired as the others she'd seen. Marc's eyes lit up and he surged out and threw his arms around her. "You're alive. I was getting worried."

"Do I have you to thank?"

Marc stepped away with a red face. "No. Ruisa. And that Graygual."

"Who are you doctoring in here?"

His face fell. He stepped aside and allowed her to enter the large room. The wounded lined the walls, many with bandages, a couple moaning. Her heart sank as she made her way around, touching a shoulder, and smiling at another. Many she didn't recognize, as they were Shadow who had not traveled with her, and a few were faces from her past, whether from her homeland or the practice yard in the Westwood Lands.

She spoke to everyone awake and laid her touch on those asleep. Finally, she arrived at Alexa, who lay with her eyes dazed and her stomach heavily bandaged. Next to her sat Xavier, a bandage around his leg and his face pained.

"What happened?" Shanti asked, wrapping her *Gift* around Alexa.

"The escaped Graygual threw a knife into her stomach. He could've killed her. Nearly did. He wanted her to quit using her *Gift*." Xavier stared at Alexa's face. "I should've done something."

"Looks like you tried to." Shanti indicated his leg. "That is more than many would've done."

"We are monitoring for infection," Marc said, standing behind Shanti. "I've done all I can do. She's a fighter, though. She's strong."

"She'll come out of it." Xavier took a deep breath. He hunched a little. "She's fierce. I've never met someone so fierce. She's got something to prove. I know how she feels. She's not like other girls."

Marc inched away. Shanti laid a hand on Xavier's arm. "Stay by her side. Give her support. Girls love that. She'll get better."

Shanti clenched her teeth and fists, willing the burning in her eyes to not turn to tears. Xavier was already close to breaking. Marc, too. They needed to see her strength and assurance. She needed to give it.

"And you?" she asked Xavier. "How is your leg?"

"It's fine." He shrugged it off.

"He keeps forgetting to change the dressings. I have to baby him so his leg doesn't get infected and have to be cut off," Marc grumbled. "That warning doesn't seem to help, though."

She moved on to Leilius, who slept soundly. He also had a bandage around his middle.

"He'll be okay," Marc said, shadowing her. "It was a deep cut, but nothing fell out or anything. His big danger was blood loss. But he'll pull through."

Shanti let out a breath she didn't know she was holding and nodded slowly, hating all the pain around her. She knew guilt wasn't logical, that they were trying to free their homes and claim vengeance, but it didn't mean she didn't feel it.

"Keep me updated," she told Marc, backing away. "If you need any help, let me know."

"There are Shadow healers that change places with me."

"I wasn't asking for a debate."

Marc hung his head. "Sorry, S'am."

Outside the door, she took a moment to compose herself. It was at that moment that she saw Burson. He was walking away from her, but stopped suddenly and looked back. Indecision crossed his face until he turned and made his way toward her.

"Shanti," he said in a soft voice. "I wanted to apologize for the part I played in all of this, while at the same time expressing to you that I acted in the way that, I believe, saved the most lives. I cannot be sure, of course, and every time I was around you, things changed dramatically without rhyme or reason, but our end goals were always the same. I want you to know that."

"When did you think you'd die, out of curiosity?"

"I've seen my death in a number of ways. I prevented those that came before you met Xandre face to face, but afterward, I chose the best way to defeat him, which often had me dying early. I was ready. I've always been ready. I've always known that you were the key to my demise."

"Yet you are still alive."

"As I said, often plans change randomly around you. I still see my death, but each day, it gets further and further away."

Shanti sighed and slipped her hands into her pockets, something she rarely did. "I don't love the part you played, you know that. Cayan hates you for it. Sanders wants to wring your neck. But that is the problem with a *Gift* like yours. You had a duty, just like I did. I've caused people to die. So have you. Neither of us had a choice if we wanted to kill Xandre. I'm trying to come to grips with that. Trying to understand the guilt, and live with it. You'll need to do that, too. It seems death will not save you from it."

"It would've been easier if it had."

She smiled. "I've thought the same thing once or twice. What will you do now?"

"Leave. Tonight. It is my turn to wander for a while. Maybe we'll meet again."

"Probably. You don't seem like the lucky type."

It was his turn to smile. "Very lucky in some ways. Not so in others. I think you have the same problem. Goodbye, Shanti. It was an honor being the one chosen to help you along your journey."

She shook his hand so she didn't accidentally lose control and strangle him with a hug, and watched him walk away. Heart heavy, yet again, she turned the other way, looking for a way down that wasn't right behind him. It wasn't until she was standing at the mouth of a large, bustling kitchen that she realized she'd taken a staff stairway. Steam rose from boiling pots, gravy splashed the table, and cooks moved around, heaping items onto plates and passing them off.

Shanti quickly moved through, apologizing.

"*Hey!*" someone shouted. "*You shouldn't be in here—*"

"*Is that the Wanderer?*" A woman rushed forward and reached for Shanti's face. Shanti slapped the hand away, but the woman was not having it. She reached again and captured Shanti's chin. "*The eyes. It's the*

Wanderer!"

"Pardon me, miss. Pardon me." A man bustled over, wiping his hands on his brown-smeared apron. *"I am sorry. Please. Are you hungry? Let's make you a plate."*

"Yes, get her a plate! What are you waiting for? Get moving." The first woman, brandishing a spoon, waved the man away and smiled up at Shanti. *"It is so nice of you to choose our humble inn. Truly, we are honored. Come. I'll show you to your place."*

The woman ushered her out, but not before yelling over her shoulder, *"She's as thin as a rake. Make sure she has enough."*

Shanti received a pat as they entered the common room from the side. To the right was a grand bar with a shining surface and a jolly-faced barman. Tables dotted the floor below a high ceiling with artful wooden carvings. In the front of the space, card tables were mostly full, but the players, men and women both, bet and lost with good grace. Shanti did not hear one boast from the latest winner.

Dazed, she allowed the woman to sit her down at the large, round table in the middle. There the woman straightened up, clasped her hands in front of her, and said in a loud voice, *"Can I get you anything to drink, Miss Wanderer?"*

The movement in the room slowed, then stopped. Heads turned her way, eyes rounded.

"No, that'll be all, thank you." Shanti could feel her face burning. It took everything she had not to reach for her sword.

"Well, look who it is." Sanders sauntered up as the cook cleared out. He had the same surly expression he always did. "The laziest one among us. How was your sleep? Restful?"

He took a seat at the table. Sonson and a tight-lipped Portolmous arrived a moment later, both with relieved expressions. That was, until Portolmous looked over her attire. His look turned sour quickly.

"You're alive," she said to Sanders. "Damn."

"Can't get rid of me that easy, try as you might." Sanders rapped on the table with his fist, happiness radiating out from him, which in no way matched his continued frown. "Have you visited the wounded?"

"*Hello!*" The barman waddled up with a beaming smile. He rested his hands on his large stomach. "*So glad you could join us, Miss Wanderer.*" He glanced around the table, nodding, but his look returned to her quickly. "*Our city is secure for you. We made sure of it. This inn is as safe as you can get, I assure you. We put great pride in maintaining our standards for nobility.*"

Sanders sniffed.

"*Is there anything I can get you?*" The barman bent toward her expectantly.

"*An ale would suit me well, thank you,*" Shanti said,

changing her mind, her face burning brighter.

"*And for your friends?*" He gestured around the table.

"*Ales all around,*" Shanti said.

"*Of course, of course.*" The man was away, still smiling.

"Usually when people recognize me, they immediately try to kill me." Shanti tugged at her collar. "Couldn't we have stayed in a less showy inn?"

"The captain wouldn't have it, you know that." Sanders leaned back.

"In answer to your question, I did visit the wounded, yes."

"We got lucky." Sanders sucked at his teeth for a moment, a wave of uncertainty rolling through. He shook his head, the only sign of his feelings. "They weren't as prepared as usual. Xandre was relying too much on his mind power."

"There is no sense rehashing what was," Portolmous said. "There is only what will be." He unconsciously rested his hand on his bandage. Arrow wounds were no fun.

"My brother, the poet." Sonson looked up as the barman showed up with their ale, helped by a young barmaid. The cook appeared directly after them with a heaping plate.

"*Thank you,*" Shanti said as her stomach growled.

"You just let me know if there is anything else," the man said, backing away. The cook hadn't budged. *"Would you come on?"* He plucked at the cook's sleeve. She yanked her arm away, but smiled and backed up. *"Anything you need,"* he said.

"This is starting to get uncomfortable," Shanti muttered.

"Starting?" Sanders asked.

THEY STAYED IN CLINTOS for another week, forcing money on the inn for accommodating them. In that time, reports came in from different parts of the land where the revolt was going strong, regardless of losses. Each victory pushed others to fight harder for their own freedom. It also inspired communities to help each other, sharing resources. The land was crippled, but it was on the first step to recovery.

Cayan and Shanti led their combined people across the land, taking the fastest route. Those who were not yet able to ride were taken in wagons and seen to by the healers and Marc. With each new city, or each person passing them, they were greeted with smiles and nods. Some went as far as to give Shanti gifts. Only very few tried to hide a scowl and hurry along. Rohnan guessed that those types didn't want to hope in case it all went bad again, but who was to say.

After a journey at a fast pace—though not fast enough for the Bastard, who kept trying to sprint at random moments—the land started to change around them. Trees became more plentiful. The air fresher. Shanti's heart became fuller.

"Is this real?" she asked Cayan as they passed the first sentry, a Shadow with a giant smile on his face. He saluted them as they rode by.

"Is what real?" he asked, his eyes flicking away from her and into the trees.

"In all that time traveling to reach this spot, we didn't see one living Graygual. Not one."

"We thought that might be the case. They are likely running and hiding."

"Now we're home." She looked at another sentry, who threw her a wave. "No more Xandre. He's dead. No more tyrant trying to find me. No more impossible duty that drags at me. No more bleak future."

"You still have a bleak future if you're going to marry the captain," Sanders called up. People chuckled.

"It doesn't feel real." Shanti patted her horse. "None of this feels real."

"I am looking forward to the day when it does," Rohnan said from behind her. "Very much so."

The closed gate loomed up ahead, so familiar and inviting. Shanti felt like she was riding on air when they got up to it, and smiled like an idiot when it opened.

Rufus, Cayan's assistant, was waiting for them, his clipboard in hand. "Good to see you home safe, sir."

"Good to be home. How is the city?"

"Well kept, well kept. I have been working with Commander Sterling to keep everything on track. Production is as good as ever, and we have the extra Shadow covered. Also, I received this."

Cayan took the note as Sterling hustled toward them, his eyes sparkling and an unexpected half-smile on his face. Cayan looked at Shanti and held out the note. "There was another group of your people who set out, right?"

Barely able to breathe, she took the note. They'd feared the third group had been lost, though they couldn't be sure. She hadn't grieved for them yet, but knew it would happen when it all sank in.

Her eyes dipped to the scrawl, too loopy and messy to be read.

"They are alive," Cayan said, clearly seeing her frustration.

"What was that?" Kallon said, moving his horse closer.

"They were surrounded by Graygual, it seems, and couldn't get free. But with the turn of control, the way is clear. They are headed to the Westwood Lands—here—hoping you will come back."

"When did you get this?" Shanti asked, hand shaking.

"That came in a week ago, ma'am." Rufus checked his notes, and then nodded up at her. "A week to the day. They were a ways west of here, so they may have had to steal horses and food along the way, which can delay travel."

"He knows your people well," Sanders said. He didn't get any argument.

"This is definitely a dream," Shanti said, folding the note and tucking it into her belt.

"Rufus, get everyone sorted. We have wounded to see to. Make sure the doctor makes space." Cayan kicked his horse forward.

"Yes, sir," Rufus said, hurrying away.

Cayan looked at her. "Shall we head home? Everything else can keep for the morning."

CHAPTER TWENTY-FOUR

"SHANTI, DO YOU have a minute?" Cayan asked as he walked down the lane toward her.

Shanti glanced away from Tanna, who was standing in the front yard only half dressed. An older man on the other side of the cobblestone street was on his third lap, walking up and down the street, staring all the while.

Cayan glanced at the problem briefly, but didn't say anything. Two weeks in the city, and this was becoming a constant problem. The Shadow, who had a lackluster attitude toward nudity, had also started wandering around half-clothed, finding the locals' reaction hilarious. Boas was the leader of the Shadow nudity campaign, of course.

"Just a moment," she said to Cayan, who nodded and stopped a few feet away.

"This will help them with their prudishness problem," Tanna said when she had Shanti's attention again.

"No." Shanti shook her head, at a loss. *"Just no. Put clothes on. That old man over there isn't walking for his health."*

"*There you go. I am helping him maintain an active lifestyle.*"

"*Until his wife tries to kill you.*"

"*And that makes three good reasons. The wife will learn how to fight in order to kill me, thus she will gain confidence in herself and her abilities. Eventually, she might learn the glory of just being one with her body.*"

"*You can be one with your body* inside *of your clothing. You don't have to wear a dress, but you do have to* wear *something.*"

Tanna shook her head as Tilas, one of the Shumas they'd met up with before the battle with Xandre, walked toward them wearing a frilly dress. It stretched wide on his upper body, was bunched in the middle, and fell to his shins.

Shanti rubbed her temples. "What the fuck?"

"*What's wrong?*" Tilas asked. He didn't speak the language, but he could understand much of it.

"*That's women's clothing, Tilas. Where did you get it?*"

"*It was on a clothesline. It gives my balls breathing room. Don't worry, I asked before I borrowed it.*"

"*I am in trouble for no clothing, and he is in trouble for wearing clothing?*" Tanna crossed her arms and shook her head. "*Chosen—I mean Shanti, this will not do. You need a clear set of rules, or how will we ever expect to follow them?*"

"What in the holy hell?" Sanders yelled from down the street. The old man, who was on another lap, caught sight of Sanders and picked up his pace, getting out of there.

"He can handle it," Cayan said, taking Shanti's hand. "He loves dealing with your people and their confusion over our customs."

"They won't understand each other," Shanti said.

"He'll get to yell louder, then." Cayan smiled, his dimples enhancing his handsomeness.

Without a second thought, Shanti let him lead her away, hearing Sanders say, "Pardon the hell out of me, but where the hell are you going? Oh great, leave me with *this*."

They left Sanders behind and walked down the street and through the large park, winding deeply into the trees. Here Cayan paused and stared down into her eyes.

"Do you remember this spot?" he asked.

She looked around, noted the area, and nodded. "The Honor Guard and I have trained throughout this park."

"This is the spot where we first fought. You were sad at the time, and didn't feel me coming upon you."

She smiled, remembering. It had been a tough spot in her life, made a little easier by his presence.

"At the time, I asked you to let me help. To let me

protect you." He brushed her lips with his. "I would like to ask again, only this time, I'm asking to protect you for the rest of time. For as long as I live. I want to continue to be beside you, and care for you. I want to continue sparring with you until we're so old we can only sit and try to hit each other with our canes. Will you do me the honor of being my wife?"

He held out a jewel-encrusted ring that was as decadent as it was beautiful. It would be a great weapon, easily able to gouge an eye should she punch someone in the face. He brought out a plain gold necklace next. "For when you fight, or don't want to wear the ring, you can keep it around your neck. With your father's."

Emotion welled up in her. She stared into his brilliant blue eyes.

He stared back expectantly.

"I realize that this is a sort of ceremony we didn't get to complete last time," she said, "but I'm not sure what happens next."

The dimples cut deeper grooves into his cheeks as his smile broadened. "You give your assent or refusal."

"I have already told you yes."

"Right." He chuckled and fit the ring to her finger before putting the chain around her neck. "I never thought I'd have to think of these things when I got married, but the chain will rip off if someone tries to choke you with it. I know that was a concern. Also, I had two more rings made, in case you are wearing the ring around your neck, you do get choked, the ring goes flying, and you can't find it after you kill your attacker."

Her heart swelled. "You've thought of everything."

"I wondered." His smile fell. "If you wanted to try for children? I know it can be difficult—"

"Of course I do! I look forward to it."

Cayan's smile blotted out the sun. He kissed her soundly before lifting her up and twirling her around.

On their way out of the park, they kept a slow pace, prolonging the inevitable. Finally, however, they could put it off no longer when they reached the edge of the trees.

"So?" Eloise jammed her fists into her hips. The entire Women's Circle waited behind her, some with smiles. "Did you tell her about her official duties?"

The captain stared down at the bold woman, his brow furrowed, with a tiny bit of fear leaking out into the air around him.

"Because she is in a leadership position now, don't you forget." Eloise raised a finger at him. Shanti could feel his small flinch. "Your mother left big shoes to fill. She would want Miss Shanti leading the way. Strong but feminine."

"Or fierce," one of the women said. "Let's not force a square peg into a round hole, here. Strong and fierce and with a vagina."

"There's no need to get crass," someone said.

"What about a dress from her land? Didn't she wear one of those, once? That would count," someone else said.

"I'm fine with nudity. I wouldn't mind airing out once in a while…" another said.

Eloise's lips thinned and she glanced behind her. After rolling her eyes, she stared Shanti down. "We will work something out, you and I. I can be reasonable." Someone sniffed. Eloise stiffened, but didn't look back. The struggle was evident. "We'll talk."

Cayan led her away, more quickly than normal. "I urge you to find a middle ground. She is meddlesome."

"Meddlesome? Or do you mean terrifying?" Shanti laughed as she felt their follower. Arsen, who had been ecstatic she'd returned, had taken up following her around the city. She let him. One day, he'd be as good as Leilius.

"What is next on your to-do list?" Cayan asked her.

"I want to check on Alexa. She is the only one who hasn't completely pulled through."

"She is close, right?"

"Close. But not there yet."

"I'll accompany you," he said.

The hospital walls were the same white as before, with a shining, equally white floor. In front of Alexa's room waited most of the Honor Guard, including

Alena, who had been with the second group of fighters, and had hated herself for it. Now she glued herself to their sides. The only one missing was Marc, who Shanti could feel inside the door.

Beyond them were Kallon and Tulous, it being their shift with the vigil. They nodded at her in greeting.

Xavier looked up, his face drawn and the bags under his eyes pronounced. "The doctor is in there with her," he said.

"How is she?" Shanti put her hand on his shoulder.

"She has a fever. Marc wasn't that worried, but the doctor is checking just to make sure."

"Whoa, S'am, is that a ring?" Rachie leaned toward her. "That's a big one."

"It's from the captain, you idiot." Leilius elbowed him. He got an elbow back and winced, grabbing at his stomach.

"Does this mean you won't be living in sin any-more?" Gracas winked before he noticed the captain's stare. His face turned red and he looked at the ground.

Shanti ignored them and pushed into the room, with Cayan behind her. Rohnan glanced over from the corner, but remained silent, as did Marc, who stood behind her bed, letting the doctor take the lead.

The doctor sighed dramatically. "Another one. Can't you people take a hint—she doesn't need you crowding around her. Go back to somewhere where you're wanted."

"Another lovely day, doctor?" Shanti asked, looking at Alexa's shining face, hot with fever.

"How is she?" Cayan asked.

"This will break, I have no doubt. She's too stubborn to succumb. Then she can just rest. We have fluids going into her, we're monitoring her—we just need peace and quiet to do our jobs…"

Marc tensed. He knew better than to talk to Cayan like that, but then, the doctor was special. He didn't care about authority.

"Her people will want to remain close," Cayan said in a tone that brooked no argument. "They stick together. Let them."

"It's not as if I could stop them," the doctor said dryly. "I physically push them toward the door, and the next thing I know, I'm being carried out. I give them a stern talking to, and they laugh. I've said it once and I'll say it again—they are a barbaric sort of people."

"I don't remember you ever saying that, doctor." Shanti grinned at him. "I think I would remember."

"Well maybe not to your face…" The doctor stood, nodded at Marc, and walked from the room with a stiff back.

"He treats you as an equal," Shanti said to Marc, feeling Alexa's hot forehead.

"Yes. I have a job here now. I don't have to train

with you anymore."

"Yes you do. Just as soon as everyone is on their feet, you'll train. It's good for you."

"Not when it always ends up hurting…"

At the very edges of her awareness, Shanti felt something that made a smile blossom on her face and tingle race down to her toes. Before she knew it, she was running as fast as she could. She could feel Rohnan and the other's longing as she raced away, shoving out of the hospital doors and sprinting through the city. At the horse stalls, she ripped open the Bastard's stall and reached in to grab him. He bit at her. She slapped his cheek.

After his consenting nod, she jumped onto his back and kicked her feet. Cayan was right behind her, having no trouble with his horse, as usual.

"Why didn't we get a warning?" Cayan yelled as they thundered out of the gate.

"Because it is a wonderful surprise!" Shanti let the Bastard go as fast as he wanted to, zipping through the trees and leaving Cayan behind.

She saw them up ahead, the horde of Shumas atop what were probably stolen horses, a ragtag crew who'd been on a journey for far too long. When they felt her, they beamed and jumped from their animals. Shanti did the same, running at them as fast as she could. She jumped into their arms and cried, so thankful to finally see them again.

"*What of the children?*" someone asked.

More horses from the city thundered toward them. The other Shumas had felt the newcomers. "*We've gotten word. They are safe. They all live. They are coming here. Coming home.*"

The rest of the Shumas piled in then. Faces wet and words coming too fast, they hugged and laughed, so happy to be reunited again. Happy to be alive and finally, finally free.

THE END

Check out KF Breene's website for her other titles:
www.KFBreene.com

Made in the USA
Coppell, TX
12 October 2021

63946120R00184